Upper Darby Public Libraries

Sellers/Main
610-789-4440
76 S. State RD

Municipal Branch
610-734-7649
501 Bywood Ave.

Primos Branch
610-622-8091
409 Ashland Ave.

Online renewals:

www.udlibraries.org
my account

Connecting you to literacy,
entertainment, and life-long learning.

FOX & PHOENIX

BOOKS BY BETH BERNOBICH

A Handful of Pearls & Other Stories

Passion Play

Fox and Phoenix

FOX & PHOENIX

Beth Bernobich

VIKING

An Imprint of Penguin Group (USA) Inc.

VIKING
Published by Penguin Group
Penguin Group (USA) Inc., 345 Hudson Street, New York, New York 10014, U.S.A.
Penguin Group (Canada), 90 Eglinton Avenue East, Suite 700, Toronto, Ontario, Canada
M4P 2Y3 (a division of Pearson Penguin Canada Inc.)
Penguin Books Ltd, 80 Strand, London WC2R 0RL, England
Penguin Ireland, 25 St Stephen's Green, Dublin 2, Ireland (a division of Penguin Books Ltd)
Penguin Group (Australia), 250 Camberwell Road, Camberwell, Victoria 3124, Australia
(a division of Pearson Australia Group Pty Ltd)
Penguin Books India Pvt Ltd, 11 Community Centre, Panchsheel Park,
New Delhi—110 017, India
Penguin Group (NZ), 67 Apollo Drive, Rosedale, Auckland 0632, New Zealand
(a division of Pearson New Zealand Ltd.)
Penguin Books (South Africa) (Pty) Ltd, 24 Sturdee Avenue, Rosebank, Johannesburg 2196,
South Africa

Penguin Books Ltd, Registered Offices: 80 Strand, London WC2R 0RL, England

First published in 2011 by Viking, a member of Penguin Group (USA) Inc.

10 9 8 7 6 5 4 3 2 1

Copyright © Beth Bernobich, 2011
All rights reserved

LIBRARY OF CONGRESS CATALOGING-IN-PUBLICATION DATA
Bernobich, Beth.
Fox and Phoenix / Beth Bernobich.
p. cm.
Summary: Sixteen-year-old Kai, a magician's apprentice and former street tough, must
travel to the Phoenix Empire, where his friend Princess Lian is studying statecraft, and
help her escape so she can return home before her father, the king, dies.
ISBN 978-0-670-01278-7 (hardcover)
[1. Fantasy. 2. Apprentices—Fiction. 3. Magic—Fiction. 4. Kings, queens, rulers, etc.—
Fiction. 5. Princesses—Fiction.] I. Title.
PZ7.B45593Fo 2011   [Fic]—dc22   2011009388

Printed in U.S.A. — Set in Latienne — Book design by Kate Renner

To Tamora Pierce, for inspiring me in so many ways,
but especially about griffins

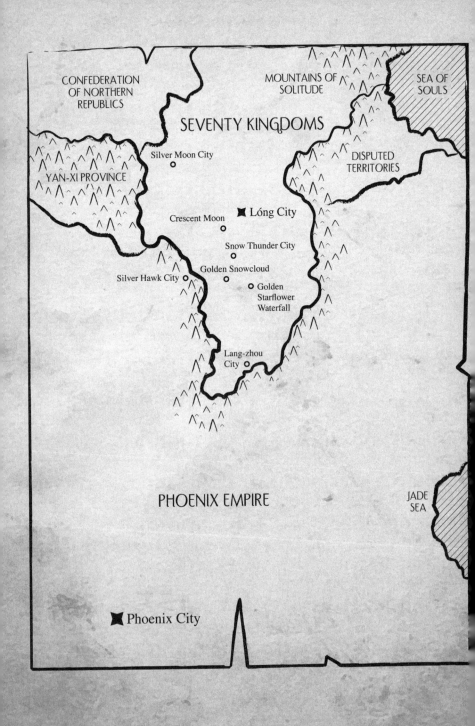

1

ONCE UPON A STUPID TIME, I LIKED FAIRY TALES.

Ai-ya, what's *not* to like? The poor kid from nowhere wins the jackpot, while the tilt-nosed snobs get turned into gargoyles. Or worse. But you know what? All those stories stop right there. They never mention what comes later. How your gang changes. How your best friend doesn't end up as your one true love. And they never tell you how your heart's desire might be a dangerous thing.

Or, in my case, just so damn boring.

I scanned the front office of my mother's tutoring shop. The room was tiny and hot. Shelves climbed all over the walls, crammed with boxes, books, scrolls, and jars, and the scent of herbs and paper dust lingered in the air. On the top shelf, a dead, stuffed griffin (miniature) curled around a glass vial that glowed faintly silver in the afternoon sunlight.

Mā mī had left me with clear instructions—review all the

homework from yesterday's beginner arithmetic class, mark any corrections, and leave the papers in her basket. I scowled at the stacks of scribbled sheets. The oldest shop cat had built her nest atop them. Hsin was ancient, her spine and haunches almost bald, and her teeth mere nubs, but she glared back at me with yellow eyes, as if daring me to disturb her.

Right. Like I want to.

With a sigh, I slapped the toggle switch on the wall. Magic flux buzzed uncertainly into life. The ceiling fan creaked into a slow circle, stirring the hot air like a spoon; our ancient radio sputtered in time with the magic flux. I fetched brushes and bottles of ink from a closet, then shooed away a grumbling Hsin and settled onto the stool behind the counter. From here I could watch for customers while I marked papers. Double duty, as Mā mī said.

I picked up the first sheet. It smelled strongly of cat piss.

This. I scowled at the papers. This *is not what I wanted for my life.*

Once upon a time, I'd been Kai, Prince of the Streets. I liked to brag about fancy dagger strikes, ghost dragons, and knowing where to get the best meat pies in Lóng City. I had my own gang of kids. I had Yún as my best friend and second-in-command.

Then the king of Lóng City declared a contest for his daughter's hand. The winner had to fulfill three impossible wishes. If he did, he got fifty thousand yuan, plus the hand of Princess Lian. Not just any man could enter, of course. You had to be a prince. Luckily, Yún figured out how to get past the prince part, and I convinced the princess I'd already done two impossible things, just by getting admitted into the palace. Just as luckily, Princess Lian didn't want a real suitor. Her heart's desire was a year or two at the famous university in the Phoenix Empire, where she could study government and politics and all those ruler-type things. That was the third and hardest wish of all. In the end, we—my gang and me—got our money and Lian got her heart's desire.

And she called us her truest friends.

All that seemed like a different story, with different people.

I pinched the bridge of my nose and squinted at the homework sheet. As bad as I thought—full of stupid mistakes, just like last week's batch and the week before. My mother ran a tutoring shop in conjuration and mathematics. Her best students got private sessions, but a couple dozen more attended classes where she drilled them in spells and numbers. Basic stuff. Now that I was her apprentice—another so-called reward from that contest—she gave me all the scut work. Thinking of all the other same-old same-old mistakes I would find, I spat on the floor, which crackled with a special cleaning spell.

If only I had stashed the king's reward in secret. But I hadn't. And I had believed Yún's wonderful description of our lives together as apprentices. We would learn magic. We would save our reward for later. And maybe, just maybe, we'd be more than friends. Okay, she didn't exactly say that, but I remembered the grin on her face as she dared me to follow her into this splendiferous new life. Except now Yún no longer had any time for anyone. And today I was stuck inside this shop.

I slid my talk-phone from my pocket. If I could buzz up Jing-mei or Gan, or even that toad Danzu, we could make a run through the Pots-and-Kettles Bazaar, stir up a little trouble. Same old, same old. After that, we could talk about the new, old days. There would be plenty of time later to grade these papers.

Before my fingers could tap out a single number, a strong piggy odor floated past my nose.

You promised Mā mī to grade those worksheets before dinner, Chen grunted.

Of course Chen knew what I was thinking. He was my spirit companion. Chen had arrived when I was six years old—two years past the usual age—but that was the first and only time he was ever late. Back in those days, he'd helped me play pranks all over Lóng City. Lately, though, he acted more like a nanny than a friend.

I didn't promise, I said silently to him. *She ordered me to.*

Does that make any difference?

It should.

But I could almost hear Mā mī's soft voice saying, "Kai-my-son, if you wish to continue as my apprentice, you must show more responsibility. The shop cannot run itself, nor can you learn your lessons by sleeping through them."

I shoved the phone back in my pocket and set about dividing the papers by name and grade. Stupid students. Stupid shop. Most days, I didn't mind the work. But most days, I wasn't stuck in the shop alone, sweating and cranky and bored. Today, Mā mī had dismissed her regular classes so she could shop for fresh magical supplies, while Yún was busy on some secret errand of her own. Again.

At the thought of Yún running around the sunny streets of Lóng City, my frustration bubbled over and I jammed my brush into the bottle. Ink squirted out, spattering the worksheets. Damn. I fetched a rag to wipe up the mess. That's when I managed to knock the bottle over, sending a river of ink over the desk and stool and floor.

A still-invisible Chen made squealing laughing noises. Cursed pig-spirit. I flung my brush at the sound of his voice. *Will you show yourself?*

The brush clattered off the wall. (More ink, damn it.) With a sputter and a pop, Chen materialized at full size in the middle of the room. He was a dark brown pig, huge, with bright black eyes and a double row of spines that zigzagged down his back, like daggers held ready. Today, he wore a pair of rimless spectacles, and an elegant calligraphy brush rested in the crook of his left front hoof. With his tusks and bristles, he was one fierce pig, but right now he looked pretty silly.

What are you doing? I demanded.

Double-checking your homework, Chen said. *Qi suggested it. Did you know you're failing advanced calculus?*

I know that. But why did Qi—*Oh, never mind.*

Qi was Yún's crane-spirit. She and Chen had become close friends, while Yún and I . . .

I threw down the rag and stomped on the ink-stained floor. Thinking about Yún had that effect on me.

You're just jealous of Shou-xin, said Chen.

Stop reading my mind! I stomped again.

I don't blame her, Chen went on, with a wicked grin. *Not after you flirted with that teahouse girl.*

Shut up!

Chen shrugged his massive shoulders and went back to squinting at my homework. I quashed the temptation to fling my chair at him. Chen would just vanish into the spirit plane, leaving me with a broken chair to explain to Mā mī. This time, she might really feed me to the watch-demons, the way she always threatened.

Still muttering, I picked through the ink-soaked papers on my desk. Ruined, all of them. Which meant no money from the students. And another lecture about responsibility.

Do you want help?

No.

I swept all the sheets into a pile and started mopping up the ink. Stupid papers. Stupid work. Stupid me for thinking I could make a good apprentice. Yún could fiddle formulae and spells better than I ever could, and that was even before she signed up as an apprentice to my mother. No wonder she was always running off to visit that stupid Shou-xin. He was Mā mī's best paying student—talented, rich, and charming.

Even Mā mī said he would end up the king's chief wizard someday.

Twenty minutes later, I wiped the sweat from my eyes. All that scrubbing and I couldn't tell a difference in those blasted ink stains. If anything, they looked blacker than before. Suspicious now, I sniffed. A faint metallic smell in the air made me think of magic, not ink and paper.

Oh, crap.

I retrieved the bottle from the counter.

EXTRA-DARK RUB-RESISTANT BLACK INK. Then in smaller characters, ENHANCED WITH MAGIC.

Some of the students cheat, Chen grunted. *The ink won't let them change their answers later and pretend they deserved a better grade.*

So I figured. I must have grabbed the bottle without checking the label first. Bad move in a conjuring shop.

By the way, have you looked in the mirror?

Why?

Then I noticed my hands. Ink all over them, of course. Extra-dark ink all over my palms, my sleeves, and underneath my fingernails. I rubbed my cheek with a clean rag. It came away smudged with black. When I blinked, my eyelids felt sticky, and not just from sweat.

Crap, crap, crap.

I hauled the bucket outside and emptied its contents into the courtyard, where Old Man Kang's chickens scolded me. The rags went into the special laundry tub. By the time I came back to the front office, Chen had discarded the spectacles and my homework. He was reading a paperback with a lurid cover, making absentminded snuffling noises to himself.

I surveyed the remaining mess. Maybe I could pull the rug over a few inches to hide the stains. No good. Mā mī noticed everything. I'd have to bribe one of her advanced students to help me clean up the mess before she came back from shopping. But not Shou-xin. Someone else. *Anyone* else.

Something poked my elbow. I glanced down.

A thin brown scroll floated in midair. It looked like one of Mā mī's older scrolls, its edges dark and crinkled. A velvety blue ribbon tied in a complicated knot kept it from unfurling.

I glared at my pig-companion. Chen feigned being absorbed in reading, but I wasn't fooled. He had probably conjured the thing from my mother's archives. We'd both be in trouble if she found out.

The scroll darted in to give me a quick poke in the stomach. I made a grab for it, but the cursed thing soared out of reach.

How can I read the scroll if it won't let me touch it?

Chen grunted and flipped a page over with his tusk.

With a sigh, I held out my hand. The scroll settled delicately onto my palm. When I touched the ribbon, it unwound itself and curled around my wrist. The scroll unfurled, showing a single densely written paragraph in the center.

And if a man or woman should wish to break a spell for unwashing such as the old wizards might put upon an enemy and his entire wardrobe, here are the words you must use . . .

It was a laundry spell, of sorts. Reading the old-style calligraphy, I wondered if some old priest or scribe had brushed those characters, all crisp and dark, like tiny black birds hopping across the rice paper. After thirteen months studying under Mā mī, I could detect glimmerings of power in the spell's deceptively simple phrases. Whoever created this scroll must have infused the characters with more magic as they brushed them, and the sequence of syllables (long and short, to be spoken with special stresses) hid the mathematical properties required to summon the magical flux. Simple and complex. Yin and yang. Chen had chosen well—a person didn't need to understand the math or the magic behind the spell to use it.

But it still required concentration.

So. Time to make all those tedious lessons in meditation pay off. The key was to eliminate distractions. Visualize the barriers to failure, then imagine them dissolving into nothing. I closed my eyes and concentrated on calming, magic-like thoughts. It was hard, especially with Chen's audible breathing, and the *slither, slap* each time he turned a page, but eventually, I managed to empty my brain of any thoughts except the here and now.

I opened my eyes and scanned the spell a second time.

(Ready?)

(Not nearly.)

Slowly and carefully I began to recite.

"Thunder and water, fire and wind, from east to west and north to south, we the unworthy call upon the sunbird and dragon to bring purity to these quarters. . . ."

The air around me shimmered as the magic flux thickened. My skin itched and a strange sharp scent filled my nose. Distracted, I stumbled over a couple syllables, but soon found my rhythm again. Was that something burning? I was galloping toward the last paragraph, when suddenly a cloud of smoke and fire exploded in front of me. I yelped and fell over backward. My head smacked against the wall, and my vision went dark. I couldn't see anything but white and red sparks jiggling in front of my eyes. There was a buzzing noise inside my skull that made me think of mosquitoes. Someone talking?

That someone seized my elbow and dragged me to my feet. "You mispronounced the third and thirty-second phrases."

I blinked. My vision cleared.

Mā mī. Oh, no.

My mother, tiny, whisper-thin Mā mī, who reminded me of a ghost dragon, the way she studied me so coolly. My mouth turned dry as she continued to gaze at me, her expression unreadable, while all around the magic flux sparkled and fizzed.

Right when I thought I might faint, Mā mī recited something in a peculiar language that sounded like a kettle hissing. The radio sputtered into silence, and a metallic smell permeated the room. I still didn't dare to move. My mother's gaze flicked over my ruined clothes, the mess of worksheets, the splotches of ink over walls and floor and bookshelves. Silently, she plucked the scroll from my hands. It obediently curled into a tight coil, and the ribbon slithered back into place, tying itself into a knot.

Mā mī uttered another incomprehensible phrase. Electric fire rippled through the air. With a loud *pêng*, all the ink disappeared. My mother held out her hand. The (dead, stuffed) griffin shook itself into life and skittered down the shelves to perch on her wrist. My mother scratched it behind its feathered ears, and its flat stone eyes narrowed to slits in contentment.

Only dead things felt safe around my mother, I thought.

She still hadn't said anything. I coughed to clear my throat. "I'm sorry for the mess, Mā mī. I'll finish the worksheets before dinner."

Mā mī nodded. She gave the griffin an absentminded kiss on its beak and set it upon the closest shelf. It shook out its feathers (plus a quantity of dust) and clambered back up to the top, where it curled once around and went still.

I expected my mother to shout. Or deliver one of those scary lectures about how her worthless street-rat son was bound for a misty hell. She did neither, and that made me nervous.

"Yún should come back soon," I said hesitantly. Mentioning Yún often made her smile.

Mā mī just nodded again and set her basket into its usual cubbyhole behind the counter. (Chen had wisely disappeared, leaving behind just a faint piggy odor.) Still not talking, she headed through the curtained doorway, into the shop's back rooms. A minute later, I heard the faint *ting* of metal from the kitchen, then water gurgling.

The curtains drifted slowly in the invisible breeze of her passage. I stared at them for a long moment, not really taking in what was going on. Deep inside my skull, an itch told me Chen had not completely left, but even he was too scared, or too surprised, to do more.

Not sure what to expect, I checked Mā mī's shopping basket. Except for a bottle of fish sauce and three packets of chewing tobacco, it was empty.

What do you think happened? I said.

You better ask her, Chen replied.

So much for my brave pig-companion.

I pushed the curtains aside. They swirled around me, ruffling against the back of my head, and enveloping me in soft shadows. I was in the main storeroom for our shop, where we kept all our supplies for classroom exercises, my mother's experiments, and the potions we sometimes brewed up for special customers. The air smelled strange and familiar, a mixture of strong herbs and black pepper, of soap from the morning mopping, of powdered metals and other rare ingredients. Hsin and several other cats napped here, keeping an erratic watch for mice. Ahead, another set of curtains marked the doorway into the kitchen, while a pair of winding stairs led to our upper floors.

I drew a deep, unsatisfying breath and headed into the kitchen.

Mā mī sat at the pockmarked old wooden table. She held a measuring spoon filled with tea leaves in one hand, in midmovement from transferring the leaves from the canister into her favorite blue teapot. The kettle sat on its grating over the coal fire; puffs of steam added to the miserable heat, but Mā mī didn't seem to notice. She had a distracted expression on her face, as though she studied something very far away.

"Market closed?" I asked.

Mā mī nodded. "Everything closed early today."

Everything?

I waited for my mother to explain, but she didn't.

"A holiday?" I said, helpfully. Royal visitors from kingdoms all throughout the mountains had crowded into Lóng City this past month—something about trade negotiations—and the king had scheduled numerous banquets and festivals to entertain them. The shops often closed early for the big celebrations.

But Mā mī was shaking her head. "The king . . ." She

stopped and rubbed a hand over her eyes, a gesture I had not seen since my father died years ago.

I was a child, almost a baby. How could I remember?

You did, you do, Chen said softly, though no one could hear us. *Children always remember.*

Even so, it had been ten years. . . .

My mother went on. "The king fell ill this morning. They believe he will not live beyond a week. They've sent for Princess Lian."

So many replies clattered through my brain. The king. Lian. My friend. She must be worried. Or scared. Those were not subjects I could discuss with my mother. Finally, I asked, "How?"

Mā mī set the spoon down on the table and frowned in its direction. I had the feeling she wasn't seeing the spoon or the table any more than she saw me right now. She said, "If you listen to the bazaar rumors, he fell by attack from angry spirits unleashed by this wretched heat. Most likely it was simply from age and overeating. He is an old man, you know. And he misses his daughter."

I knew that. I also knew it was my fault that Lian was far away in Phoenix City. *And now her father is dying.*

"I am thinking I should suspend classes," was my mother's next unsettling announcement.

"Close the shop?" My voice squeaked up.

She gave me a sharp look, almost like usual. "Not entirely. You and Yún shall have your lessons. But the tutoring can wait. A week or two, not more. Things should be decided by then."

Things? Like the king dying?

The teakettle rattled. Mā mī pushed herself to standing—stiffly—and fetched it from its hook. "You need not finish the worksheets," she said quietly, as she poured the boiling water over the leaves. "Go. Find your friends. Just come back by nightfall."

I stared at her, not believing what I heard or saw. Mā mī telling me to goof off? Mā mī acting quiet and bothered by what went on in that "golden egg crate they call a palace"? I waited another minute, but she never glanced in my direction. She rifled through the cabinet and extracted a honey pot, which she set beside her cup. My mother never took honey, not that I remembered. She liked her tea strong and bitter. Like her.

Unnerved by all the strangeness, I backed through the

curtains into the dimly lit corridor, where Chen waited. He'd taken a smaller form, the size of a formidable cat. His bristles stood out in worry.

I'm going out, I whispered.

He tilted his head.

She told me to, I added.

Chen made a soft, pig-whistle noise. *Do you want company?*

I . . . I don't know yet.

He nodded. *I will listen for you, then.*

I turned the shop sign to CLOSED and headed down to the Golden Market. It was the oddest walk I'd ever taken through Lóng City. Sure, there were festivals where the shops closed early, but that usually meant people thronged the streets, laughing and dancing and buying grilled kebabs or bowls of rice and curry from street vendors. And in the main squares, the public radio speakers always played loud old-time music, while jugglers tossed batons and acrobats flipped around in heart-stopping handsprings.

Today, the streets were quiet and empty. In the bazaar itself, the noodle shops had closed their shutters, and their brightly colored awnings were rolled away. One scrawny mutt lounged in the shade, panting. An old man swept the steps in front of his house. He stared at me as I passed by.

Two or three kids wandered around, with confused expressions. Probably their parents had told them to go play, too.

I took a roundabout path to the nearest wind-and-magic lift. Iron shutters blocked the counter. Chains hung across the entryway, and a hand-brushed sign informed me the lifts weren't running. A big placard with an arrow pointed at the stone stairs nearby.

Seven hundred years ago, Wei Lóng, our first king, had ordered staircases built all over the city as part of its defense. He wanted to make sure his soldiers could always reach every corner and terrace of Lóng City, even if the wind-and-magic lifts stopped working. Whenever a king or queen expanded the city, they added another flight, or reinforced the existing ones. It was a fine accomplishment—one I could appreciate better when I wasn't trudging up those same stairs in the lingering heat of a late summer's day.

There were six flights between me and the top of the city. Guard posts marked every landing, and every intersection with a major boulevard. Some of those guards stared at me as I passed, their electronic eyes whirring as they recorded my image. I stared back, scowling.

I reached the topmost terrace, then bent over, wheezing. Behind me stood the city's outermost wall. More architecture. Above that the mountain shot up another *li* to a snow-rimmed peak.

Once I regained my breath, I scrambled up the wall, using chinks and knobs as handholds, until I reached a narrow ledge. There, I settled onto my perch and braced my feet in two handy niches below. A nest of ants, disturbed by my arrival, swarmed away in all directions. The air smelled of dirt and pine and a rank scent that spoke of mice and beetles and magical creatures.

Lóng City spread over the mountainside in steps and tumbles and folds. From here I could see the Golden Market, the Pots-and-Kettles Bazaar, the warehouse district where my old gang liked to meet, and off to one side, its fat towers shining bright and yellow in the late afternoon sun, the king's palace.

I slid out my phone and stared at it unhappily. How many weeks had it been since I talked with my friends? More than I wanted to admit. Gan worked in his uncle's stables and attended a special academy for the king's guards. Jing-mei spent her days flirting or buying expensive clothes and trendy gadgets. Fun, but she and Gan argued all the time, him saying she wasted her money, her saying he'd turned into a big, ugly stick. And Danzu had started up his own gang, but there were strange rumors about what that gang was up to.

What about Lian?

My fingers hovered over the keys. The talk-phone was the princess's gift to me after our adventure, and she had coded it with her personal number. She didn't give that number to many. Me, Yún, a handful of others. Ordinary talk-phones needed a land connection, which you could find in any tea or noodle shop; mine was different. Special connectors drew the magic flux into a knot at the talk-phone's receptor port. More wires and resistors translated the flux into a braided current, strong enough to carry voices to the nearest transmitter tower.

But if Gan was busy, Lian would be ten times busier, arranging for her long journey home. In spite of the baking sun, I shivered. Autumn rains would make travel difficult through the mountains. An early snowstorm would make it dangerous, if not impossible. The Guild Council had to be nervous to send for Lian now.

As I tucked the talk-phone into its pouch, I noticed a dark smudge on my wrist. Ink. And just underneath my sleeve, where I might not notice it right away. A quick survey of my clothes showed presentable trousers above my knees, spatters of ink below. When I wiped at my forehead, my hand came away stained. No wonder those guards had stared.

I muttered some bad words. *Can you help me?* I asked Chen.

But either Chen couldn't, or he had stopped listening, because I heard no answer.

Or maybe he thinks he already has helped me.

Inside everyone, the scholars said, there existed a quiet place, where everything was possible. The old wizards, the magic workers who first climbed the mountains to commune with gods, must have known about it. They were able to work miracles. All I wanted was to clean my face and hands. With a whispered apology to those old and holy priests, I closed my eyes and recited the spell from Chen's scroll.

". . . from east to west and north to south, we the unworthy call upon the sunbird and dragon to bring purity to these quarters. . . ."

I recited the spell, taking care over the stresses and the pronunciation. As I spoke the last word, the air went taut for one long, silent moment. Then . . .

Magic snapped and crackled over my skin, which felt raw, as though a fire burned too close. The air rippled bright and tense, like the moment before lightning strikes. I drew a breath, tasted the strong scent of incense on the back of my tongue. Only when the smell faded away did I open my eyes. With a leaping pulse, I saw the ink had vanished. My skin and my clothes were clean and soft, shining with a residual brightness, which even now was trickling away.

So. I have worked my first spell by myself.

I felt strange. Like something had dissected me, plucked my feelings outside the shell of my body. For a time, I could think of nothing except this peculiar sensation. Then my thoughts wandered back to Lian and her father the king, and from there to my own father, dead these past ten years. When my thoughts returned to the now and here, I noticed the sun was dipping toward the horizon. Soon it would be twilight, and the watch-demons would swarm from their lairs to patrol the streets.

I clambered down from my perch and loped homeward.

Mā mī had locked herself in her private workroom. In the kitchen, I found soup, rice, and tea warming over the grate. Yún had left a note for Mā mī propped upon the counter. She had come and gone, apparently, while I was out.

Kai?

Chen's gruff whisper sounded inside my skull.

Not now, I answered.

I dumped the soup and rice outside for Old Man Kang's chickens, then stacked the dishes in our sink and went to bed.

2

THE KING DIDN'T DIE, BUT HE DIDN'T GET BETTER.

After a while, the shops reopened their doors, and the craftspeople and street vendors and other common folk returned to their work. As the old saying goes, it's the heart that grieves, not the stomach, and without business, we would all starve. But it wasn't the same as before. Most of the tea shops closed early, the temples held prayers twice daily for the king's health, and the city bells were wrapped in cloth by their keepers.

Most important, at least to me, my mother had not reopened her tutoring shop.

Unfortunately, that didn't mean I was free of lessons.

"Students, attend."

Mā mī stood behind a lectern in the shop's drafty classroom, just like always, as though nothing had changed. As though she had not wiped tears from her eyes ten days before. Yún and I both dipped our brushes in our ink bottles and waited, ready to take down her words.

"Man is within the *chi*, the *chi* is within the man. From heaven and earth down to the myriad creatures below the soil, there is not one thing that does not require *chi* in order to live."

Yún bent over her notepaper and wrote swiftly—down stroke, cross stroke, swooping stroke, and dot—small, perfect characters that marched down, then up the page. She had changed a lot since our street-rat days. She wore clothes bought new from Lóng City tailors, not begged from servants in rich houses, and she'd moved from that tiny set of rooms into a real house along with her mother and aunt. But it was more than that. She spent all her free hours reading dusty old books or memorizing lists of herbs and compounds and all the other useless things my mother gave us to learn.

One lock of her hair had worked loose and curled around to tickle her cheek. With hardly a pause, Yún tucked the lock behind her ear and kept writing. One last dot, one last line and she glanced up. I quickly turned back to my blank paper.

"Kai-my-son, have you done with the writing?"

Mā mī's tone was dry.

"Almost." I dashed off three columns that might or might not have had anything to do with her lecture.

Yún gave a tiny smile, dimpling her cheeks.

"And do not copy from your classmate," Mā mī added. "Listen and transcribe the words upon your heart and mind, as well as the paper, as Wu Cheng the philosopher writes. To continue, my students . . ."

Off she went, reciting page after page from some old text about the parallels between *chi* and blood and air, and how knowledge of the body aided the student with the *chi*, which everyone knew was another word for magic flux.

Or at least, that's how it sounded to me. Most likely Mā mī would announce a surprise test, and insist we recite the words exactly. That was the main reason I was flunking both advanced calculus and magical philosophy. Well, that and she subtracted points for illegible handwriting. If she couldn't read it, she said it didn't count.

You could practice your penmanship, Chen offered, speaking quickly. (Our spirit companions were not supposed to talk with us during class.)

I do practice, I replied.

A faint squeal. A loud crack. Chen vanished.

Attend, said a familiar voice inside my head, while out

loud, my mother's lecture continued ". . . but people use the *chi* every day and do not understand it . . ."

Damn straight, I thought, struggling to keep up. At one point, I shot a glance at Yún. She pretended to ignore me, but her eyes were bright with amusement as her brush skimmed across the page. Maybe she'd let me read her notes, just this once. That wasn't exactly copying . . . more like refreshing my memory.

Just as my hand cramped up, the clock chimed the hour. Yún made one last dot and waited. I scribbled the last few characters, trying not to drop my brush. Mā mī surveyed us, her lips pursed, as though considering another hour of misery for us.

"Students dismissed," she said at last. "Kai, you will take the second afternoon shift of watching the store. Three o'clock. Remember you must also review our accounts this evening. Please consider that when you arrange your studies for today."

I nodded, as though I always planned my studies.

"And Yún. You will take first afternoon shift. Please review the inventory against this list. Mark the items we need and provide a written account of the cost."

She handed over a tightly wound scroll. Yún tucked it into

her pocket and made a sitting-bow, her face wiped clean of anything but obedience. *Hypocrite*, I thought. I choked back a snort before my mother could suspect it, and made my own sitting-student bow. Mā mī's eyes narrowed with suspicion. She said nothing, however, merely swept from the room with the dignity of a queen.

Yún screwed the cap onto her ink bottle and began to stow her books and writing materials in her satchel.

I stuffed my own books into my satchel. "Say, Yún?"

Her eyebrows lifted, reminding me of swift elegant question marks. "Yes?"

"I, um, was wondering . . ."

". . . if you could read my notes?"

"Well, I thought I could . . ."

"Kai." She made my name sound like a sigh. "You know what your mother said."

"She said *no copying*. Not *no reading*—Oh, never mind."

I slung my satchel over my shoulder and stalked from the classroom. Mā mī stood behind the counter at the front of the shop, paper and basket in hand, frowning. Before she could say anything, I pounded up the stairs to my bedroom and flung my satchel into one corner. Just in time, I stopped myself from letting out a howl.

Last year. Everything had changed since then. Last year Yún and I had been friends. Last year we'd run pranks in the marketplace. We'd plotted together how to win the king's challenge. It was Yún who tricked Mā mī into giving us the magical spells we needed. And it was Yún who stood next to me when we faced down watch-demons and ghost dragons. Sure, Lian was with us, too, but it was Yún I remembered.

But Yún had turned into Little Miss Proper. She had no time for pranks, only her studies. Even worse, she lectured me the same way Mā mī did. I wasn't smart enough, steady enough. Oh, sure, she didn't say those words exactly, but telling me I had "lots of potential" was just another way of saying I was too stupid right now.

Ai-ya, how I wish we'd never won that stupid reward. We wouldn't be friends with Lian, but at least we'd be friends with each other.

Chen materialized next to me, large and spiky. *You forgot a few things downstairs.*

He set my ink bottle (capped) and a pile of smudged notes on my desk.

Thank you, I said through gritted teeth.

You also forgot to say good-bye to Yún.

Who cares? She doesn't.

Chen grunted in a way that could mean "you stupid boy" or "I know lots more than you do but I'm not telling." Pigs were obnoxious like that, and Chen the worst of all.

Why don't you call Gan? he asked after a few moments.

He's busy, I snapped.

Not today. Tao says Gan went on night shift last week.

Tao was Gan's ox-spirit companion.

Cursed nannies, I thought. Always gossiping about their humans behind their backs. But I punched Gan's number into my talk-phone anyway.

Fizzle-sizzle-clickety-click.

Gan answered on the second chime. "Kai."

His voice was deeper, quicker than last year.

"How did you know—"

"New talk-phone with ID circuitry," Gan said. "Last week. Standard issue."

Aha. That meant he'd passed his entrance exams for the king's guards. Trust Gan not to mention it. Well, knowing how the royal wizards spiked the lines regularly, we were better off talking in face-time. "Uptown shiny hotspot," I said. "If you have time."

"A couple hours, sure," Gan said. "They put me on night shift duty last week. What about the others?"

Meaning Jing-mei and Danzu.

"Yeah. But you better call them."

Before he could ask about Yún, I clicked off.

Old habits are hard to rub clean, as the saying goes. Even if we weren't a real gang any more, we still used our codewords. "Uptown shiny hotspot" meant the new tea shop in the palace square. It had silk screens playing music videos from local bands, and it served rare teas and snacks imported from the Phoenix Empire and beyond. That was another thing that had changed between last year and this one—we all had plenty of money.

Speaking of which, I tucked some bills and coins into my shirt and smoothed back my hair.

Chen appeared in a fuzzy pig-shaped cloud and grinned at me. *Pretty.*

"Shut up," I said. "And move your ugly snout from my mirror."

His only reply was a snorting laugh before he popped out of sight.

The wind-and-magic lifts were running on half schedules, but even so, most of the front cars were empty. I tossed a ten-yuan piece at the fat counterman, hopped over the railing and into the front seat. A whistle shrieked. I buckled myself in just in time. Magic crackled around the lift. A second whistle split the air. The next minute, the cars dropped down two heart-stopping levels to Lóng City's main terrace.

An attendant handed me a double-strength chai—standard issue for all express passengers so we could recover our heartbeat. I slugged down the cup and staggered through the gates into the main square. The tea shop stood on the corner between the palace and the city's largest avenue. Jing-mei and Gan had taken over the biggest table by the ceiling-high glass window. Jing-mei played some complicated solitaire game, while Gan watched from half-lidded eyes. Two miniature teapots and matching cups were already in use.

I slid into the seat next to Gan. "No marble eyes?"

Royal guards had special surgery that gave them artificial eyes with all kinds of wiring and special connections into the palace's magic currents. Gan shook his head and gave me a slow amused smile. "Not yet. Check again in seven years."

Jing-mei flipped her cards into a new pattern. She wore a filmy blue tunic that glittered with sparks of magic flux pulled in from the surrounding air.

"Nice threads," I told her.

She rolled her eyes. "That slang is so old, it died before my ancestors did."

"It was a joke."

"An awful one. Hey, Deming."

She beckoned to a passing waiter, a sleek young man with a shaved head and spectacles that glittered with magic and electricity. "More ginger tea," she said. "Oh, and some of those pepper pastries you told me about."

The waiter blinked. Bright specks flowed over his lenses. I'd heard of the new micro-receptor-transmitter technology, but I'd never seen it before outside the royal palace, and even there it was new stuff. With a smile both polite and condescending at the same time, Deming glided away to fill our order. Jing-mei shuffled her cards anew. "He's their best waiter," she said. "We're lucky to get his service."

Gan snorted. Jing-mei shot him a sharp look. "It's true."

"I never said it wasn't."

Jing-mei's mouth stretched into a thin, unhappy smile, but all she said was, "You said you liked those pastries."

Deming returned with a tray stacked with cups, teapots, and a platter bearing small white pastries. They were fancy ones, dusted with red and black powder, and arranged to look like Lóng City's highest bell tower. I snagged one from the top, ignoring Deming's pained expression at my lack of appreciation for art.

"So, where's Danzu?" I asked.

"He's coming, but he might be late," Gan said. "He's checking over a special shipment."

"What kind of shipment?"

Gan shrugged. Jing-mei glanced away. All those stories about Danzu and his new gang being smugglers were true, then. Embarrassed, I stuffed the pastry in my mouth. Deming had continued to hover around our table. When I scowled at him, he just sniffed.

That's when I realized why they were called *pepper* pastries.

Fire exploded inside my mouth. I choked, spraying pastry bits all over the table. Jing-mei poured a cup of ginger tea and emptied it down my throat. I swallowed and wiped the tears from my eyes. Oh, joy. Everyone in the shop was staring at us. How nice.

Jing-mei poured a second cup. I waved it away. "No more," I croaked. "I'm fine. Thanks."

She frowned, but then glanced up. I followed her gaze to see Danzu, grinning at all of us. How much had he seen? Too much, I guessed.

"You haven't changed at all," he said. He dropped into the seat opposite me, still grinning.

I grinned back, though it made my teeth hurt. "Hi, Goat Boy." Danzu's companion spirit was a scrawny goat with mismatched horns.

Danzu made fake grunting noises at me.

Gan grabbed my arm before I could smack Danzu. "Shut up. No fighting." Under his breath he added, "I wish Yún were here. She could make you both behave. Why didn't you invite her?"

"She was *busy*, okay?" My gut cramped from guilt and the pepper pastries. I drank another cup of ginger tea, slowly. "When she's not studying, my mother gives her extra work in the shop."

"Really? I heard your mā mī closed the shop."

I hesitated. "Not completely. We're doing some astrology readings for old customers. Some special conjuration orders. Things like that."

"*Hü.*" Danzu studied me with a speculative look. "Does that mean you're doing magic?"

Remembering the ink disaster, I shook my head. No use talking about working magic myself, all alone on the city walls. That was just an accident. "Mā mī does the real magic. Yún and I do inventory and accounting books. And lessons. I think I might die doing lessons."

Jing-mei snickered. "I still don't know why you signed on as an apprentice. You hate that stuff."

"Oh, but I love my health," I assured her solemnly.

"Oh, yeah," Danzu said. "If he refused, his mā mī might lay a curse on him, turn him into a gargoyle. Not that being a gargoyle would hurt your looks," he added.

He grinned. I grinned back. This time my teeth didn't hurt so much. Gan just shook his head. Then Jing-mei started a long story about some old rich merchant who bought magic infused shirts because he wanted to impress his beautiful young wife. Gan followed with stories about early days in the academy and pranks they had played on their officers. It wasn't exactly like old times. No Yún, for one thing. But the talk itself was good, and underneath, I could hear Chen's snorfling and the faintest replies from Jing-mei's monkey-spirit, Gan's ox, and Danzu's miserable goat.

"So," Danzu said, pouring more tea into his cup, "what is going on with the king?"

Gan was just reaching for the last pork dumpling. He paused and gave Danzu a suspicious look. "He's ill."

"I know that, stone-face. But I hear rumors. Thought you might have the real story."

"Me? I'm just a grunt in the academy."

"Not anymore. I heard you graduated last week."

"So? That only makes me a different kind of grunt."

Danzu gave a quiet chuckle. "You are one careful Ox Boy. Okay, forget I asked. I was just curious."

My skin itched, uncomfortable at how the mood had changed so quickly. Jing-mei must have felt the same way, because she scrunched her face. "We're all curious, Danzu. You should know that."

"And what makes you think we know more than you do?" Gan said.

"I *don't* think so. But I ask, just in case. The more I know, the better I can figure plans for some special deals."

"Smuggling," I said, without thinking.

Danzu made a rude gesture. "No."

"Then what kind of special deals do you mean?" Gan said. "You don't talk to us anymore." His glance slid toward Jing-mei. "At least you don't talk to some of us. All we can do is guess."

"Well, you guessed wrong." Danzu stood up and dropped a bag onto the table. It landed with a noisy *clank*. "Here. My treat. See you later. Maybe."

He stomped out the door and slammed it shut.

I blew out a breath. So did Jing-mei. Gan stared out the

window. I followed his glance, and saw Danzu emerge from the tea shop. An older man and two young men crossed the square to join him. They all conferred a few moments, then melted away into the crowds.

"I have heard stories about the king," Gan said softly. "But I didn't want to—I wasn't sure."

Jing-mei laid a hand over his, then plucked it back and started fiddling with her cards, shuffling them in different patterns, over and over. I watched them both and thought how our good hour was just an illusion. The truth was, our gang had broken apart, and none of us felt comfortable talking about anything but fluff.

"I heard . . ." I said tentatively.

Both their gazed flicked up to mine.

I cleared my throat and tried again. "Mā mī told me yesterday that things weren't good in the palace. I don't know where she heard it, but she says the court physicians can't figure out what's wrong. They bled him, stuffed him with pills, read his latest astrology charts. Nothing helps. Even the potions cooked up by the royal wizards did zilch."

"That's what I heard, too," Jing-mei whispered. She started another shuffle, stopped, and set the pack aside. "And it started so quick—right in the middle of a private talk with those tilt-nosed muckety-mucks from Lang-zhou City."

"Diplomats," Gan murmured.

"Same thing," Jing-mei said.

She was right. Lang-zhou City was the biggest and richest of all the mountain kingdoms. Some claimed it was too far into the lower hills to count. No matter. Lang-zhou City guarded the main passes into the Phoenix Kingdom. Anyone who wanted to transport goods into or out of the mountains had to use their roads, just like anyone who wanted to trade with central and northern kingdoms had to go through ours.

Gan cleared his throat. "They say some of the nobles are plotting—I mean, planning what might happen if the princess doesn't return in time."

"She will," I insisted. "You know Lian. She's probably on her way now."

Again, their gazes swerved up at the same time. Gan glanced at Jing-mei, then said, "Didn't you hear? Lian hasn't answered her talk-phone, or the letters, or—"

"—it's like she's vanished," Jing-mei said. "And that's why the nobles are, well—"

"—plotting," Gan finished for her. "There's talk about problems with the magic flux, or the empire being so far away, but the royal wizards have private lines for urgent communications. Besides, we haven't had any trouble with magic since the Interregnum Wars, and those were three hundred years ago."

My mouth went dry. I knew Lian. She'd never run away from her duties, no matter how terrible. Sure, she had fought her father to study at the Phoenix University, but that was only so she could learn how to rule properly. Remembering her face as she stared down the king of the ghost dragons, I shivered.

"Have you talked to her?" Jing-mei asked me.

"No. I thought she'd be too busy."

Too busy for a street rat who failed advanced calculus. Maybe Gan could read my thoughts, or Chen had a word with Tao, because he shook his head. "Never mind all that. Call her. Just in case. She'd want to hear from her friends."

Hü. I found that hard to believe. Still, I tapped Lian's private number into my talk-phone.

Click-click-tick-a-tick.

The magic flux hissed loudly as it switched over to connect-mode. Then a flat, mechanical voice announced, "Sorry. No such number."

OUR PARTY BROKE up quickly after that. No one wanted to speculate about Lian or why her number no longer worked. We paid our bill from Danzu's stash, including a hefty tip for Deming, and silently scattered our separate ways. Me, I took the long route home, walking instead of taking the wind-and-magic lifts, and arrived just as the tower bells chimed half past three o'clock.

Yún waited for me behind the front counter. Hsin the queen and one of her sisters dozed off to one side. A thick book lay open in front of Yún. Its pages were crammed full of old-fashioned, hand-brushed characters—one of the ancient histories Mā mī had special-ordered from a northern university. One of our assignments?

"You're late," Yún said. "And I thought you had homework."

I was still scared about Lian and wanted to yell that my homework was none of Yún's business. But Yún looked cranky and tired, so I swallowed hard and shook my head. "Sorry. Any new business?"

"Two astrology readings and one Elixir of Eternal Happiness." She shuddered. "I don't know why anyone would order something that nasty."

The Elixir of Eternal Happiness was our shop's best-selling product, brewed from licorice, black pepper, and fermented rice—plus whatever magic kick Mā mī added that week. Like Yún said, it was nasty stuff.

"People are strange, that's all I know," I said. "Is my mother back yet?"

Yún frowned. "No. She said something about visiting the herb markets. Here." She handed me a sheaf of papers. "Tell your mother I finished the inventory. Here's what we need for restocking. I've marked the items we can buy in the city markets. The rest we need to order special from merchants up north or from the Phoenix Empire."

I scanned the top sheet. Lots of items had checkmarks, but lots more had none. "We need all that?"

Yún rolled her eyes. "What do you think? I have better things to do than make these things up."

"It was just a question."

"So nicely asked, too. By the way, I hope you had fun with Gan and Jing-mei and Danzu. Thank you so *very* much for inviting me."

"You were *busy*."

"And no one can ever change their plans to later."

"They might if you—"

I stopped myself before I said anything truly unforgiveable. Yún still carried her knife from our gang days, and she knew how to use it. Besides, her eyes were shining. If she didn't stab me, she might start crying.

We both glared at each other instead.

"I have to get home," Yún said. "Auntie needs me."

She stomped out the front door. I threw the bolts and flipped the sign around to CLOSED. BACK SOON. Mā mī would peel the skin from my butt for closing early, but it wasn't as though clients were banging on our door. A part of me wondered why she needed so many new magical ingredients, but my head hurt too much to think about it.

With a sigh, I shooed Hsin from her perch and pulled out the account books. They made a huge boring heap on the counter. *But I promised,* I told myself.

You didn't promise, Chen said. *She ordered you to.*

Where have you been? I asked.

Around. Looking in corners and holes.

Chen, being cryptic again. I set about sorting through our students' accounts. By the time I finished with them, my brain would start working more clearly. Maybe.

Once I settled into the routine of checking numbers, the hours slid past like oil. Yún had turned the radio station to something dull and meditative, which suited me just fine. Once or twice, someone rapped at the front door, then cursed loudly when an invisible pig poked his snout into their backs.

When I couldn't read the numbers anymore, I switched on the wall lamps. Brown shadows spilled away from the light. Outside, the skies were violet and shading into gray. A few stars speckled the clear skies of early autumn, but I noticed a fringe of clouds by the horizons. Soon the rains would start.

Very slowly, my brain clicked over a few key thoughts.

Dark. Watch-demons. Mā mī.

Once the sun set, and twilight poured over the horizon, the royal guards released the watch-demons of Lóng City to patrol the streets. They were better than any human sentries, and twice as dangerous. Only the bravest thieves dared to venture out after dark. Most of them didn't survive. Yún and I had once, along with Princess Lian, but that was a different story.

I poked my head into the kitchen. "Mā mī?"

No one there.

My heart thumping double-time, I ran up the stairs to the second floor, where my mother had a private workroom. No one answered my knock. I pressed the latch down, sure it would be locked.

It wasn't. The door swung open onto a dark and empty room.

All Mā mī's dire warnings echoed through my brain as I stepped inside. *No trespassing, Kai-my-son. Unless you like a three-year itch.*

No itch. No spells at all, so far as I could tell. Just a shadow-dark room made strange with abandoned vials and beakers and the white-dusted coals of a dying fire. That pricked my curiosity. Why did Mā mī need a fire so early in autumn? I lit a candle and scanned for more clues.

The vials were all empty. The beakers were coated with a thin silvery residue that emanated magic, both potential and unleashed. Now I knew where all those special ingredients had gone. Dozens of empty boxes and canisters and stoppered vials littered her desk. Among them, I found stacks of scribbled sheets and astrology readings, but none of them made sense.

By now I was scared. Sure, my mā mī was stronger and fiercer than any human I'd known. Maybe even fiercer than a watch-demon or two. But never, ever, had she failed to come home at night, without leaving word.

Vanished. Just like Lian.

I hurried from the workroom, across the landing, to her small bedroom. It was empty, too.

A nudge at my arm recalled me. The griffin hovered in midair, its golden wings glittering in the faint light from the hallway. When it saw it had my attention, it leapt on my shoulder.

"How did you get up here?" I asked.

It gave an odd keening sound and butted my head.

"Go on. You're dead."

The griffin nibbled at my ear. Just as you might expect for a pet chosen by my mother, it was not gentle.

"Ow! Okay, not quite dead."

It butted me again and keened. Cautiously, I scratched the griffin behind its ears. It gave a rough trill that sounded like a purr.

"What's the matter?" I said. "You miss her?"

The griffin tucked itself under my ear, its tail curled around my neck. Its feathers were cold and stiff, its tiny paws hot. I could feel its nervous heartbeat against my skin. For a dead thing, it was acting very much alive.

"It's okay," I whispered to the griffin. "She's just visiting a friend. She'll be back tomorrow."

I could only hope I wasn't lying.

3

Monsters swarmed through my dreams that night, making me twitch and shiver and sometimes bolt upright, positive that something was eating the flesh from my bones. Each time I woke up, I heard the whispery tolling of the temple bells. Softer still came an eerie, slithering noise, like fine, metallic chains being drawn over stones—the watch-demons making their rounds.

I had finally fallen into a blank, dreamless sleep when Old Man Kang's rooster sang out its morning cry. I buried my head under my pillow and groaned. The next minute, a weight thudded onto my back, driving the breath from my body. Four sharp points dug into my back.

Chen . . .

Chen jabbed me underneath my right arm—hard.

I yelped and twitched away. "Stop that! I'm not in the mood for any jokes."

A sharp jab in the sole of my left foot jerked me awake.

Chen, you stupid—

I threw off my bedclothes and sat up.

Chen crouched in the far corner of my bedroom, between the open door and my washstand. His spines were slanted back, his bristles, too, and he had an odd expression on his piggy face—as though he wanted to laugh but didn't know how, and besides he wasn't really in the mood. When he caught my eye, he tilted his head and stared pointedly at the foot of my bed.

There sat the griffin, chewing holes in the blanket.

"You," I growled. "Look, I told you—she's not here."

It shot me a disbelieving glare, then fastened its beak on a loose thread and yanked.

"Stop that!" I tried shooing it away.

It snapped at me and hissed. I flung my pillow. With a shrill cry, the griffin launched into flight, scattering feathers and dander and bits of blanket all over the room. It circled twice around, just missing my head, then soared out the open door.

I swiped the feathers and dirt from my face. My head felt thick, and my mouth tasted like old vinegar. My room smelled musty. I couldn't tell if that was the griffin or the clothes I'd dropped on the floor yesterday, before dropping myself into bed.

You look awful, Chen remarked.

Yeah, and I feel *awful.* I stumbled from the bed to my washbasin and splashed water over my head. Rinsed my mouth and spat out dust and feathers. I wondered if the griffin had been swimming in my washbasin. On second thought, I didn't want to know.

Is she back? I whispered to Chen.

No.

What about—

Gone. Then he added, *I checked everywhere. Nuó is gone, too.*

Nuó was Mā mī's companion spirit, a smoke-gray mountain cat. Nuó scared me even more than Mā mī did. She scared Chen, too. That Chen had deliberately gone looking for her meant he was truly worried by Mā mī's disappearance.

I pulled on last night's shirt and trousers and pounded down to Mā mī's bedroom. It was empty, of course. I'd known it would be, but scanning the room, swept clean just yesterday, and the blankets neatly tucked around the bed, I felt a pain tugging at my gut.

I told you she wasn't back. Yet.

I know. I just—

I swallowed hard. Chen made soft snuffling noises in my ear, as though I were a baby piglet that needed comforting.

Go away, I said. *I'm fine.*

I checked the workroom again. No change there either.

I hate nightmares that don't stop when you wake up.

In the kitchen, the sight of last night's dirty dishes (one plate, one teacup, not two) checked me harder than my mother's deserted workroom or bedroom. I spun around, ready to run and run until fright and anger bled away.

Chen blocked my path.

Eat first, he said. *Then we make plans.*

I'm not hungry.

He lowered his head and presented his tusks. *You will be.*

With Chen prodding and poking me along, I stacked the dirty dishes in the wash basin and filled the teakettle from the courtyard well. While I waited for that to boil, I fed the shop cats and cleaned out their sandboxes. The sun was well up before I finished. I brewed a full pot of tea and chewed on some leftover dried fish cakes from the pantry. There wasn't much else. Other than a few more packets of salted fish, our pantry was nearly empty. I'd have to visit the farmer's markets soon, however, or I'd be eating dust.

(Only if my mother doesn't come back.)

(She will.)

(But when?)

A small hard skull butted my hand. The griffin.

The flat stone eyes gleamed black, and its metallic feathers glittered in the thin yellow light. When it saw it had my attention, it opened its beak and keened. All the cats scattered at the noise.

"You can't be hungry," I said.

With a quick dart, it nipped my thumb.

"Ow!" I sucked at the bite and tasted blood. Were there such things as vampire griffins?

The griffin keened again. I tossed a spare fish cake in its direction. It pounced and tore the cake into bits with its beak. Being dead and stuffed didn't seem to stop it from wanting meals. Or attention or comfort, I mentally added, when it butted my hand again, demanding a scratch behind its feathered ears. I wondered what kind of magic Mā mī had worked upon it.

Thinking of my mother made my stomach churn. I tossed the griffin my last fish cake and bolted up the stairs to my room. There I picked up the leather scroll case with my special certificate, proclaiming me to be a prince of the streets.

On second thought, I stopped long enough to scribble down a note for Yún, explaining that Mā mī had cancelled our classes for the day. She and I would be at the special import markets to order the exotic goods from Yún's list. Yún was to spend her free hours alone in the nearest temple, practicing meditation.

A faint odor warned me that Chen watched over my shoulder.

You should tell Yún, he said. *Or she'll worry.*

She'd worry more if I told her the truth.

She is your friend. Friends tell each other the truth.

Easy for him to say. Yún would only have questions. So did I. I wanted to ask mine first.

I galloped back down the stairs and flipped around the sign that said CLOSED UNTIL FURTHER NOTICE. PRESS RED BUTTON TO LEAVE A VOICE MESSAGE FOR EMERGENCIES. Then I locked all the doors and windows, dumped the new dirty dishes into the washbasin, and poured the remaining hot water over them. Outside, I sealed Yún's message into an envelope labeled YÚN: READ ME and stuffed it into a crack where she would find it.

Make another sweep for Nuó, I told Chen.

Where are you going? Chen's tone sounded more anxious than usual.

To the palace.

"PLEASE LET YOUR Highness be assured we shall exert ourselves mightily . . ."

The bland young officer sitting across from me was using all the pretty phrases he must have learned in bureaucrat school. More, I thought, because I'd come waving around my special certificate. In spite of the official seals, and the fancy wires and circuits embedded in the scroll's leather container, the business of me being a prince was all a big ugly lie, and we both knew it, but the young man was good at his job, so he didn't say anything.

And that's the problem, I thought, scowling at him. He wasn't saying *anything*, just the same-old same-old excuses.

His name was Meng Li Guo, and he was the tenth official I'd visited today. Like all the others, he was dressed in sober gray, with the screaming dragon insignia embroidered over his heart, and except for an honorific here and there, his speech sounded the same as all his brother officials. I'd noticed that each time one handed me off to the next, it was always to a smaller room, with chairs more uncomfortable than the last. Now I perched on a rickety wooden stool in a cramped cubicle, on the second basement level of the palace wing dedicated to police and royal security. Meng Li Guo's eyes were an ordinary black, nothing like the mechanical eyes with wires and connectors you saw in the senior guards. That alone told me no one was taking me seriously.

I scowled and thumped a fist on his desk. "Right. Thank you. Very well. You *would* make every effort. Oh, except my mother is an ordinary old woman, and not some important noble in His Royal Majesty's court, so I should not express great surprise if you are unable to spare the guards or wizards to search for her."

The guard allowed himself a brief glare. However, he was an experienced diplomat, despite his youth, so he suppressed whatever curses rose into his throat. Instead, he coughed politely and referred to the papers on his desk. "You say you last spoke with your mother, the widow Shen Zōu, yesterday at twelve o'clock. You left her shop in the West Moon Wind District and spent several hours—"

"Two hours," I said, testily.

He smiled. Scribbled a notation on the paper. "Two

hours with various acquaintances, whose names are listed below . . .”

On he went, describing my pitiful morning and afternoon in more detail than I wanted to hear. But I listened hard, nevertheless, to make certain he had not omitted, or worse, altered, any details. Of course, I had not mentioned Danzu’s possible connection with smugglers, nor the speculations I shared with my friends about the king’s health and doings at court. Those didn’t matter. What mattered was that my mother had walked out one fine bright autumn afternoon and never returned.

“. . . and the second apprentice, one Yún Chang, informed you upon your return that your mother had departed at two o’clock, with the intention of visiting certain markets where one might obtain herbal and magical ingredients . . .”

I wanted to choke him, to make him talk faster, to find my mā mī *that instant*, but I knew throwing a temper tantrum wouldn’t accomplish anything.

So I squashed my impatience, and listened to the miserable toad assigned to handle my complaint. After ten hours of waiting in antechambers and shuffling through the palace corridors, I’d heard enough to realize the chief wizards and ministers were more concerned with troubles in court. Oh,

I didn't hear anything outright, just whispered innuendoes, and the names they used were all nicknames, which only insiders could recognize. Still, I knew the smell of rumors, and these all stank of intrigue.

At last, the young man finished off his report, signed it, and placed it under a coiled gray lamp. He pressed a button. Blue light flared, making me blink.

"Done," he said. "That will transmit the report to our outer guard posts. If you wish for regular updates on our progress, you will need to submit form number 34A-732, with appropriate identification and signatures, to the district oversight department." He eyed me with some doubt. "Or not. However, please be aware we have fulfilled our usual obligations for such a case. Extraordinary measures . . ."

". . . would require extraordinary commands." A phrase Princess Lian often quoted with a scowl. "Yes, I understand. Thank you."

Outside the palace, I released a long unhappy breath.

You were nice.

Chen, invisible, but very present.

I didn't want to be, I told him. *I wanted to throw bricks at his ugly face.*

But you did not.

I blew out another breath, no better, no easier than the first. *It wouldn't do Mā mī any good. Maybe I'll come back tomorrow. Be like water on stone.*

Chen grunted an indecipherable comment that had to be rude, or it wouldn't be Chen. Ignoring him, I trudged across the square to the nearest fountain and splashed handfuls of water over my hot and dusty face. All those hours in the palace had left me feeling dried up, like a withered prune, and it wasn't until I dunked my whole head in the fountain that I felt human again. A breeze made my wet skin prickle. It carried hints of wood smoke and pork roasting in a nearby kitchen. The stronger scent of pine and old frozen snow from the mountain tops. A hint of wet chill that spoke of the coming autumn rains.

I wiped the water from my eyes, only to get an unhappy surprise.

The public square in front of the palace was always crowded, but in the few moments I'd taken to wash, it had emptied out. Sunset burned bright red across the gray and white peaks above the city. Shadows flickered through the narrow streets. Night was fast approaching.

Hurry. I hear the demons are hungry these days, Chen said, before winking away himself.

I shook the water from my hair and jogged to the closest wind-and-magic lift. Just as I reached the counter, the temple bells rang out the hour. Immediately, the old hag behind the counter slammed down the shutter. At the same time, the warning whistle screeched, the gates snapped together, and the lift shot upward.

I cursed.

No reply from behind the shutter except a wheezing laugh. Well, she might have a room nearby, but I didn't. And I didn't care to spend the night in a cramped (and expensive) dark-time shelter. Without wasting any more curses on counter clerks, I jogged even faster toward the next covered passageway. Those wouldn't keep me safe from watch-demons either, but they did lead to the nearest entry into Lóng City's Hundred Sewers. Most people stayed out of the sewers, and not just for the usual reasons, but I had special privileges, courtesy of my adventures with Lian.

You just like the muck, Chen said.

Ignoring him, I levered the metal plate off to one side, then scrambled down the metal ladder.

Magic lamps clicked on as I landed on the stone platform at the bottom. Their light reflected off the damp brick walls, casting a sheen over the thick oily stream running down the center of the tunnel. My eyes watered from the stink. The old kings had built these sewers as escape routes, but that didn't stop them from being used for all the usual reasons, too.

A narrow ledge ran alongside the stream. I held my nose and set off at a trot, watching where I set my feet.

Once, I hadn't cared.

Once, I was a street rat.

Maybe not anymore.

On I jogged, my thoughts jumping between the old days and the new, how Jing-mei and Gan had changed, how Danzu hadn't, how I had been sent to younger and younger guards, in smaller and smaller rooms, as though they were trying to wear me out, or maybe they were distracted by all the plots and schemes inside the palace. Lian had told me that every glance meant six or ten or even a hundred different things. There were probably a gajillion hints I'd missed during those tedious interviews. . . .

A hiss, like a teakettle starting to boil, yanked me away from my thoughts. I stopped. My throat squeezed shut, as I remembered the last time I'd heard this same noise.

An enormous ghost dragon materialized in the tunnel. Its length coiled above and around and to either side, making the sewer walls appear wrapped in fog—a silvery fog patterned in scales, from the huge ones for belly and tail to thumb-size ones that lapped the dragon's narrow snout.

It wasn't just any ghost dragon. This was the king of ghost dragons, who ruled over his own subjects in a realm that existed alongside our human one of Lóng City. I had met him a year ago, when Lian and Yún and I were running from watch-demons and palace guards. He had granted me free passage throughout the Hundred Sewers, a rare favor, but seeing his great head a few feet from mine made my mouth paper dry.

"Your Majesty?" My voice came out in a whisper. I licked my lips and tried again. "Your Majesty?"

My friend is ill. He needs his daughter.

"Friend?" I croaked.

The ghost dragon's eyes narrowed to slits as he regarded me coldly. *Have you forgotten your king so quickly?*

My skin crawled at his otherworldly voice. I opened my mouth, but my voice refused more than a squeak.

Still glaring at me with those cold silvery eyes, the king ghost dragon uncurled one forepaw, pad upward. A seemingly innocuous gesture, but the ghost dragon's claws were longer than any executioner's sword. In terror, I flinched and started to babble like an idiot. "No, sir. Your Majesty. I haven't—I didn't—"

The ghost dragon huffed, cutting off my gibbering in a second. *See your king.*

He spoke a word in some strange harsh language. A strong metallic smell filled the air, and a bubble of light gathered between those terrible claws.

Still terrified, but curious now, I bent closer. Specks whirled over the bubble's surface. Gradually, it cleared, showing an image inside. Small figures darted about—palace servants in their liveries, the royal physicians and their attendants—everyone hurried in and out and around a richly appointed chamber. Everyone, that is, except one thin old man, who lay in the center of a vast bed. His hands rested limply on his chest, which rose and fell in slow shallow breaths. His eyes were like bruised plums in a pale sweating face.

My friend is dying, the ghost dragon whispered. The image faded. He folded his claws into a fist and breathed out a rattling sigh.

"Can you save him with magic?" I asked. Any ghost dragon could work magic, and surely, the king of them all—

I have tried. I cannot. There is a blank, a void, where the sickness eats at him.

The anguish in his voice made my chest ache in sympathy. "I'm sorry. I wish I could—"

He brushed away my concern with a gesture. *You must go to Phoenix City. You must find Princess Lian and tell her of her father's illness.*

"Me?" I squeaked.

He nodded. *You. The king is my friend, the princess is yours. You are the only one I can trust. Even the best of the king's ministers are taken up with plots and their own security. You must go. Find out what is wrong.*

I gulped, tried not to think about the ghost dragon's deadly whiskers, his terrible claws, his breath that could poison any human with excess magic, or so the legends claimed. "I can't go," I said. Then louder, "I'm sorry, I can't. Not with Mā mī missing."

Another faint wheezing, as though the dragon were laughing at my plight. He set both front paws upon the ground and leaned closer. Though it made me go stiff with terror, I did not flinch back.

You are stubborn, he observed, still wheezing. *Like your friend the princess.*

True enough, though I privately thought that Lian could win any contest if it came to stubbornness. Her and Yún.

The ghost dragon nodded, his whiskers swaying in counterpoint with his great head. *I shall look after your mā mī. I promise. Now go. Find the princess. Return as quickly as you may, if not sooner.*

Whenever had a ghost dragon needed a human's aid? I wondered, gazing upward into those luminescent eyes. Especially the king of ghost dragons? I nearly asked him that same question, then snapped my mouth shut. Lian was my friend. Besides, you didn't argue with ghost dragons, however large or small.

I bowed low before him. "I will leave tomorrow, Your Majesty."

4

EXCEPT I DIDN'T.

Oh, sure, the ghost dragon king had promised to look after Mā mī, but he never said anything about her tutoring shop. I didn't want to travel nine hundred *li* and back, just to have Mā mī feed me to the watch-dragons because I let her shop go to ruin—or to the tax collectors which, according to her, was the same thing.

I crouched in front of my mother's safe, where she kept her most important papers. Chen hovered off to one side, like a massive brown shadow. The griffin perched on the counter above my head, watching with a curious expression on its narrow, feathered face.

Are you sure this is a good idea? Chen asked.

Of course not. What a stupid question.

I squinted at the combination lock, then double-checked my conjuration workbook. If only I had taken Chen's advice and practiced my handwriting, this would be easier. Maybe.

After another double-check, I recited the simplest open-me spell on the page. Right away the air fizzed with magic flux. The room turned dark and ugly yellow lines squirmed over the safe. From behind me came the sound of someone chuckling to himself.

Chen . . .

Chen snorted. *Not my fault. That was your mother's protection spell.*

Right. I could believe that. I checked the next entry on the page. Another simple spell, one I'd learned on my own before I turned ten. Not one I expected my mother to use, but you could never tell. She always taught us the trickiest magic was the easiest to guess.

Two syllables into the spell, my ears popped and a thousand invisible fire ants swarmed over me, biting and nipping and stinging. I yelped and beat my clothes. The griffin screeched and vanished. Somewhere, an invisible Chen wheezed with laughter. I wanted to beat him, too, but I was too busy with the cursed ants.

The swarm vanished. I fell to my knees, like a string puppet dropped by its master.

Chen nosed me with his giant snout. I swatted at him, still angry. *I'm fine. Go away.*

She knows good magic, your mā mī. Do you want my help?

I eyed the safe and shuddered. *I think we'd better check the other papers first.*

There were a lot of them—lists of students, special tutoring schedules, lecture notes for her more advanced students, including Yún and me. (Wait, *I* was advanced?) Most important of all, a scribbled list of expected expenses for the next quarter. As I read through that last one, my eyebrows climbed up into my hair. I'd had no idea there were so many fees required by Lóng City's bureaucrats. Taxes, garbage collection and composting fees, sewage fees, teaching license renewal, import fees, something called a magic containment surcharge, the usual monthly bill for magic flux . . .

I wrote down a few sums, got the items mixed up, started over, then lost track of what I'd been looking at. I was about to cram all the papers back in their slots, when I felt a gentle nudge at my shoulder, a whisper of warm piggy breath at my ear.

We can do this together, Chen said softly.

He materialized next to me, once more wearing those foolish spectacles, with a brush tucked in the crook of one foreleg. I wanted to laugh, but my head hurt too much. *Do what?* I asked. *Catalog a mountain?*

His bristles quivered with amusement. *Something like that. Here, you take a look at each of these papers. Tell me what kind they are. Then you put it in a pile. One for each kind. After that we can decide what comes next.*

We settled down to a good routine. I'd read a few columns from each scroll. Chen recorded what kind of thing it was. Then we'd argue which pile it belonged in. We'd sorted half the papers, including all the taxes and fees, and were think-ing of taking a break for tea, when the front door opened and Yún walked inside.

Chen winked from sight. I swept my notes and list under a pile of scrolls.

"Good morning," I croaked.

Yún shook droplets of early-morning rain from her hair, scanned the shop. "Good morning, Kai. Where is your mother?"

"Out and about," I said airily.

Her gaze traveled down to my hands, lying atop the messy pile of scrolls. "What about our classes?"

"We don't have any today. Mā mī's orders."

Yún's eyes narrowed. "Two days in a row? What about the supplies she bought yesterday?"

"All fine. I took care of it."

"Really? When is your mother coming back to the shop? I want to ask her—"

"She's not coming back," I said quickly. "Not right away. She went to visit a cousin. Up north. Family emergency."

Which was true enough, in its own way.

But Yún was studying me suspiciously. "For how long?"

"A week."

"What about the shop?"

"I'm watching over it. You're—" I nearly said, *You're to get a holiday,* but Mā mī never gave holidays. Quickly, I snatched up a bundle of old books, tied together with a string. "Here," I said. "Mā mī said you were to deliver these to Shou-xin today. He needs extra tutoring and she wants you to help him. Take as long as you need."

Yún's gaze dropped to the top book. An odd expression crossed her face, something between laughter and puzzlement and exasperation. Inside me, Chen's laughter tickled at my brain. *You gave her that stack of old books about love philters for old men,* he grunted. *The ones your mother wanted to sell to the junk man.*

Gah. My face burned hotter than before. When Yún glanced up, I held my breath.

"Okay," she said, her voice trembling slightly. "Whatever she wants."

She *was* laughing at me. Never mind. At least the trick worked.

We muttered a few more words at each other—I doubt either of us was paying too much attention to what the other person said—then Yún left with the books in hand. I let out a sigh of relief. It seemed too easy that she believed my stupid explanation. Unless it was true what I thought about her liking Shou-xin . . .

You don't look happy, Chen commented.

I am. I just . . . Oh never mind. Let's get back to work.

We finished totaling up the bills and taxes. I picked up the next folder, which turned out to be a list of extra-special, super-private students. Rich ones, who paid exorbitant fees for special tutoring. Curse it, I had forgotten about them. Hurriedly I scribbled out a note, saying that their teacher was called away to a special conference and so would be unavailable for the next month.

You won't be back in a month, Chen said.

I might, I said.

More like three. Or five.

Ignoring him, I took out a dozen sheets of our best rice

paper, copied the note over twelve times, and set the sheets aside to dry. Then I rooted around in the stationery box for the special gold-edged sheets Mā mī always used for her best customers. Curse it again, there were only six left. I'd have to add the stationer's to my list of ten thousand errands. Now it was ten thousand and one errands.

Meanwhile, Chen had not stopped watching me with those big disapproving eyes.

What? I said. *What's wrong?*

You should tell Yún.

I slammed the brush onto the desk. *We talked about that already. I can't tell her. If I do, she'll try to stop me.*

She won't stop you. She might even help you.

Only so she can boss me around.

Chen laughed and grunted. A horrible stink filled the air.

I pinched my nose shut. *Chen.*

What? You are farting with your mouth, stupid pig-boy. Yún is your friend. She's Lian's friend, too—

Stop nagging me! I shouted.

Why? So I can watch you stomp all over your friends?

Without warning, the griffin exploded into sight, snapping and squawking at me. Its beak fastened on my hand. "Ow!" I grabbed it behind its head. It tried to squirm free, but I wrestled the horrible creature into my jacket and sat on it. Still panting, I said, "I mean it, Chen. I don't want to hear anything more about Yún or Lian or anyone else. And no sneaking behind my back and telling her, I mean, them. Swear it."

The whole shop went quiet, even the griffin. Chen stared at me with bright black eyes, all the mockery wiped clean away. A dangerous beast. One who knew all kinds of powerful magic.

You want me to swear? he said, still fixing me with that unblinking gaze. *A companion oath?*

My brain went blank with dread for a minute.

There is an oath, as awful and terrible as the old folk tales say, which a human can use to bind their spirit companion to their will. It's not written down, of course. Spirit companions show up when a child reaches four years old. Chen was two years late, but I still wouldn't have understood something like that from a book. But he spoke the words directly to me, heart to heart, and I knew that we were bonded. And I knew that such an oath existed.

Yes, I croaked. *Swear you won't tell Yún where I'm going, or why.*

Chen slowly dipped his massive head. *I swear.*

He looked so grim, I almost wished I could take back the oath. Almost.

I stood up, still holding the griffin. *I think I'll go to the markets now. Buy supplies for the trip. We can finish here this afternoon.*

No answer except a gradual fade into invisibility.

A tremor passed through me. We'd never quarreled like this before.

I couldn't stay here. If I did, I might throw up. Or cry. I didn't want Chen to see either.

I blew out a breath. To the markets, then. That meant another list of what I needed and money to buy it with.

The griffin gave a feeble croak. I released him from my jacket.

"What's wrong with you?" I whispered. "Hungry?"

But when I loosened my grip, the griffin launched itself into flight and vanished in a glittering puff of magic.

I DECIDED I didn't need any lists. I knew what I needed. If I forgot anything, I could buy it along the way. Besides, the shop felt too empty, too quiet right now. So I locked all the doors and left a message for any customers to come back the next day. Then I hurried to the banking district.

Mā mī did all her banking with a *piaohao* run by two partners, Bin Chu and Hai-feng Lo. They did business from a hole-in-the-wall office, tucked between two bigger, fancier *piaohao*. I'd come here once or twice over the past year, ever since I won the king's reward, but it was Mā mī who handled the investments.

It was dim inside, except for a bright lamp over the counter. The air reeked of tobacco and the electric tang of magic. No one was in sight, but I heard a tap-tapping, followed by the scratch of a metal pen on paper. Then someone coughed.

I leaned over the counter. Hai-feng Lo crouched behind it, bent over a thick book and an antique calculor. He was sucking on a hookah and writing down columns of numbers. Now and then, he tapped the calculor's keys. The magic flux hummed in time to his tapping.

I cleared my throat.

Hai-feng Lo spat out the hookah pipe and smiled. A horrible sight, because his mouth stretched wide like a monkey's, and his face crinkled in a thousand different directions.

"Kai Zōu, hello. You have business with us today?"

"For my mother," I said, using my best grown-up impersonation. "We would like to arrange for some automatic payments."

The old man made a noise, halfway between a cough and a laugh. He held out an ink-stained hand and took the list of bills and taxes from me. His eyebrows danced up, then down, then tied themselves together over his nose as he glanced over the papers. "Already done," he said.

"What do you mean, already done?"

"Three days ago. She came to us with a list—very thorough, very neat." Here he frowned at my own messy writing. "Very neat. She made arrangements for us to handle all payments until she returned, or sent word otherwise. Do you wish to see her request?"

Without waiting for me to answer, he tapped out a few keys on the calculor, then rose creakily to his feet to pluck a scroll case from one of the thousand pigeonholes. I recognized the style of the case. It was leather, tooled with official guild patterns, and capped with gold-plated discs at both ends.

Just like the one she made for me and Yún to fool the royal wizards.

Hai-feng Lo was still talking, something about how my

mother had made additional arrangements. I heard the words "emergencies," "main account," then my name and Yún's.

"Say what?" I said.

"An emergency authorization," Hai-feng repeated with admirable patience. "Granted by Shen Zōu to her son Kai Zōu and to Yún Chang, to make special payments for expenses connected to the tutoring shop owned by the aforementioned Shen Zōu. You are each authorized to name a representative for yourselves, in case of unforeseen absences."

So she had expected to vanish. But why make all those arrangements and not tell me?

"Any more questions?" Hai-feng Lo asked.

Oh sure, I had a mountain of questions, but right now I had to hurry to buy supplies and run errands before sunset. "I need money. From my own account."

Hai-feng nodded. "Very good. How much?"

I'd worked out the amounts beforehand. "One hundred in paper cash. And, um, six hundred in personal notes. Do I have enough in my account?"

"Oh, yes. Your mother made an extra transfer, just for you."

That gave me another jolt of surprise. I wanted to ask him

if my mother had given any reason for all these mysteri-ous transactions, but I knew better. You didn't bank with Hai-feng Lo and his partner for the shiny offices. You did it because you wanted reliable money handlers who knew how to keep secrets. So I took my bag of cash and notes and didn't ask any questions.

For the next couple of hours, I spent money, picking up this and that for my journey. It was late afternoon, and the temple bells were ringing, before I collapsed onto a stool in the nearest noodle shop. The waiter set down a pot of hot tea, then handed me a menu to read. "Garlic dumplings," I told him. "Curried rice. Spicy meatballs. And more tea. Lots of it. Oh, and get me a brush and ink, please."

Unlike Deming, this waiter didn't sneer at my order. He whisked himself and the menu away. Two minutes later, he'd refilled my teapot and plunked a ready-writing-kit on my table. As he disappeared back into the kitchen, I heard a banging of pots, and someone swearing in a thick, lowlander dialect. The swearing stopped suddenly, replaced by whin-ing music.

I took out the package of gold-edge rice paper, wrote off the addresses as neatly as I could, then folded them around the letters. The waiter soon returned with several steaming platters. I ate absentmindedly, picking at tidbits from one then another, while fiddling with an extra sheet of the fancy paper. The argument in the kitchen had started up again, joined by a woman's high voice. Meanwhile the other customers had paid and left. The waiter slowly made his circuit of the room, cleaning off tables and humming tunelessly along with the radio.

Clearly, Mā mī had planned to disappear. Just as clearly, she hadn't forgotten about me and the shop. That made me feel a little bit better, except . . .

. . . *except she would never forget a chance to tell me exactly what to do and how to do it.*

So, it wasn't all right, as much as I wanted it to be.

All unaware, I'd folded the sheet of paper into a hexagon. On impulse I unfolded it and scribbled a note to Yún, telling her about the *piaohao* and Mā mī's special instructions about payments. It wasn't a real explanation, but it was the most I could say right now. At least someone would be in the city to watch over the shop, and Mā mī clearly trusted her.

When I'd finished, I dusted the ink dry, folded the paper around my key to the shop, and enclosed everything in two more layers of paper, which I sealed with wax from the writing kit. Across the front I wrote Yún's name and address.

I sent the waiter off for another pot of tea and dialed up Jing-mei on my talk-phone. "Yo, pretty girl. It's me, Kai."

Her answer was a noisy raspberry. "Kai, my friend. Word said you had died in a garbage pail."

"Have you been talking to Danzu?" I asked suspiciously.

She laughed. "Every day. What's up?"

"Business. I need a favor. Could you meet me at that fancy tea shop of yours?"

"Sorry, I can't. Oh, wait." I heard a brief muffled conversation, then, "Come over to my apartment. It's a new one—in the Silk Merchant quarter, second lane over from the wind-and-magic lift. Number three-oh-nineteen."

Once Jing-mei had lived with squatters, in the poorest quarter of Lóng City. After we won the reward from Lian's father, she had moved at once into an apartment of her own, but apparently that wasn't good enough, and she'd moved again a month ago. Eyeing the mansions and houses of the silk merchants who lived in this district, I wondered again what Jing-mei was up to. Oh, well. It wasn't my money or my life.

I came to number 3019, a three-story building for those merchants who weren't quite rich, but who wanted to look it. Jing-mei answered her door on the second ring, which told me she'd been waiting for me. She smiled and led me through a series of rooms, all of them stacked high with trinkets and gadgets and other expensive toys.

When we got to a small room in the back, I was in for another surprise. Gan sat there, dressed in a crisp palace uniform. "Hello, Kai," he said.

"Um, yeah. Hi, Gan. I thought you were on night shift."

"So I got up early today."

He grinned. Jing-mei grinned. I felt my ears go hot.

"So what's your favor?" Jing-mei said.

I pulled the packet from my tunic and tossed it to her. "For Yún. Something I can't trust to the post. But don't hand it over for three more days."

She accepted the packet gingerly. "What's inside?"

"A love letter," I growled. "Look, it's important. That's all I can say. Just promise to do exactly what I ask."

Jing-mei glanced at Gan. "Well, okay."

I stayed to share a cup of tea, no longer. It was hard to sit with my friends when we had so many secrets between us. Gan and Jing-mei had made those scary steps from flirts to something more serious. And Danzu . . . It was hard to say what Danzu was up to. Knowing Goat Boy, he had probably turned smuggler or worse. Whatever it was, I could see plain as a dumpling that this new game involved Jing-mei, and Gan didn't like it.

Back home, I set to work, packing my new clothes and gear for the journey. The temple bells were ringing midnight before I finished.

Only then did I sit down and pull out a sheet of cheap paper from my desk.

Dear Yún. I'm sorry. I had to—

No, that wasn't right. There wasn't anything I could tell her, not unless I wanted Yún to come haring after me. (And I didn't want that. Right? *Right?*)

Scowling, I crumpled up the paper and tossed it into the corner.

THE SKIES WERE still dark when I dragged myself from my lumpy bed. Breakfast consisted of leftover rice and a tin of salted fish from the pantry. Chen showed up to nag me about washing dishes and taking care of the cats' morning feeding. After that, I scribbled another note for Yún, telling her about the griffin and asking her to feed and water the beast, along with the cats, until I got back.

Knowing she might not show up until much later, I set out

a dish of beef kibble and whistled. "Beastie," I called. "Here, beastie, beastie—"

It's not here.

Chen appeared as a semi-visible apparition, in the darkest corner of the kitchen.

How do you know? I asked. *Have you seen it?*

Not since you scared it yesterday.

I winced at the memory. Probably for the best.

I hoisted my backpack over my shoulder. Checked the knives in my boots and belt and at my wrists. Locked the doors and set the alarm. A few of Old Man Kang's chickens clucked at me as I left the courtyard and set off through the gray-lit city. The air felt damp and cool; the paved streets were slick beneath my feet. I breathed in the scents of wood smoke and stale garbage. A few wisps of fog swirled through the alleyways. Ghosts or demons? The spawn of watch-dragons?

By the time I reached the main gates, the sun had jumped above the horizon. I took my place in line among the traders, freight wagons, and others waiting to depart. As the gates swung open, I glanced over my shoulder at the city leaping up the mountain in a gold and gray jumble of towers, walls, and winding stairs. This was the first time I'd left Lóng

City—truly left it—and my heart was dancing to a strange fast rhythm. An old man, a trapper from his looks, prodded my back with his staff. I hurried through the gates and onto the open highway.

At the first fork of highways, I took the smaller branch leading south. An hour later, I came to the first of the monster suspension bridges hanging between Lóng City's mountain and its neighbor. I glanced back and took in the great green and gray expanse of the mountain, the dark sprawl of Lóng City itself. For a moment, I thought I saw the outline of a great translucent dragon hovering above the mountainside.

I turned back to the bridge and the road. That's when it started to rain.

5

THE FIRST TWO OR THREE DAYS ON THE ROAD weren't so bad. The winds were still warm and mild, and the rain showers were more like a dog shaking water from its coat than a real storm. Now and then, the sun poked through, making the wet grass glitter and shine.

But as the drizzle turned into real rain, the crowds of travelers thinned, then disappeared. I trudged on, alone except for a set of blisters and Chen's occasional rude comment. Every once in a while, I passed a clump of miserable goats. Once a shape-changer galloped past, making my heart jump into my throat. Luckily, watch-demons didn't live outside cities, and the bigger monsters kept to their tunnels and caverns. In the wild parts of the mountains, though, I expected to come across stranger, more dangerous creatures. Maybe even a wild ghost dragon.

Right now, all I cared about was the mud and rain. Rain

dripped into my eyes. Rain trickled between my collar and hat, running down my back. It rained so much my special wet-proof clothes gave up and soaked up the water, making my pack ten times heavier. And every step was like a battle, as I yanked one foot free of the mud and staggered sideways, regained my footing, then struggled to work the other foot free.

Squelch. Squoosh. Splat.

Danzu would love all this mud, I thought sourly, as I slithered down a particularly steep section. It was my tenth day on the road. *Stupid Goat Boy. Stupid . . .*

Thinking of Danzu, dry and comfortable in Lóng City, I stomped extra hard. My foot hit a slick patch and sent me sliding all the way down the slope to the two-foot-deep puddle at the bottom.

Splat.

I spat out a mouthful of mud and yelled curses at the gods, the sky, Danzu, the ghost dragon king, anyone and anything else I could think of.

Are you done? Chen said calmly.

No, I said, and yelled some more, until my throat went hoarse.

Eventually, I ran out of curses. I picked myself up and wiped my face.

Mud coated my boots and trousers and hair. Mud had ground itself underneath my fingernails, and I was sure there was mud inside my ears.

"I hate mud," I muttered.

Then, because you can't curse the gods without them hearing you, lightning flashed across the steel-gray sky, the earth rumbled, and a mother of all storms broke loose. I nearly drowned in that first minute. Rain sluiced over my face and washed all the mud away from my clothes and skin. Wet-proofing didn't matter to this storm. Deep inside, very faint, I could hear Chen's chuckling.

I rubbed the water from my eyes and trudged on.

Three hours later I reached a small, flea-ridden inn, tucked between the trail and a rocky cliff. The innkeeper took one look at me, streaming water all over his floor, and charged me double for the privilege of standing out of the rain. "Storms are very bad this year," he said, helpfully, as he hurried me through the common room, into a closet-size backroom, where a grinning serving girl tried to help me out of my clothes.

"Stop it," I growled. "I can undress myself."

Still grinning, the girl left me alone to bathe and change my clothes. Soon after that, I had a hot meal and felt more like a real human being again. *It's temporary,* I thought. *Surely it can't make a difference if I spend just a day here.*

BY THE AFTERNOON of the third day, I'd stopped asking when the storm would blow past. *Never,* I thought, as I stared at the blank shuttered window. Bits of ice and hail ticked against the wooden slats.

Inside, two dried-out women and a younger man spent their hours tossing spirit-bones and betting on the outcome. Two other men who looked like ex-caravan guards drank mugs of steaming hot beer and fed bits of bread and meat to the hairy dogs at their feet. A handful of others wandered restlessly between the common room, the stable, and the stuffy loft upstairs where we all slept. We were all bored, even the dogs. The radio had died two days ago. A vid-silk-screen stretched across one corner of the common room, but it was an old model, and it only played static movies, and the flux here ran in spits and spurts, making the vids even harder to watch.

Once the rain lets up, we go, I thought.

It won't let up for another month, Chen grumbled. *Then it snows.*

We go anyway. The storm's almost past. Besides I can't stand it here—

The inn's front door banged open, and a huge mountain of a man stumbled into the room.

I glanced over, back to the shutters. Then my gaze clicked back in amazement.

Water dripped and dropped from the man's voluminous overcoat and wide-brimmed hat, but nothing *stuck* to him. His clothes looked crisp, his gray and white streaked hair remained neatly tied back into its queue, and even his boots were clean of mud and muck. I sniffed and smelled magic. He had to be a rich merchant. Who else would spend a fortune on so many spells to keep himself dry?

A crackling noise sounded from underneath the floorboards, and some invisible force sucked away the pool of water. One of the ex-guards twitched. I coughed to hide my laugh—it was just a standard spell laid by a commercial magic worker to keep the inn dry and clean. Oblivious to the magic underfoot, the man glared around at everyone. "I need a room," he growled. "Immediately." Oh, yes. He was a rich merchant, all right. One with lots of minions.

The innkeeper ran forward, skipping around the damp patches. "We have no room," he said. "Sorry, no room at all."

"There is *always* room. Besides, I spoke to you—to *you*, you miserable worm—ten days ago by talk-phone. You promised rooms for me and all my caravan. Were you lying?"

The poor innkeeper was almost weeping. "Storms have been very, very bad," he whined. "The worst in ten decades, and the hospitality laws say I must not—"

"I know all about hospitality laws," the old merchant barked. "That means you give me and all my train rooms, too. You can't send us back on the road. Two of my own donkeys drowned, and the roads are knee-deep in mud . . ."

He went on, howling about some special cargo that a very special customer had demanded by express delivery—one so precious the merchant himself had to oversee its transport. I groaned quietly. It was easy to see where this argument would go. The innkeeper truly had no more rooms, but the merchant was right. Those same hospitality laws said you must not, could not turn away travelers in life-threatening weather, except for extraordinary circumstances. I already shared a room with two stinking men. By tonight, I'd share it with at least two more.

". . . please, honored sir."

". . . extra expense, calling direct from Crescent Moon . . ."

More sobs and weeping. One of the old women griped

about the weather workers not doing their job properly. The other one blamed everything on the kings hereabouts, saying they hadn't paid the magic guild yet.

The young man spat onto the floor. Magic sizzled and drank up the thick yellow gob. "And they won't. Not with the king of Lóng City falling sick like that."

"You mean dying like that," the older of the women said.

My stomach pinched tight, remembering the sight of His Royal Majesty, Wencheng Li, lying limp and sweating in his bed. No matter how rich he was, no matter many attendants he had, he was dying.

Why did that idiot ghost dragon think I could do any good?

I drank back the rest of my spiced chai and stood up, feeling queasy. Maybe I could take a nap before the innkeeper gave away my bed.

The door swung open again, and a new stranger trudged inside. Water streamed over the floor, more water dripped from the wide-brimmed hat and the backpack slung over one shoulder. But like the merchant, the stranger's clothes appeared unaffected by the rain, and only a scant inch of mud stained his trouser hems.

The newcomer stopped in the middle of the inn's common room and dropped his backpack onto the floor. (A strange muted squeak sounded from deep inside.) Then he wiped the water from his face and turned to observe the room.

Not "his." My breath came short, of a sudden. *Yún.*

Yún's gaze stopped at me. She did not smile. She didn't frown. It was more like she couldn't decide how she felt either.

"Hi," I said. My voice was barely louder than a whisper.

Yún nodded, then turned to the innkeeper. "A room, please," she said quietly.

The innkeeper began his litany about no rooms, no rooms at all, and how all the hospitality laws in the world and its Seventy Kingdoms could not alter that fact.

Yún held up a hand. "You have stables," she said. "Let me have a corner there, next to the pigs and goats if necessary. And tea, please—as hot as you can make it. Thank you."

Without even waiting for his reply, she sat opposite me. "Kai. Hello."

"How, um, did you find me?" I said.

"Jing-mei gave me your letter. It didn't make any sense . . ." She dropped her voice to an almost whisper. "It didn't make sense why or how your mother had disappeared. So I went to the palace guards, and they told me how you showed up three days before I did and reported your mother missing."

A flicker of lightning in her eyes reminded me of the storms outside. But Yún didn't go crash and thunder. She just sighed and shook her head. "Why didn't you tell me?"

"I-I was too worried to think. Then the ghost dragon king . . ."

"He told me the rest," Yún said.

Ah, so. That explained a lot.

"But how did you know which road to take?" I asked.

And how did you know to stop here?

A muffled squawk interrupted us. Yún's backpack rocked back and forth. She was just reaching down to the strings, when a small golden beak poked through the cloth.

"Silly monster." Yún grabbed for the strings, but the backpack rolled away from her reach. Another, louder squawk sounded. Now everyone in the common room stopped what they were doing. The merchant hissed. The innkeeper took two quick side-steps away from the backpack and made a sign with two fingers—a gesture the old women in the Pots-and-Kettles Bazaar used whenever they saw a ghost dragon, or something equally scary. Both dogs rose onto stiff legs and growled in their throats.

A small, rumpled griffin crawled out of the pack. Quick as a curse, it launched itself toward me and bit me on the ear.

Three things happened all at the same time.

"Ow!"

"*Wa!* Monsters!"

"*Āi-āi!* My clean floors!"

The innkeeper shouted. Two bear-like men thundered from the back rooms. Before I could figure out what was going on, they'd hefted me and Yún into the air. I had one glimpse of a steaming pile of griffin crap on the floor, then they'd wafted me through the common room and tossed me out the door.

I landed in a mud puddle with a *splat*.

A second later, Yún landed next to me.

"And don't ever come back," the innkeeper shrieked.

He said more, but a burst of thunder drowned out his voice. I scrambled to my feet and ran to the door just as he slammed it shut. "Let us in!" I demanded. "Hospitality rules! You can't just—"

The door swung open. Two heavy backpacks hit me in the chest, knocking me back into the puddle. "Extraordinary circumstances!" the innkeeper shouted. "Your magic is bad for my magic!"

Yún slithered to her feet. She grabbed for my hand. I swatted her away and wiped the mud from my eyes, cursing the rain, the innkeeper. Most especially I cursed the innkeeper. All my rainproof gear was inside my packs, leaving me soaked and coated with mud. Yún herself didn't look much better. Clumps of mud stuck to her hair, and the water streamed from her clothes. *Ha-ha!* I thought, obscurely pleased.

She made another grab for my arm. That's when I saw she was laughing. Whoops and squeaks of laughter. "Stop that!" I growled.

"I'm sorry, it's just too—"

Yún whooped again and bent over.

I tried again. "We can spend the night in this toad's stables," I said. "He can't stop us. He's lying about magic. I don't have any—"

"It's the"—Yún gulped down a breath—"the griffin, Kai." Her voice still shook with suppressed laughter. "And don't bother with the stables. He keeps a couple of guards on watch. Besides, it's stuffed full with mules and cargo from that merchant's caravan."

"How do you know?"

"How else? I went into his stables first."

She whistled. A pack pony thudded toward us from the direction of the stables. Yún captured its reins. She hoisted our packs onto its back and fastened them onto the frame, alongside several other packs and bundles. The pony gave a rattling sigh, as if to complain, but when Yún rubbed its neck, it leaned against her. I felt a twinge of jealousy.

"We can make the next shelter if we hurry," Yún said. "Where's your griffin?"

"He's not my—"

A horrible screech made my bones shiver. The griffin reappeared from nowhere and landed on top of the packs, still screeching. The pony swung its head around and snorted at the noisy creature, but it didn't shut up until Yún laid a hand over its head and murmured something that made the air tingle with magic. The pony shook its head, as though disgusted by the griffin's behavior.

Yún handed me the pony's reins. "Come on. We need to set up camp before dark."

"Where? Yún, it's dark and wet and—"

"—and there's a way shelter two *li* from here, according to the map."

The two *li* felt more like ten before she called a halt. It wasn't much of a campsite, I realized with a sinking stomach. A wide shoulder of dirt and rocks stuck out from the mountainside. Another, bigger hump, crowned with lots more rocks, loomed over the first one. Someone had built two crude walls out of logs to make a square, and roofed them with branches. Several pine trees huddled close to the entrance, looking as tired as I felt.

The griffin sailed into the shelter. Yún led the pony inside and started to unload the packs. "At least we have plenty of water," she said.

"Very funny," I said. Then I remembered how her clothes had been as dry and clean as the merchant's. Now they were wet and filthy like mine. "What happened to your magic, Smart One?"

"Oh." She actually looked embarrassed. "I can only do that for a short while."

"You were showing off."

Her teeth made a white flicker in the gray light. "A little. Come on. We can build a fire and cook something hot. You'll feel better."

I mumbled something about how I'd feel better if someone hadn't brought a certain griffin, but Yún ignored me. She ordered me to finish unloading the pony while she laid sticks and tinder from the shelter's wood supply into a neat pyramid. The wood was damp, but between a few magic drying spells and a lot of patience, Yún coaxed a fire to start. Soon we had changed out of our wet clothes and into ones that were merely damp, and the pony was happily eating warm mash.

One of the gear bags had a neat folding iron cooking grate. Yún set pots of water on the grate, then measured out rice into one and tea into a second one. She even had a packet of dried beef for the griffin, which the horrible beast flung itself upon with screeches of joy. Yún was like a street trickster pulling a gajillion things out of his hat. I nearly expected to see her pull out a monkey next.

For a while we didn't say anything. We were both too busy guzzling hot tea in between mouthfuls of rice. My toes and fingers stopped feeling numb, and my damp clothes steamed from the fire. My brain stopped churning around all the bad luck thoughts of the past few days, and I felt more hopeful.

"So what else did you bring?" I asked.

"Passports," she said. "We won't need them in the mountains, but the Phoenix Empire is different."

She rummaged in another pack and handed them over to me—two thin leather tubes with the usual gold-plated caps with electrical magical connectors underneath. One had my name burnt in thick characters along one side. I unscrewed that one and slid the parchment scroll into one hand.

"Are these real?" I asked.

"Yes and no," Yún said. "Gan sneaked some of the official seals and connectors. I did the rest." She shot me a quick glance. "I couldn't hide that you and I and your mother had left Lóng City, but I didn't want to let everyone in the palace know *where* you and I had gone. Just in case."

Ah, yes. All those plots and schemes the ghost dragon king had mentioned.

"About my mother . . ." I swallowed and tried again. "About the tutoring shop. What did you—"

"Locked and doubled-locked," she said. "I notified the watch that the shop's owners were away. I said you'd traveled north, to Silver Moon City, to visit family. Then I bribed the watch captain to patrol twice as often in the neighborhood. That was Danzu's advice."

"You told *Danzu*?"

She snorted. "Of course not. He got the same story you told me. He won't believe it any more than I did, but the shop ought be safe. Jing-mei and Gan promised to check every day, too. They'll take care of the cats and make sure everything is fine. Oh, and I gave Jing-mei authorization to handle any business emergencies."

At that, I nearly fainted. "But, but Jing-mei is an—"

"—extremely intelligent and capable young woman. Have you actually talked to her since last year?"

"Um, some. You really trust her?"

"Completely. So does Hai-feng Lo."

I felt as though I'd walked into a magical mirror where everything had turned into its reverse. In the old folk tales, the hero always came up with some clever trick to overcome the problems of talking and fighting and thinking in reverse, but right now I didn't feel very clever. I just felt tired and faintly queasy at the thought of Jing-mei running my mother's tutoring shop.

Mā mī can only kill me once.

Unless she brings you back to life, Chen said helpfully. *Like she did the griffin.*

As if the beast had heard us, the griffin hopped down from its perch and waddled over to Yún. It butted its head against her hand and keened softly. Yún smoothed back its feathers and rubbed the back of its skull. The griffin leaned into the caress, humming oddly.

The air around me trembled.

Magic. I could smell it, taste it. If I closed my eyes, I could imagine myself back in my mother's tutoring shop, with all the jumble of herbs, sharp-smelling potions, and the ever-present scent of magic. It was as if my mother had left her imprint upon me and the griffin both.

This creature might be the last spell my mother ever cast.

I furled the papers back into their scroll, and sealed everything into its leather case. By now I felt pretty stupid. Grateful but stupid. All those things I'd forgotten in my rush to start my journey. If Yún had not decided to chase after me . . .

"Thank you," I said carefully. "You were very smart to make these. And to track me down. You didn't need to go to all that trouble."

Yún's hand stilled over the griffin's head. "Your mother is my teacher, Kai. And you are my friend. Of course I want to help."

Friend. Yes. Well, that answered another question.

"Thanks," I mumbled.

As if by common agreement, we decided it was time for sleep. Yún packed away our passports and other papers, then checked the pony one last time. I laid out our blankets and wrapped myself up tightly in mine. The wind had died off, and the rain had turned to drizzle. Every once in a while, one of the branches of the pine trees shifted, and water cascaded over the shelter's roof and walls. A soft silvery patter-ing that would have soothed me any other night.

The griffin crawled over to me and poked its nose into my face.

Go away, I thought. *You're dead.*

The griffin sniffed and crawled over to Yún's side. I lay there, listening to its complaining chirps, Yún's soft murmur as she soothed the beast into quiet. I told myself I was ner-vous, sleeping outside, even though I knew watch-demons didn't patrol any roads outside the cities. It had nothing to do with Yún herself, lying a hand span away from me.

She's my friend. I'm glad she's here. What else could I pos-sibly want?

It took a long time before I could fall asleep.

6

NOT ONLY DID YÚN BRING PASSPORTS AND GEAR, she also brought maps. Expensive maps, drawn with colored ink on thick parchment, and spelled against rain and rot and mice, just like those used by merchants. She hauled them out one by one—maps of cities and towns and wayside stations, maps that showed highways and side roads and even the tiny goat tracks criss-crossing the wild middle regions, maps for every part of the Seventy Kingdoms. Everywhere except the Phoenix Empire.

When I asked about that, she shook her head. "We'll buy those at the border. Just in case someone got curious."

"You think someone might?"

"Yes, I do. Things are *wrong*, Kai. All kinds of wrong. I think . . ." She sent me a sidelong glance, as though she wasn't sure how I'd take her next words. "I think we ought to take some precautions."

Precautions was a polite weasel-word for "let's do everything my way, stupid boy." Ever since Lóng City, I'd kept to the main highways. Yún changed all that. *Ai-ya*, did she change it. Over breakfast, she laid out a complicated zig-zag route, from this side road to that one, up and down the mountains. It was like charting the wandering path of a drunken gargoyle.

"That makes no sense," I told her.

"Just so," she replied.

As if that explained anything.

I told you she was bossy, I said to Chen.

Chen snuffled. *You could argue with her. Explain why she's wrong.*

She's not wrong. Not really. Just . . . bossy.

Chen didn't even bother to answer me, but I could hear him laughing, oh so quietly.

Stupid pig-spirit, I thought, not for the first time.

STILL GRUMBLING TO myself, I helped Yún pack up our belongings. The rain had eased up during the night, but as soon as we set off, it came down harder than before—a steady soaking rain that never stopped for the next ten days.

No matter how much I argued, Yún refused to give up her crazy ideas. So up and downhill we slogged through the mud. The mountains turned into great looming walls of granite, streaked and capped by frozen snow, like colossal silent guards standing watch. There were days when the clouds thinned out and we could see patches of sky overhead. Other days, the clouds sank low, and our world turned into a cold, gray, wet mist, and we could hardly tell where the path ended.

We had just crossed over the pass into Snow Thunder City when sleet started to fall along with the rain. We stumbled onward, half-blinded and numb, until we came to a small inn huddled by the side of the road. It looked more like a jumble of rocks than a real inn, but at least there were stables for our pony, and pots of scalding hot tea waiting for us in the common room.

"They charge too much here," I said. I was beating my hands together. Water streamed from my clothes, which had given up their waterproof spells a couple days before.

"We don't have much choice," Yún replied. "We can get more money at the next *piaohao*. Your mā mī arranged that—"

She broke off as the serving boy approached with a pot of butter tea. The boy filled our mugs, then held out a hand and announced the price. Twice what we'd paid at the previous place. Ignoring the choking noise I made, Yún counted out the outrageous sum into his palm.

"You say you serve good curry here," she said. "How much?"

He named a sum three times higher than what we paid for the tea.

I gulped. Yún never flinched. "Two bowls, please. And send a third one to the stables."

We'd lodged the griffin in the stables with our packs and pony. The innkeeper had argued at first. He didn't like monsters under his roof. It upset the customers and terrified the staff. Yún had patiently argued back that there were no other customers, and was he saying that he and his serving boy were afraid of a tiny fluffy creature? Before the innkeeper could invent a new objection, she had pulled out her purse and smiled. That ended the argument. It always did.

The serving boy apparently didn't like the griffin any more than his master did, because he scowled when she mentioned the stables. Yún silently added another coin to the pile. The boy grunted, scooped the coins into his palm, and slouched away.

"Why are you wasting money?" I hissed. We had counted

our funds the night before. Even with camping in shelters, we were spending a lot more than we both expected.

"I want to make sure he gives the stew to the griffin and doesn't eat it himself. Did you see how skinny he is? He's like one of those runty trees we passed coming up the trail, the one that had lost all its needles. I wonder if the innkeeper feeds him at all."

"I bet he does feed him. I bet he and the old man murder all their customers and eat them. That's why no one else is here."

Yún's only answer was a snort of laughter.

We drank down our tea, wincing at its bitterness. Gradually the warmth spread to my toes and fingers. I swallowed a yawn and looked around for our serving boy and the curry. No sign of him or the innkeeper, though I heard a crash and clatter from the kitchen.

Yún unfolded one of her maps and frowned. She didn't answer my next question, so I wandered over to the windows. An icy wind leaked around the shutters. I heard a far-off booming, like the dull echo of thunder. Yún said the kingdom's name came from all the avalanches in the region. We'd have to be careful once we set off again.

I glanced over my shoulder. Yún and I were still the only

ones in the common room. I pulled my talk-phone from inside my shirt. My heart tripped faster as I tapped in the special code for Princess Lian's talk-phone, the one she had entered herself the year before. Deep inside, I heard Chen snuffling—anxious—but he wisely did not say anything. He knew I'd tried this same number last week.

A weird hissing noise echoed from the talk-phone. I heard a clicking, then nothing.

Āi-āi, *where are you, Lian?*

"No use," said a voice next to my elbow.

I jumped and hurriedly tucked my talk-phone into my pocket. "What?"

The serving boy jerked his chin toward my shirt. "That. Your talk-phone." He dumped a tray with my bowl of goat curry on the nearest table. "It's no use trying to call anyone. We got no magic flux, not until spring."

That got my attention. "Why?"

"Don't you know? It's because—"

"*Hēi!* Boy!" shouted the innkeeper. "Get your lazy bones over here."

The serving boy snapped his mouth shut and scurried away. The innkeeper grabbed the boy's arm and dragged him to the far corner of the common room, where the two of them squabbled at each other in low tense voices. The inn-keeper glanced toward me once—his eyebrows flashed down to a point over his fleshy nose—then back to his hapless serving boy. He hissed something in a wordless undertone, and the boy scuttled away through the kitchen doors.

Nosy old man, I thought.

He's angry, Chen grunted. *No, he's afraid. But I don't know about what.*

Maybe he thinks the storm will knock down his miserable inn.

Chen snorted a laugh. *Maybe.*

He did a quick fade from my mind, leaving me to my bowl of curry. It wasn't so bad, I thought, chewing a cautious mouthful. Whoever did the cooking knew a lot about spices. Or they'd bought a package of standard kitchen spells. But then I remembered what the serving boy said about the magic flux, and that meant no spells, pre-packaged or not. I chewed another mouthful, thinking hard. I'd heard how a magic well could go dry, or how a disturbance might alter the currents the flux followed through the air, but how could anyone predict the magic would return next spring?

I finished my curry and yawned. It was only mid-afternoon, but the light slanting through the shutters was dim and gray. Outside, the wind blew stronger, keening like a ghost. The inn shuddered and seemed to shrink around me. I cleared a spot in front of me and rested my head on my hands.

The next thing I knew, someone was shaking me roughly. "Kai! Kai, wake up!"

I bolted upright and nearly fell over. Yún grabbed my arm and shoved me back into my seat.

It was pitch-dark outside. We were alone in the common room, which shimmered with an eerie yellow glow from an oil lamp overhead. As Yún turned toward the light, I could see a strange wild look in her eyes. "What is it?" I whispered.

"The griffin. Come with me."

She hustled me through the corridor that connected the inn with the stables. Even though I told myself that nothing could be wrong, Yún's urgency and the howling of the wind had infected me. My throat squeezed tight as I undid the latch and entered the stall, where we had stowed our animals and our gear.

Our pony cowered against the far wall, its dark eyes wide with reproach against us and the gods who had brought him to this terrible spot. Between us, a small feathered creature lay motionless in the straw. Next to it was a small smelly heap of half-digested stew.

My heart stopped at the sight, then lurched into motion again when the griffin stirred. "Did the serving boy—"

"I don't think so."

It's not poisoned, Chen said. *I would know. So would Qi.*

"Poisoned or not, it's dying," Yún said flatly. "Kai, we must leave as soon as possible. The innkeeper tells me there's a famous magical physician in the next valley, in Golden Starflower Waterfall. It's nearly on our way."

Wind slammed against the stable. Ice water spattered the stall, and more leaked through the cracks between the bowed wooden planks. I opened my mouth, ready to say we should wait until the storm passed, but then Yún laid a gentle hand over the griffin. The beast lifted its head. It opened its beak wide, like a small chick begging to its mother.

Our little monster.

"Tomorrow," I said. "As soon as it's light."

"Thank you," Yún whispered.

We packed our gear and paid the innkeeper for an early breakfast. At dawn, we set off through the sleet and freezing rain. The innkeeper himself had cooked us a breakfast and gave us directions on the fastest route into the valley. If we took the next fork heading downward, he told us, we could reach Golden Starflower Waterfall before nightfall. From there, he confirmed what Yún's map told us—that we would have an easy trek along the river road to Lang-zhou City and the border hills, where we could take the magic-powered freight lifts into the Phoenix Empire.

If Lang-zhou City still had its magic. If we didn't freeze to death in the mountains. If and if and if. I shoved those thoughts aside. Our whole journey was a chain of ifs. Like the old philosophers said, we had to forget the limits of our selves, even as we understood them.

By late morning, we reached the fork. The road split in three different directions. The main segment continued along the mountainside, a fat pale worm of stone that wriggled in and around with the hillside. A second, smaller track climbed up toward the snow caps. A few villages perched on the heights above—the inhabitants mostly goatherds, but there were wilder folk who lived in those cold heights—demon hunters, ghost trappers, and the like.

Our path was the third track, which looped down to the valley below. The sleet died off, to my everlasting gratitude. Eventually the skies cleared enough that our world changed into a glittering jewel of silver and white. We had to pick our way carefully to avoid slipping over the side into the depths below.

Hours later, we had reached a truly scary point along the path, which had narrowed as it curved around a bulge in the mountain. The wind had kicked up again, blowing a thin gruel of snow powder down from the snowfield and glaciers above. We stopped beneath a rocky overhang to rest the pony. Yún pulled out her map and checked it again. "We can reach the next way station by dark."

"An inn?" I asked.

"No. A shelter. But at least we'll be dry and out of the wind. And I can try another spell with Xiǎo Yāo-guài."

Xiǎo Yāo-guài? "Little Monster?"

Then I realized she meant the griffin.

Name a thing and you promise it your heart, went the old sayings. Well, I had promised a lot of things these past few weeks.

We both lurched to our feet. The pony grumbled as I looped the reins around my arm and tugged. Yún had ventured forward a few steps. She stopped, edged back and beckoned for me to lean close.

"Did you hear something?" she whispered.

I listened.

There was a thin whistling noise—the wind singing over the knife-sharp edges of boulders cut by ice and snow. My own heartbeat thumping inside my chest. The *tick-tick-tick* of gravel sliding over the mountain face.

I hear something, Chen said. *Another spirit. No, lots of others.*

Pêng! A ghostly spider materialized in front of us. Chen popped into sight and the two plunged over the side in battle, just as a squad of six armed men surged around the bend. I glimpsed swords in their hands. The next second, Yún and I had our belt knives out.

Yún caught the first sword near the hilt and shoved it aside. Her second knife slid from her wrist sheath. She struck. The first man fell. Yún ducked down to finish him while I fended off the next who surged forward. Inside my mind, I heard Chen's furious roars, Qi's bone-shivering cries, the rasping howl and cough of wild cats and dogs from the spirit world.

Block and slash, duck, thrust. Yún and I worked together, moving as quick as thought to keep those bright blades away. The narrow path kept them from overwhelming us, but still they had swords and we had nothing but daggers and terror. In spite of the cold, sweat rolled down my back and dripped into my eyes. I had to blink it away—I didn't dare pause to swipe my face with my hand.

"Not right," Yún panted. "They aren't—"

"Don't talk. Save your breath."

But she's right, came the next thought. These men didn't fight like bandits. Their blades were expensive blue-tempered steel. Each attack and counterattack was like a dance of murder, precise and deadly.

They fight like soldiers.

The pony squealed and lashed out behind. I heard a meaty thump and a groan. Someone cursed in a thick southern dialect. I glanced back to see six more men scrambling down from a ledge above the trail. My stomach went cold. We could never win against so many.

No time to think about that. Yún darted forward and jabbed the nearest man. He doubled over, making a horrible gagging noise. Yún tugged at her knife, trying to work it free. Another attacker slashed at her eyes. She flung up her arm and deflected the blade. With another hard yank, she had her blade free and staggered back. At first, I thought she'd escaped unhurt, but then I saw the blood streaming from her scalp.

"We'll give you our money!" I shouted. "All of it! Just let us—"

Their leader answered with a quick thrust with his sword. I blocked his blade—barely. Yún tried an undercut, but I could see how awkwardly she moved. I edged past her, even though it meant facing all those bandits or soldiers or whatever they were alone. At least I could die fighting, I thought fiercely.

Behind me, Yún dragged herself to standing. She drew an audible breath and shouted. No, that wasn't right. More like she trilled a waterfall of notes, high and clear. Magic. I recognized it right away. Just like the ghost dragon king's but hers was beautiful, while its had been harsh.

The air shivered and drew taut. No one moved. Then, I felt a puff of cold air against my face. The faint metallic scent faded, even as I noticed it, and the tension leaked away. One of the men grinned, his jagged teeth white against his sun-darkened face. "Magic, is it? You think that will help?"

"I don't think anything," Yún snarled. "I *know*."

She shouted the words again. Her voice was breaking. I could hear the edge of a sob. *The magic isn't working*, I thought. *Why not?*

Chen! I called out. *Help us!*

With a roar, Chen popped into this world, followed by Qi. Just as quickly, they both vanished. The air rippled. Inside my shirt, the griffin roused and scrabbled at my chest with its claws. And then, and then . . .

. . . and then the mountain shouted back. I felt a rumbling at my back and under my feet. . . .

A river of snow roared down the mountainside. It hit the rock overhang and exploded into a burst of sparkling white. Our attackers scrambled to escape. In a heartbeat, the river of snow swept them all away.

Yes, I thought, then froze in horror.

Yún was slipping over the ledge. I grabbed her arm, started to fall with her. The pony bit my shirt and hauled me back. I fell to my knees and dragged Yún to safety. A part of me noticed that her sleeve had turned dark with blood. More blood streaked her face, and her mouth pinched shut against the pain. Without even thinking, I wrapped my arms around her. "Yún. You almost—"

"So did you. I thought—"

Her lips brushed against mine. We stopped, breathless. Our hearts were beating fast—I felt hers thumping in time with mine against my chest. Then I leaned forward and kissed her again.

Her lips were chapped from the wind, but warm and dry. She tasted of blood and sweat. Underneath the scent of damp wool and the metallic scents of blood and magic, I caught a whiff of the herbs she used to pack around our clothes.

"Yún."

"Kai."

Her breath hissed in suddenly and she flinched, eyes wide. She was staring at a point far behind me. Slowly, I swiveled my head around.

There, suspended above the valley, was a ghost dragon, a long, skinny creature, like a coil of gray smoke in the cloud-streaked skies. Every thought inside my head evaporated into nothing. This dragon was not nearly as large as the king ghost dragon in Lóng City, but that didn't matter. Its fangs were just as sharp, and its breath just as poisonous.

Yún whispered something.

"What?" I whispered back.

She whispered again in that wordless language. This time I could almost tease its meaning from the rise and fall of each syllable. A dim memory of some lecture six months before fluttered through my brain—Mā mī telling us about ancient languages once used by wizards of all kingdoms, all kinds.

The ghost dragon tilted its head, as if trying to decide whether to rip us into shreds or eat us whole. Yún spoke in a firmer voice, a new series of tones that sounded like a command. The ghost dragon's lips curled back from its fangs. Its breath—like puffs of magic flux made visible—hung in the air between us. If I squinted hard enough, I could see the valley and distant mountains through its body.

Then, without a sound, it plunged downward to the valley.

7

UNTIL THE GHOST DRAGON VANISHED, WE HAD NOT dared to twitch even one muscle. Now, I was suddenly very much aware that I still had my arms around Yún. Our bodies were pressed close together; even through the double-layer of our clothes, I could trace the warm outline of her arms and legs. Embarrassed, I loosened my hold, only to have her go limp.

I caught her under her arms before she could slide over the cliff again. "Yún, what's wrong?"

"My—my arm."

Carefully, I eased her onto the ground and examined her. Her knife arm—the left one—was clean, but her right sleeve was dark and wet. I cursed softly as I cut through the cloth to take a closer look. Just as I thought—a deep slash ran along her forearm. She'd taken a wound in the shoulder, too.

Without warning, Yún lunged to one side and threw up noisily.

"Sorry," she wheezed. "I'm sorry. I thought—"

"You forgot you weren't immortal," I said.

She managed a smothered laugh, then shivered. "Kai . . ."

"*Shī, shī.* We'll make that shelter down the trail. I'll take care of everything."

We made it to the next way station before dark. Yún immediately slumped to the ground. I spread out the tarpaulin and blankets and made her lie down. Then I covered her to keep her warm while I did all the rest—building a fire, rubbing down our pony and giving it extra feed, and constructing a small nest for the griffin.

Once I had water boiling for tea, I turned to Yún. "Now for you."

Yún's mouth trembled in a smile. "Are you going to heal me?"

"Maybe." I hadn't told Yún about that strange moment on Lóng City's outer walls. It wasn't healing, but at least it was magic.

The cut along her scalp had stopped bleeding. I cleaned it gently with warm water mixed with herbs from Yún's pack. She bore that well, gritting her teeth. So far, so good. But the wounds along her forearm and shoulder brought a curse to my lips. Both were ragged and deep. One was festering already—that man must have used a dirty blade.

"'S my fault," Yún mumbled. "If I hadn't bribed the watch, no one would have known."

"*Shī, shī, shī.*" I brushed her hair back from her forehead, which felt warm to my touch. Once more I cursed those mercenaries and wished them into the coldest depths of hell. "You did right, Yún. You made sure the shop was safe."

"But I—"

"You did right," I repeated. "You always do. Always. It's those others. The ones plotting against Lian. They sent spies to chase us down. But you were smart, you figured that out. If you hadn't come after me, I'd be dead and frozen on a mountain top."

Still babbling whatever came into my head, I gently washed away the blood and dirt. Yún lay there sweating and shaking, even after I stopped.

(Now what?)

(We try something else.)

I laid my hands gently on her shoulder and her forehead. Closed my eyes and drew one long breath, held it long enough to hurt, then released it slowly in time to my heartbeat. Again. It was hard. Little things kept distracting me—the spit and pop of the fire, our pony whuffling, the sting and itch of my own scratches and cuts.

Nothing.

Not even a flicker of magic flux.

Frustrated, I drew my hands back and thought. Sure, I'd never claimed to be a wizard, but I'd always been able to sense the magic flux. But now I felt as though the air had vanished around me.

(What did I think? That I would wriggle my brain and make everything better?)

Shī, whispered Chen. *Stop thinking. Breathe.*

His voice boomed in the space between my ears. Underneath it, there was a faint whispering, whistling voice—Yún's companion, Qi. *Spirit magic,* I thought. I placed my hands back on Yún's shoulder and forehead and breathed as Chen had commanded. My pulse slowed, my thoughts dropped away, and the whine of my fears dissolved. It was like swimming in a pool of quiet. A stillness, an emptiness. An everything.

It was nothing like the magic flux. Not weaker or smaller—different. As different as water is from sunlight. As salt is from sugar. For the first time, I had an inkling what my mother meant when she lectured about yin and yang, then even that inkling vanished into infinity.

When I opened my eyes, dark had fallen and a cold wind blew across the shelter's outer edges. Yún lay with her eyes closed, breathing easily. The fire had died away to glowing coals; its ruddy light limned her face like an artist's paintbrush. Had she meant that kiss? Or was it just because we were both terrified and amazed to be alive?

She stirred. Her eyes blinked open. She looked faintly astonished.

"I feel much better. What do you think?"

I think I love you.

But that was impossible to say.

THE NEXT MORNING, I checked Yún's wounds again. The cut on her scalp had closed. Only a raised pink scar remained, a tiny ribbon mostly hidden underneath her thick hair. When I laid my hand on her head, the last traces of magic buzzed against my palm, telling me that healing continued. The scar might even disappear by day's end.

Her other wounds had not healed as much. You could still see an ugly ragged line along her forearm. Her shoulder wound wept a clear pinkish liquid. The skin around both felt warm to my touch. Not so dangerously hot as the night before, and not as inflamed, but still not good.

"We'll wash you up and bind everything fresh," I told her.

"Doctor Kai," she murmured. "You saved my life. Thank you."

I covered up my embarrassment by acting very busy. I built up our fire and set pots of water to boil for tea, and for mixing up more antiseptic to wash her arm and shoulder. Yún shuffled over to the griffin's nest of blankets and knelt awkwardly by its side. When I happened to glance around, she was frowning.

"Is he—"

"Alive." Her voice sounded subdued. "But weak."

I knelt beside her and laid a hand over the griffin's chest. Yāo-guài stirred uneasily, but its eyes did not open, and its body felt thicker, stiffer. *Stuffed*, I thought, cold washing over my skin.

"Let me try a spell," Yún said.

She recited a series of those mathematical incantations, the ones that sounded like ice trickling in the spring thaw. This time, there was not even the faintest sense of magic flux in the air. "That's not right," she whispered. "There's always magic. Always. You used it last night to heal me. How?"

"I'm not sure," I said. "Chen helped me. All I know is that it wasn't magic flux."

I gave you our magic, Chen grunted. *Qi and I both. You made it easier than I expected, but now we have headaches.*

"Can you do it again?" I asked, aloud and to Chen. "Can you save the griffin?"

Voices doubled within my mind. *We tried last night. We couldn't. The griffin lives upon the flux and nothing else.*

Yún rubbed her hand over her forehead and shivered. "How can there be no magic flux? And what about the ava-lanche? I didn't summon that. I tried but—"

"The ghost dragon," I said suddenly. "Maybe he heard you and wanted to help."

"*Hü.* Maybe." But she didn't sound convinced. "At least I knew the right words to send him away. The ghost dragon king insisted I learn them. I didn't see why at first, but I'm glad he did." She rubbed her forehead again, winced, then frowned at her injured arm, as though it had disappointed her somehow. "That still doesn't explain about the magic flux. How can it disappear like that?"

The idea that magic could just vanish made me go cold inside. "I don't know. But wait a minute. That boy at the inn told me they had a drought here. Or something like that." It was hard to remember the exact words he used. "He said the magic flux would come back in the spring."

"How could he know that?"

"I have no idea. That nosy old innkeeper interrupted us."

We stared at each other, Yún looking as troubled as I felt.

Yún released a long breath. "It doesn't matter how he knows, or what that means. Not now, anyway. First we have to find a city-kingdom that does have wells or currents. But we'd better be careful which one. Those men who attacked us, they didn't act like bandits. You saw their weapons."

Exactly what I had thought. "Do you think that innkeeper sent them after us?"

"I don't think so. But someone did. Someone rich and powerful who wants to keep us from telling Lian about her father."

Assassins. I shivered. Gan had talked about plots and machinations. I hadn't realized that plots sometimes meant death. I should have.

Yún's always been the one who figures everything out. That's not enough. We both have to be clever.

Yún herself looked weary and pain-wracked. I ordered her to sleep a few more hours while I cooked breakfast and tended our pony. Yún didn't even argue. She curled up with the griffin and didn't wake up until late morning. We ate our breakfast while poring over our maps.

"No more Golden Starflower Waterfall," I said.

"And no more Lang-zhou City," Yún said. "Whoever sent those soldiers will have more spies and soldiers in the valley."

She stared at the map, chewing her lip. "We need magic and we need money."

And Lang-zhou City had had both, not to mention those powerful wind-and-magic lifts that could take us up over the mountains and into the plains of the Phoenix Empire.

"West," I said. "They won't expect that."

Yún stopped chewing her lips. "You're right." She pointed to the next kingdom over, northwest of our own shelter. "Here. At least for starters."

GOLDEN SNOWCLOUD, said the legend. According to the symbols, it had a *piaohao* and magic flux wells. "Looks small. And will it have a doctor?"

"It's tiny," Yún said. "But it has some of the deepest magic flux wells in the whole Seventy Kingdoms. *They* won't have any droughts. With all that magic, they have to have doctors as well. We can fix up Yāo-guài, buy a few more supplies, and plan the rest of our route."

Her voice was stronger. Her manner was matter-of-fact.

Nothing like yesterday evening.

(Or yesterday afternoon, when you kissed her.)

I chewed that thought into small bits and spat them aside. We didn't have time for me to play lovesick kid. We had to reach Golden Snowcloud before Yāo-guài died. Again.

We broke camp and doubled back to the fork in the roads. Our map said Golden Snowcloud was a three-plus-day march. We covered the distance in half the time. Up the goat-trail, over the hump-backed mountain, and along a gorge so deep, shadows covered its depths. By late afternoon of that second day, we reached the border stones of the next kingdom.

Here the road stopped at a cliff. Again we consulted the maps, and we didn't like what they told us. Golden Snowcloud lay at the bottom of an even deeper gorge, surrounded by walls of mountains. There were two ways to enter the kingdom—by wind-and-magic lift and goat path. The wind-and-magic lift—a big sturdy platform with ropes and winches that looked like they could haul a gargoyle—was closed. When I pounded my fist against the shuttered gates to the lift, a pre-recorded voice whined that the lifts had stopped running because of imminent storms.

Leaving us that impossible goat track.

Our pony, the poor creature, bleated just one protest at the top of our descent. We had to slither and slide our way down, gripping the handrails that some later kind soul had installed. (Most likely after all his near relatives had died trying to enter this thrice-damned city.)

The path dropped us and our trembling pony between two iron posts that marked the city's outer walls and the entrance to a wide market square surrounded by tall stone buildings. Twilight was falling, and the guards herded us through a carved gateway that led directly into the mountainside. "There's a monster blizzard coming," said one, in answer to our questions. "Hail and sleet and ice, the wizards say."

Inside the mountain, a vast cavern held another city, complete with its own market square, this one crowded with goats and sheep being herded into their winter pens. Shafts and vents cut into the mountainside let fresh air inside and carried the wood smoke away. Mirrors reflected the dimming sunlight. Even as I watched, a series of lamps flickered on, like stars against a stony sky.

That's when I noticed a difference in the air—a scent that tickled my nose and sent a rippling excitement over my skin. Magic. It was like drinking water after a long drought.

Yún plucked at my sleeve. "Over here."

She elbowed her way between the goats and sheep and shepherds to the vendor stalls that lined the market square. One, tended by an old woman smoking a pipe, had a strange stone chimney beside it.

"How much?" Yún asked.

The old woman puffed out a mouthful of smoke and named a price.

It was so high I squeaked, but Yún didn't even hesitate. "Kai, let me have Yāo-guài, please."

I drew the limp griffin from its pouch.

The griffin huffed. Its eyes were dull. Its feathers had turned a tarnished yellow. Several floated to the ground as I handed it over to Yún. The old woman watched us with narrowed eyes, especially the griffin. "Better hurry," she wheezed. "It'll die more easily the second time."

"How do you know?" I asked.

The woman shrugged. "How could I not know? Magic is my business. Take this for the flux," she said to Yún, handing over a tall stone beaker. "Your tin cups won't do."

Yún accepted the beaker and counted out the sum into the old woman's palm. Following the woman's directions, she held the beaker underneath a spout beside the well. The old woman tossed the coins into her moneybox. With her pipe still between her teeth, she leaned close to the chimney, muttering a series of words I recognized from our long-ago lessons. A mathematical sequence. A magical one.

Magic flux streamed into the beaker, filling it to the brim. Yún carefully brought the beaker around to the griffin's half-open beak. "Yāo-guài," she whispered. "Drink."

Magic flowed from the beaker over the griffin's beak, like a stream of concentrated mist. Yāo-guài panted, snapped at the silvery cloud, then opened its beak wide, drinking in the mist until the beaker ran dry.

Yún handed the empty beaker back to the woman. She cupped her hand over the griffin's head in a caress. With a weak squawk, it fastened its beak onto Yún's finger. Yún winced and smiled. I could see her joy in her face, and my heart danced around. Our griffin would live. And Yún had smiled.

THE WIZARDS WERE right—the storm roared over the mountains at nightfall. Safe inside the cavern, I saw nothing but I heard everything. *Ai-ya*, did I hear it. Those heavy iron doors shuddered with every blast of wind, and their massive hinges groaned and creaked, while from outside came a horrible grinding noise, as though a giant gnashed its teeth. The magic flux lamps burned steadily, but ordinary candles and lamps flickered. We spent most of our funds for supper and a double-sized stall in the cavern's stables.

The pony gave a great rattling sigh as soon as I unloaded our packs. One of the old market women sold me hot water and mash, which I gave to the long-suffering beast to munch on while Yún rubbed him down. I went off to fetch a bucket of water from the common well so we could drink and wash and make tea. Like everything else, the water tasted and smelled of magic.

But when I got back, I found Yún sitting on the ground. The pony stood over her, nuzzling her hair. As I hurried forward, it jerked up its head and gave a scolding whuff.

I dropped the bucket and fell to my knees next to Yún. "What's wrong?"

"Nothing." She tried to stand up, fell back with a groan.

"It's your shoulder, isn't it?" I said bluntly. "You were so busy worrying about Yāo-guài, you forgot to worry about yourself."

I unbuttoned Yún's shirt and pulled the bandage away. The wound had closed completely since I last examined her, but sure enough, the scar puckered angrily and the skin surrounding it had turned a bright red. I cupped my hand gently over her shoulder. Thank all the gods in heaven, her skin wasn't fever hot, just overly warm.

Oh but there were all kinds of warm in the world.

Yún turned her face toward mine, eyes wide and dark. Her lips were a few inches away, no more. Her breath feathered my cheek. Blood rushed into my face as the world dropped away from everything except the two of us, alone in the stall. *No ghost dragons,* I thought confusedly. *Nothing to interrupt us now.*

Without me thinking, my hand strayed down even as I leaned forward to kiss her.

"No." Yún jerked her face away. "No, Kai."

All the warmth vanished in the sudden chill. Yún closed her eyes tight, and her face went deadly still. As if Yún herself had vanished deep inside.

I rocked back onto my heels and stood. Swung around so Yún couldn't see my flushed face.

She's embarrassed. She never meant to kiss me back that first time. And now she's scared of what I might do.

"The water has magic," I said, trying to keep my voice level. "You should drink some."

Whether she did or not, I had no idea. Yāo-guài chirped loudly, demanding attention. I gathered him into my arms and carried him to his nest of blankets. Still too weak from lack of magic, he squirmed and protested in soft complaining warbles, but he didn't do more than nip at my hands as I tucked the cloth around him. Chen said nothing. He didn't need to. By the time I finished, Yún had already curled up in her blanket, her back toward me. I did the same, ready to pretend sleep until it came for real.

8

I WOKE TO THE SMOTHERING GRAY HALF-LIGHT OF morning. The air was chilly and close; it smelled of wood smoke and a hundred leftover meals.

Yún was still asleep. I resisted the impulse to touch her wrist, her cheek. *I'm sorry,* I thought. *I'm sorry I'm such a horrible, selfish friend.*

A soft, snuffling piggy inside my head. Then, *You are too hard on yourself.*

Maybe I'm not hard enough. That's what my mother always said.

Chen snorted, but he didn't say anything else. I fed the pony and, picking up a sling basket from our gear, headed out to the indoor market to fetch something for breakfast.

Snow trickled down from the smoke vents. The magicians had extinguished the lamps, leaving only the pale, pale light from the openings, and a dank breeze drifted through the cavern. I bought a flask of hot tea from one vendor, a bowl of spiced noodles from another, and tucked them into my basket. Radios played in the market square. The flux ran strong here, I could tell, because there wasn't the usual crackle and sputter. A few even relayed news and vids from kingdoms as far away as the Khamsang provinces, way up north, but most were tuned to local weather stations. I listened as I poked around a few more stalls, looking for something the griffin might eat.

". . . weather wizards predict five more days of heavy snowfall . . ."

". . . bursts of dangerously high winds . . ."

". . . all freight lifts closed and magic-locked by royal decree . . ."

Five days locked underground. I shuddered at the idea. Sure, we could eat well, but nothing in this underground city was cheap. As I counted out more and more coins, I thought we would have to visit a *piaohao* soon.

One of the vendors sold grilled lamb mixed with rice. I bought enough for one small but hungry griffin (recently dead), then headed back toward our stall. Yún would be awake by now. Whether she was talking to me was something else.

Golden Snowcloud's cavern was laid out like a checkerboard, with different squares for markets, others for ware-houses, livestock pens, guard barracks, offices for the royal bureaucracy, and anything you could imagine, plus a lot more. There was even a palace of sorts. Small, but then the Golden Snowcloud outside was tiny as well. In the middle lay a wide open square with the city wells, which the royal wizards had dug into the rock centuries ago.

I was crossing the center square, when I heard an uproar—shouts, the clatter of boots, and then the shrill cry of some unnatural beast.

Trouble, Chen grunted in my ear.

He didn't need to say more. I knew that screech. It was Yāo-guài. The crowds were already streaming toward the quadrant where the livestock and stables were located. I slung the basket of food over on shoulder and thrust myself into the middle of the swarming, milling mass of bodies. Another screech launched my heart into my throat. All kinds of explanations tumbled through my head, none of them happy ones.

Hands grabbed me by the shoulders. "Kai!"

Yún. I nearly fell over in relief. "Yún, what happened?"

"Where were you?" she demanded, ignoring my question. "You left. You didn't even—"

"You were asleep. I went to buy—"

"You should have said something. I thought you—"

A bone-rattling shriek interrupted her. Yāo-guài again. Yún threw an angry hiss at me and plunged into the mob. I shouted at her to stop, but she ignored me. Cursing, I shoved my way after her. There was a tense, panicked air to everyone we passed—tough old men, even tougher old women, stout men sweating in spite of the chill. Only as we got closer did I understand. The air was alight with a strange white glow, and a stream of electric sparks arced overhead.

Finally, one after the other, we staggered clear—and nearly turned around again.

A dozen royal soldiers stood before our stall, swords drawn. Their faces were stiff and blank, but the way they gripped their weapons, all white-knuckled and furious, plainly said they were scared.

What in the name of the heaven's king was going on?

A man shouted from inside. At once, a chorus of chants rolled through the air—voices timed precisely in pitch and strength. Magic workers, chanting a spell of exorcism and containment. Yún and I exchanged glances, our argument forgotten. Behind us, the crowd muttered.

Chen? I whispered.

Your little monster lost its temper, he said.

The stall door opened. The crowd went silent.

Two soldiers emerged from the stall, a limp body slung between them: A man, barely covered by his scorched and ragged clothing. His bloody head lolled to one side. His eyes were wide, rimmed with white, like a ghost's, and staring at nothing at all. Dead? My heart froze inside my chest. Then the man's eyelids slowly sank shut, and I found I could breathe again.

The men staggered away in the direction of the palace quadrant. They didn't have to say anything. The crowd opened a lane for their passage at once. An old woman made a warding sign. Others clutched their robes close, as if a mere touch could scorch them, too. The lane closed after the soldiers, and muttering welled up, louder than before.

". . . magic blasting everywhere . . ."

". . . guards and wizards . . ."

". . . man almost dead . . ."

". . . that monster savaged him . . ."

Without waiting to hear more, Yún stalked toward the door. One of the soldiers grabbed her arm. She bared her teeth and growled. The man snatched away his hand and recoiled. Seeing my chance, I ran after her and slid through the half-open stall door.

And nearly ran smack into three wizards just inside.

They stood with their backs to us, palms lifted upward as they chanted in low rhythmic voices. Our pony huddled against the opposite wall. Yāo-guài crouched in the middle of the stall, surrounded by our scattered gear. His wings were spread wide and stiff. All his feathers stood on end, like spikes. His eyes glittered with fury and magic.

"What happened?" Yún demanded.

All three wizards spun around. "What are you doing here? Get out before that monster—"

"That 'monster' belongs to us. He was protecting our belongings and our pony. Anyone with two good eyes could see that."

She glared at the wizards. The oldest of the three wizards folded his arms and glared back. "We are responsible for keeping peace within the kingdom," he said evenly. "Your little monster is clearly dangerous. Do you have a permit for importing magical beasts into our jurisdiction?"

"Legal talk." Yún spat on the ground.

The man's lips tightened into a satisfied smile. "Which

means you do not. I need you and your companion to come with us to the palace for questioning."

"Us?" My voice squeaked up. "We didn't do anything—"

"You imported a dangerous creature. You did not notify the authorities of its presence. And whatever the provocation, your monster attacked and almost killed a man. You will come with us for questioning."

Yún drew herself into a straight line. "We refuse."

"Then we will arrest you for threatening the safety and tranquility of our king's domain. Do not think," he added, "that we cannot. Our chief wizard is more powerful than you can imagine."

More glares. More hisses from Yún. The wizard, however, was taller and older, with the immovable patience of a mountain. If we had a century to wear him down, like rain wearing through rock and metal . . . But we didn't. And this mountain had two wizards and a bunch of armed soldiers on his side.

"What about that thief?" Yún said reluctantly.

"He will be questioned. Do not worry."

Easy for him to say. He wasn't facing any fines or jail sentence.

I touched Yún's arm. "We have no choice."

She flinched away from my touch. "I know," she said in a low voice. "But"—she rounded on the senior wizard—"we bring our griffin with us. It's not safe otherwise."

His eyes narrowed, but he only shrugged. "You are probably right."

"And our stall," she continued. "You must set a guard here so no one else attempts to rob us. Understood?"

He grunted, which I took to mean *yes*.

I scooped up Yāo-guài. He shivered in my arms and made small chirruping noises. It was hard to imagine this small feathery creature attacking anyone. (Killing them. Admit it. He almost did.) The griffin nibbled at my shirt. I offered him a chunk of lamb from the basket. He gobbled it down so fast he almost choked.

They tried to smother him, Chen said.

What do you mean, 'they'?

There were three. Two remained outside to keep watch. They ran away when their comrade screamed. Their companion spirits were very strange. Not from around here.

For Chen to call a companion spirit "strange" meant something.

The wizard coughed. Right. Better to get this questioning

over with. Besides, it made more sense to tell the chief so-and-so about the thief's friends.

They hurried us through the crowds to the miniature palace, and down winding stone steps to an underground (more underground) hall with doors and corridors leading off in all directions. Our wizards directed us down the widest of these corridors, to a set of double doors with guards on either side.

The senior wizard stepped forward and presented credentials. He and the two guards spoke in low tones.

". . . taking care of that other one now . . ."

". . . really think it's necessary . . ."

". . . unauthorized magic . . ."

The guard must have agreed we were terribly dangerous criminals because he stared at us nervously before tapping on his wrist talk-phone. It beeped right away, and the doors swung open.

Our wizard keepers herded us into a small room covered on all sides by stone fitted to stone. A striped carpet blanketed the floor—all greens and browns and brass-bright yellow. A steady golden light illuminated everything without any sign of lamp or candle. And though there was no fireplace in sight, the air was as hot as a summer day, and smelling of crushed herbs and sweat. All around us magic flux flickered.

An old woman dressed in dark blue sat behind a desk. Her hair was snowy white and so thin that her skull showed through. Her eyes were shining black buttons in a nut-brown face, thick with wrinkles. In spite of the heat, she wore layer upon layer of woolen robes.

The chief wizard observed our approach. "I hope you have not misjudged the importance of interrupting me," she said mildly.

Our wizard bent low. "A matter of a magical disturbance, Your Honored Worship."

"Ah. That." She beckoned him closer and they conferred. Her expression never changed, but at the end of two minutes, she nodded briskly. "Good enough. Leave them with me."

"Your Honored Worship—"

"I am not in danger, Captain."

Though her voice was low, he snapped back with a salute. "Of course. I just—"

"—wished to articulate your concern. Good. You have done so. Now go."

She dismissed the wizards with a flick of one tiny prune-hand. Once the door closed behind the men, she turned to us. "Sit."

There was a bench in front of her desk. We sat. Yāo-guài wriggled in my arms. His eyes were brighter than before, almost alive. I tightened my hold and prayed to all the gods in heaven that he would behave.

The chief wizard studied us a few moments with an unreadable gaze. "You possess an interesting creature," she said. "He was dying when you brought him here, no?"

Yún nodded mutely. Her anger had drained away. She looked shaken and her wounds were probably bothering her. I wanted to take her away and let her lie down to rest, but when I made the slightest movement, Yún shook her head.

"Hmmmmm." The woman hummed, as if trying to recall a song. "You haven't trained him very well."

"We didn't know how," I said, irritated.

"Not a good excuse." She hummed again. Yún's expression eased, and her cheeks flushed with better color. "Now then. About this matter of theft and attack. You admit the creature nearly killed someone."

"Yes, but—"

"No more excuses."

I swallowed. "Yes, ma'am."

Her face wrinkled with a passing smile. "And no more false modesty. You were both furious with our wizards. Can't say I blame you. They are pompous fools. However, they were right to bring you here. We must guard our tranquility, especially when our kingdom is barricaded under the mountain. So I will question you both. And you, you will tell me the truth."

"About everything?" I burst out.

She tilted her head. Her ancient eyes narrowed to black slits. "Have you something to hide?"

I gulped. "Um, a little. Nothing bad."

Another smile, like the shadow of a brighter one. "I doubt that. However, I concede your argument. My duty to ensure tranquility does not give me the right to frolic through your thoughts and memories with abandon."

The image of this tiny old woman frolicking anywhere had me snorting. I tried to stop myself and went into a coughing fit. Yún thumped me on the back—harder than she needed to. I subsided into hiccups and wiped the tears from my eyes. "Sorry."

The woman wheezed. "Also doubtful. I can see on your face that you are seldom truly sorry. One day you must learn to speak honestly and from your heart, or you will regret the wasted years. So, the questions." She held up a hand. The air stirred around us, settling into a deeper and denser silence than before. "You have the features and accent from the mountains north of us. You have been traveling several weeks, then. Is this the first trouble you've encountered?"

I opened my mouth. Felt my tongue squeeze into new and uncomfortable shapes. Yún was massaging her throat, her expression unsettled. She worked her jaw as though testing her ability to speak. "No," she whispered. "A few days ago. Bandits—" Her throat spasmed. "Assassins. Soldiers. Not bandits."

The woman nodded. "Who sent them?"

"We don't know. We-we guess but we don't know."

"Are they dead, these not-bandits?"

"Yes. Died in an avalanche."

"Hmmmmm. More and more interesting. And now a thief breaks into your belongings." She turned to me. "Have you done anything to attract such attention?"

"Yes," I said. "No. Nothing wrong."

"Everything right," Yún said.

"You work for yourselves?"

"For our—for the—" Yún struggled not to speak. The griffin whistled and keened in distress. The woman waved a hand, and Yún slumped into her chair. "Perhaps that detail is not necessary. I can decide later. Tell me this, however. Does your work have anything to do with Golden Snowcloud? With our king or our kingdom or anyone else here?"

No, and no, and no. We traveled south. To the Phoenix Empire. To bring news to a dear friend. We answered a dozen more disconnected questions—none of them as nosy as I had feared. I was just beginning to relax when the desk beeped. The chief wizard touched a metal plate and the door hissed open.

A guard hurried to the chief wizard's side and whispered in her ear.

"When?" she said sharply.

"Moments ago. No more."

"And those fool wizards could not prevent it?"

"They tried—"

She dismissed the excuse with a gesture. "Never mind. I shall attend to the matter myself." Her attention swung back to us. "What would you say if you learned that thief died? Not from his wounds, but from magic?"

I stared. Yún did the same.

"Someone," the chief wizard said, "did not wish us to question him." She tapped her fingers against her desktop, clearly distracted by the news. Yún and I shifted nervously. All I could think was that no matter who was to blame, they'd sentence us to jail for the man's death and we'd never get to Phoenix City to find Lian.

"I see only one solution," she said at last. "You brought these troubles to our city, therefore you must take them away. You must leave Golden Snowcloud tomorrow morning and no later. If we detained you, we would only draw more violence upon ourselves. Better if you take it away with you."

"You can't throw us out into a storm. Hospitality says—"

"There is no more storm."

"What?"

Yún and I spoke at the same time.

"You had no idea?" She stared at us a moment longer. "An even stronger reason to send you away as quickly as we might," she murmured. To us, she said, "Your griffin extinguished the storm with its magic. Now do you see why you must go?"

I was too shocked to argue. Yāo-guài? Our little monster? Yún appeared equally shaken.

The chief wizard shook her head. Ran a hand through her wispy hair. Her fingers were like small brown sticks. How many of her enemies underestimated her, thinking her old and weak and fragile?

"I wish I knew more about the reason for your journey," she said, "but that is not my concern. Now, before you depart, let me remove the spell for truth. You might find it inconvenient."

She spoke a word. I had the sense of a cloak falling away from my skin. Yún touched her throat. Her color had improved in the past few moments.

"You will find your injuries trouble you no more," the chief wizard said. "You will also find the shopkeepers more accommodating. And when the gates open tomorrow morning, they will open earlier than usual. That is not a kindness, you understand. The easier you equip yourself, the faster you leave Golden Snowcloud. You should make good time before others notice your departure," she added.

Her attention dropped to the desk and a stack of papers. Yún released an audible breath. Relief? Despair? I could hardly tell how I felt myself.

No time to wonder. The guard laid a hand upon my shoulder and pointed to the door. We were dismissed.

W_E SPENT THE REST OF THAT DAY REPACKING, repairing, and generally refitting for our journey.

It wasn't a happy time.

"I don't care what magic spells that old wizard worked. You should rest," I told Yún, once we returned to our rented stall. "Watch over Yāo-guài, and let me take care of everything."

"No." She snapped off the word.

"But you're—"

"I'm fine. Great. Never better."

She faced away from me, just the curve of her brown cheek visible, framed by wisps of black hair. Her shoulders were hunched high and stiff, and she'd wrapped her arms around her chest, like chains around a treasure box. Whatever words came rising up in my thoughts would be the wrong ones, I could tell.

I just wanted to do the right thing. And I am sorry. I am.

"Shall I go to the *piaohao*?" I asked.

"If you like."

It took a mighty effort not to stomp away, cursing. Instead, I blew out a breath (quietly) and counted to a hundred. "I would like that. And would you like to pack our gear?"

"Yes."

One small word, as cold as an entire blizzard.

What did I do wrong? All I did was kiss her. Twice. I thought she liked kissing.

Chen didn't even bother to say anything. Deep inside, I felt his presence, but nothing more. Maybe he didn't understand girls either.

In spite of our not exactly speaking to each other, we were awake and ready long before dawn the next day. One vendor had opened his stall early, and from him, we bought a hot breakfast, which neither of us felt like eating. As soon as the royal watch opened the doors, we left.

Crews of workers had cleared away the snow our griffin had not melted with his magic. More snow trickled down from the leaden clouds, but already patches of a silvery sky showed through, and a faint sunlight glittered off the remaining ice and snow. The magic flux ran stronger, too, because the lifts were running smooth and quick, taking us up to the highway in moments instead of hours.

We headed south in cold and determined silence. Three hours later, we reached a point where the highway split into five different directions. One large black stone pillar marked the main highway south. Three smaller tracks looped back toward Snow Thunder City and other points east. The fifth one wound up the mountain slope to the next narrow goat trail heading almost directly west.

"South?" I said.

"No. East."

"Won't they expect us to head east? I mean—"

"West then. I don't care."

I glanced over. Yún glared back, tight-lipped, her eyes unnaturally bright.

"West," I said. "Sounds good to me."

The pony whuffed horse-curses under its breath, but didn't balk, even when the goat trail vanished into an expanse of bare rock. Hours later, we'd gained a point high above the same highway. Yún called for a stop, and I wasn't going to argue.

I'm tired of arguing. I'm tired of this trip. I just want to find Lian and go home.

We rubbed the pony down and fed Yāo-guài dried beef. I

pulled off my boots and massaged my feet. How many weeks since I'd left Lóng City? Five, at least. Maybe six. I'd lost track through all the storms. Meanwhile, Yún was staring over the edge of our cliff at something far away. She'd found a new way to ignore me, I thought. Then, she gave a muffled exclamation.

"What is it?" I asked.

She motioned for me to be quiet.

I crept quietly to her side and peered over the ledge. The cliff dropped straight down to a jumble of snow-whitened rock and dirt and scrub below. It was hard to make out anything in the patchwork of gray and brown and the bright glare of sunlight on snow. I wiped the tears from my eyes and stared harder.

Then I saw it. The highway marker we'd left three hours before. A few spots along the highway itself were visible farther along. But what snagged my attention were the five black figures circling around the marker.

Yún rummaged in her pack and took out a long round cylinder fashioned out of a dull gray metal. Both ends were capped with glass lenses. Brass rings circled the cylinder all along its length. There was a whiff of magic and science about the thing. She set the glass against one eye and aimed its other end at the stone marker. With her free hand, she twisted the brass rings, then hissed with satisfaction.

"May I see?" I whispered cautiously.

She shot me a glare, but handed me the cylinder.

It took me a few tries, but all of a sudden, the stone pillar leapt straight at me, large and crisply clear. All its markings were as easy to read as if I stood right beside it.

Without warning, a dark brown shadow blotted out the pillar. I jumped.

"What is it?" Yún asked quietly.

"I can't tell yet."

With more trial and error, I found the black pillar again. Adjusted the brass rings until the pillar seemed to recede into the distance. Another blur obscured the pillar, but only for a moment. Then a second one blocked my view. Without taking the lens from my eye, I twisted the smallest brass ring just a hair.

And saw a dark brown face staring upward.

I yelped, nearly dropped the cylinder. Yún grabbed for it, but I yanked the device away and hunkered down to try again.

Of course the man below didn't see me. It was only an illusion that his gaze drilled into mine. Still, my heart was thumping hard and my hands shook as I adjusted the lens to draw back a few more feet.

Five men stood around the black pillar. They were dressed in gray woolen cloaks with hoods, over leather armor. One man pushed his hood back and adjusted his steel helmet. They were pointing at the stone pillar and the different roads leading away.

Silently, I handed the cylinder to Yún. Waited for her to make the same discovery I had.

These were not bandits. And I would bet the rest of my reward from Princess Lian they weren't soldiers from Golden Snowcloud. They were mercenaries. Assassins, Yún had called them. And they were looking for us.

Someone wants to find us, I thought. *To stop us.*

If they had magic, they could. The ancient wizards could see through all the roads of time, according to my mother's lessons—past or present or even the possible futures. Cold crept over my skin. It had nothing to do with the winter winds scudding down from the mountain peaks.

Chen? I kept my inner voice to a whisper.

No. No magic.

Can you tell where they come from?

Too dangerous. Their companions are watching for us, too.

Through Chen's eyes, I glimpsed a raven, a giant rat, a scorpion, and other, stranger creatures I couldn't identify. They weren't magical—there were few humans with those beasts as their companion spirits—but ones that made me think of foreign lands, far away from these mountains.

Yún laid down the cylinder. "Not good. But not so bad."

"What are they doing?"

"Going the wrong way," she said. "Qi is distracting them with a false trail."

But her tone was plainly unhappy.

"Why is that not good?"

"Because whoever sent these men probably sent more."

Right. Like those mercenaries we'd already met.

A dozen last week. Five here. No, wait. There had been six, counting the thief in Golden Snowcloud. The number six teased at my memory. Weeks and weeks ago, when we were ordinary apprentices, Mā mī had given us a lecture about the magical properties of numbers. Some of those properties were genuine, some the heartfelt delusion of certain practitioners. The key to dealing with any opponent, she said, was to tell the difference.

"Six of them," Yún murmured. "Twice six before."

So she had noticed, too. "We should go," I said.

And for once, Yún didn't argue.

It took us three days, battling unnaturally fierce winds, before we crossed that pass. Neither of us had the strength to bicker with the other. If the griffin hadn't nipped us bloody, we might have forgotten to feed him. Six more days creeping along foot-wide paths brought us to the final pass, where the mountains spilled outward into the plains.

I paused. So did Yún. Seeing a chance to rest, our pony dropped its head and blew out great steaming gouts of breath into the chilled air.

All my life, I'd lived with soaring walls of stone around me. The skies reached up toward infinity, but left and right, with hands outstretched, you always felt as though you could touch the next mountain, not so very far away. All that had vanished. Before me lay an impossible stretch of brown and gray—so flat, I felt as though I'd lost my balance, and I was falling sideways.

Well, not exactly flat. The land undulated toward the horizon, interrupted here and there by rivers and their valleys, fringed by thin stands of trees. Farther north, a line of blue hills rippled outward toward the horizon. In the other direction, gold mottled the brown fields. Beyond that, I could just make out a few blotches of dark green, and some larger, darker spots that might be cities.

It was the Phoenix Empire.

10

WE TOOK AN EASY ROUTE DOWN THE LAST MOUNtain slopes. Our goal was Silver Hawk City, a neutral territory that sprawled between the foothills and the plains. Old-time legends said its first ruler was a bandit queen who got tired of fighting for her gold. She retired from the road, promoted all her sergeants, and negotiated fearsome treaties with the Seventy Kingdoms and the Phoenix Empire. All the caravans that passed between the mountains and the empire paid a road tax, a water tax, a guard tax, and taxes on anything else the queen could imagine, as well as high tariffs on all their goods. In return, Queen Bao-yu and her descendents ensured the highways and railroads remained well maintained and peaceful.

The last mountain pass had left us all exhausted. Even our ill-tempered pony had turned docile. Yún didn't argue with me, but she also wasn't talking much, except to mention necessary things. We'd left snow and sleet behind. The rains had slacked off to a drizzle, and we trudged through a blanketing gray mist. Luckily the roads were good. Our goat track widened to a regular highway road, marked with white painted stones touched with magic flux, which glowed like lamps in the fog.

We reached the border of Silver Hawk City by late afternoon, only to find a wall of soldiers armed with electric stun guns guarding the gates. They waved us off to one side, where we joined a never-ending queue of caravans, mule drivers, trappers on foot, and even a string of camels laden with goods. Neutral or not, Silver Hawk City guarded its borders. No one passed in or through without showing papers and paying their tax. We stood in line, passports in hand, for hours, while our pony stamped its impatience and our griffin stalked up and down the lines.

"How much longer?" I grumbled. "It's almost dark."

Yún sighed like the wind. "Soon."

"You said that last hour."

"Kai, shut up. I can't—"

"Next!" called out the guard.

We shambled forward, one cranky pony, two humans, and a dead stuffed miniature griffin, recently re-restored to life. The snow and sleet had died away in the southern passes, but rains had overtaken us. We were damp to our bones, our clothes stank of mildew, and even Yún couldn't do more than scowl and shove our papers at the guard.

"Kai Zōu," he said.

I grunted.

"Yún Chang."

Yún waved a weary hand.

"Anything to declare?"

With a squawk, Yāo-guài materialized in a cloud of sparks.

"One magical creature," the guard intoned. "Special tax and form A401-3 . . ."

Yāo-guài rose onto his hind legs and trilled loudly.

"*Shī*," I told it. "Hush!"

The griffin trilled louder. Was it my imagination or were there syllables and stops in between those clear high notes?

"What's wrong?" Yún whispered.

"I don't know."

Chen? I asked. *What's going on?*

A brief pause followed before Chen replied. *I'm not sure. But there is something strange here.*

What kind of strange? No answer. *Chen! Say something!*

With a *pêng* and a *p'ong*, two distinct presences crowded

into my mind—Chen and Qi. Dizzy, I sat down in the dirt.
Yún staggered and grabbed the pony's neck; it started back,
snorting and whuffing. The mists around us had turned
thick and dark, and my ears buzzed with magic. The griffin's
trills pierced through, loud and emphatic.

Go on ahead, said a whistling voice. *We have something we
must investigate.*

What kind of thing?

Yún's voice doubled with mine. We both sounded frantic.

Magical, Qi said.

Something I've never seen before, Chen said. Then he added,
*It won't take us long—a day or two at most. Don't worry. We'll
find you along the road.*

Then they were both gone, more completely than if their
bodies had vanished. Inside my thoughts, Chen's last words
echoed weirdly, like a ghost's unearthly prediction. "Yún?"
I said, uncertainly.

"I'm here, Kai."

"What do you think?"

"Application granted," the guard said crisply. "Transport
fees paid at the next station."

"But—"

We had no time to discuss the situation. Two much bigger guards hefted us to the nearest counter, where a wizened scribe laid out the fees we owed: entry fee, overnight residency, stabling fees, import fees, and an even larger sum they claimed was an estimated magic usage tax. Yún handed over the sum, in spite of my arguments. Once we had our stamped visas and receipts, the guards chivvied us through a pair of gates and into the city.

"Now what?" I muttered to Yún.

"We . . . we find a room and wait?"

She didn't sound all that certain herself, but she was right about one thing. We couldn't stand in the middle of this muddy road for long.

We headed down the road, into the main settlement of the kingdom. The only settlement. Hundreds of people jabbered at each other in different languages and dialects, all mixed together. Everywhere was the stink of magic and grease and steam. And soldiers. Hundreds and hundreds of soldiers patrolling the streets, or marching in drills in fields outside the city, next to the garrison. Holding tight onto our pony's lead, we threaded our way through the chaos and took rooms at the first inn we could afford.

Once we had our pony settled, and our bags stowed, it was evening verging on night. Chen and Qi had not returned.

Yún and I sat in the common room to plan our next move. We'd ordered a large pot of a strange new drink, supposedly imported from lands across the sea. The drink was strong and face-scrunchingly bitter. I spooned in a helping of honey. Tried it again. Bleh, still horrible.

Yún stared in her cup, the drink untasted. Her mouth was pinched with unhappiness. We hadn't talked much (at all) these past two weeks, but I couldn't help asking, "What's wrong?"

She shrugged. "Worried. About Qi and Chen. About . . . everything. All those soldiers, too." She shuddered. "There's trouble between the mountains and the empire. Maybe it's something to do with Lian, or not. Doesn't matter if we're caught in the middle."

Worry likes the sitting man, the old saying goes. And I couldn't blame Yún. We'd spent a month dodging mercenaries and thieves and snowstorms, and we still had more than five hundred *li* to go before we reached Phoenix City.

And it was the first time in two weeks that she'd answered me without frowning or glaring or muttering something afterward. My insides warmed a bit, and not because of the hideous coffee drink. Picking up my courage, I asked, "So what do you think we should do?"

Yún hesitated visibly, as though she weren't so sure about my reaction. "I think we should go. Right away. And not by horse caravan. We need a wind-and-magic train. We'll have to sell our pony and all our things, but we should get a good price for both. The second-hand dealers would be glad to buy our gear."

I eyed her suspiciously. "You planned all this today?"

Another hesitation. "No. Days ago."

And hadn't told me until the last minute.

(You told Chen she liked to order you around.)

(And being right is so wonderful.)

At the same time, Yún was right, too. We had to reach Lian as soon as possible.

"What about Chen and Qi?" I asked.

"They'll find us," she said quickly. Too quickly.

"Are you sure?"

"No. All I know is that we have to reach Lian as soon as possible."

I sighed. My head ached and my heart was empty. And yet, and yet . . . As much as I wanted to argue, she was right, curse her. "Okay. We hop on the fastest train tomorrow. What about our passports? Won't that tell our spy friends what we're up to?"

Yún looked startled, as if she'd expected me to start a fight. "I don't think that is a problem," she said at last. "After all, it's not the emperor who wants to stop us. It's someone in Lóng City, in the court. Someone who wants the crown."

Maybe. It seemed too simple. But like a lock-spell, the simplest explanations were often the true ones.

WE SOLD OUR pony and gear the next morning and headed to the train junction on the southern edge of the city. There we bought two first-class tickets, nonstop, for Phoenix City.

"How much money do we have left?" I whispered when I heard the price.

"Never mind," she whispered back.

She shoved a brochure at me, while she handled the paperwork.

. . . *unlimited meals, private bath, luxury and security in a single package for the discriminating passenger* . . .

Yāo-guài poked its beak outside my shirt and chirped. Unlimited meals, huh. With our hungry little monster, maybe that was a good thing. Not to mention the extra guards. And maybe, if we were sitting in a private compartment, I could talk to Yún about what happened in the mountains.

We boarded our train late that afternoon. As soon as we reached our cabin, Yún disappeared into the private bathroom with our griffin. I stowed our packs in a cabinet and scanned the compartment. It was huge—big enough for two couches and a table. Buttons along the window let me change the glass from transparent to gray to absolutely dark. More buttons and switches controlled the seats, how much air flowed through the cabin, even what perfumes got puffed from hidden dispensers. A special combination (explained in tedious detail by some bureaucratic technical writer) explained how to transform the seats into beds.

Purely by luck, I pressed a combination that made a vidscreen pop out from its slot. A tap or two on the controls, and the picture snapped into focus. A man's face filled the screen—his eyes were dark slits, his skin the color of weak tea, his hair a thin skein of iron gray over his skull. His face was unlined, but I could tell he wasn't young. He stood, as the saying goes, on the far side of the mountain. How far, I could not tell.

I was fiddling with the controls, trying to find out what

kind of vid was playing, when the screen blipped and a long menu written in hand-lettered characters appeared. Food. Real tasty food, cooked by gourmet chefs—not weeks-old provisions warmed over a smoky campfire.

Yún would like these, I thought, scrolling down the list.

I punched in whatever sounded tasty, or interesting, or even just different. Candied prawns, gingered shrimp, twice-cooked beef with scallions, a very strange dish called magic crabs. The only thing missing was the rude commentary from Chen. I paused and listened, certain he would pop into hearing or sight, but . . . nothing.

Oh, well. He's still off investigating with Qi.

The rushing water had stopped inside the bathroom, but still no Yún, either. A serving boy soon arrived, his cart piled high with dishes. With a flourish, he swung a table out from its hidden slot, then laid out each dish with another flourish and a bow. He reminded me too much of Deming, back in Lóng City. In spite of that, I paid him an extra large tip.

Only after the door closed did Yún peek out from the bathroom.

"Is he gone?" she asked.

She wore a silk robe, rose-colored and embroidered with

lilies and hummingbirds along its borders. Her dark hair was damp, and braided into a loose queue draped over her shoulder. She smelled faintly of rose petals. All my good intentions vanished and my face went hot.

"He's gone," I mumbled. "Let's eat."

We ate for a while in a silence thicker than wool. Just the *click-click-click* of the wheels as the train rattled on its tracks, the *shī* and hiss of the wind in the train's sails, and the crackle of magic when the engineer adjusted his levers to maintain the speed.

Only once did I try to say something. "Yún, about Golden Snowcloud. I'm sorry—"

"No," she said right away. "I mean, not now. Please, Kai. Later. After we find Lian."

Right. A good excuse, a true one. But would *later* ever get here? Or would Yún go back to Lóng City, earn her conjuration license and set up another shop, far away from a stupid street rat named Kai Zōu?

My appetite vanished. I clicked the vid screen on again. Six old men in dark tunics sat around a table, jabbering on about economic stimulus packages, future shares in magic flux, and how the trade negotiations in Lóng City might affect them. It was dull, but right now I wanted dull. Everything else hurt too much. Yún. My mother, missing or worse.

Yún set her chopsticks down. "That's not a video. That's real-time broadcast."

I blinked at her words. Sure, I'd seen fancier real-time broadcasts in Lóng City's vid-parlors, but never before in a train rattling along at thirty *li* an hour. I started to ask Yún how she could tell the difference, but she shushed me.

My questions were unimportant, I thought. I poured myself a mug of tea and punched the window controls. The swirling patterns vanished from the glass. Outside, the countryside flashed by. Fields and fields and more fields. Herds of swine and cattle and sheep. A larger market town. A broad sluggish river. Tiny villages that were hardly more than dots as we sped past. Dark clouds smudged the gray skies. Even as I watched, a white streak jumped from the clouds to the soggy fields below. It was raining again.

EIGHTEEN HOURS.

Ai-yi, they were the fastest and slowest hours of my entire life.

The griffin slept and ate and chewed up blankets. Yún did nothing but watch the news broadcasts, switching from channel to channel for no reason I could figure out. After a while, I gave up and stared out the rain-smudged windows at the countryside as the train shot over the rails. Chen never did make an appearance, though I called to him once or twice. It felt strange to be so alone inside myself. Worse than alone—empty.

Six hours into our journey, Yún switched channels again. I recognized the man who reminded me of a vid-screen actor. "Who is that?"

"Kaishan Zhu," Yún said. "The emperor of the Phoenix Empire."

"And those others?"

"His trade ministers."

The gabbling onscreen sounded like the same gabbling as before, except that now the emperor was explaining how recent purchases of magic flux supplies from various neighboring kingdoms would ease this temporary shortage in the empire. He went on to reassure us that new negotiations were underway in the central mountain kingdoms to ensure a permanent solution.

"How can it be temporary and permanent at the same time?" I said.

Yún didn't answer. She punched a few buttons on the keypad. Most of the windows on the screen closed, replaced by one filled with text. Yún kept tapping at the keyboard. More text scrolled by, too fast for me to read. It was obvious she didn't want to talk.

The rest of the evening passed in dreary silence. Yāo-guài fell asleep in a small snoring heap. I ordered another meal of cooked beef and packed all the dishes into cartons and stowed them in our packs. Yún was still studying the screens when I finished picking up all our scattered belongings from around the cabin and packed them away, too. As the hazy disc of the full moon rose above a bank of clouds, I rolled myself in my blankets and fell asleep.

A LOUD SQUEALING woke me. I bolted up.

"Yāo-guài?"

The squealing came from outside the train. The griffin darted around the cabin, adding squawks and trills to the noise, while the squealing went on and on. Yún must have turned the windows to opaque, because a smothering darkness enveloped our compartment. Groaning, I switched the window to transparent. A flood of bright sunlight poured through the glass, blinding me and sending Yāo-guài on another frantic circuit. Late morning, my bleary mind calculated.

Yún sat up rubbing her eyes. "What is it?" she croaked.

"I don't know."

Our vid-screen chimed. A woman's voice announced, "One hour to Phoenix City. Please make ready for departure."

We had plenty of time to wash and eat breakfast. As the train slid into the station, Yún and I were already standing by the doors. The griffin had not protested once when Yún tucked him into her backpack, but I could see him squirming around inside.

The doors hissed open, letting a wave of warmth roll into the train. Dry air, tinged with smoke and grease and the electric scent of magic.

I nearly lost sight of Yún in the first two minutes. We had to grab each other's hands to keep from getting separated as we squeezed our way past hordes of travelers trying to board the train. Overhead, signs glowing with magic flux showed arriving and departing trains by platform number. Children shrieked. Voices from the loudspeakers announced changes to the schedule. Vendors hawking spiced rice, roasted chicken, and grilled squid shouted out their wares. An old woman carrying a live chicken in a cage stomped past us, both of them screeching at each other. We might have introduced ten noisy griffins and no one would have noticed.

By the time we squeezed through the last doorway into a wide square outside the station, I was sweating. It was far warmer than I'd expected. More like late summer than almost winter—a very damp summer where rain clogged the air but never fell.

"Do you remember Lian's address?" I said.

"She has a set of rooms near the university. Used to. She said something about moving when we last talked, but she didn't say where. But the university should have her new address. We can ask once we get there."

We exchanged our money at a small kiosk next to the station. Yún asked the man for directions to the University Quarter. He grunted and waved his hand toward the opposite side of the square, as if that answered our question.

We did the squeeze routine again, sweating even harder than before. Eventually we popped out of the crowd next to rows of shops and vendors. And one strange, six-sided tower.

It was short, barely taller than I was, and painted a dull black. Each side had a big slot, a little slot, and a metal plaque with instructions. On top was a mesh cage. As I squinted at the instructions, a gnarled old man elbowed me aside and shoved a coin into a smaller slot. He jabbered into the slot in a thick southern accent. I heard a whirring noise. *Poof.* A flame shot up from the mesh cage, followed by a cloud of sickly-sweet-smelling incense. A minute later, the old man pulled a small square of paper from a larger slot and hurried off.

Yún planted herself in front of the machine and inserted a coin. "University Quarter," she said briskly. "Headquarters for student dormitories. First year students. Political science and magical studies."

More flames and smelly incense. The tower clicked and whirred and spat out another square of paper. Yún crammed it into her pocket.

We ducked into a nearby alley and examined the paper. Flowing script covered one side—directions to the University Quarter. On the other side was a map of the square where we stood. Magic flux flickered over its surface in the shape of an arrow pointing southwest. As we turned to see what lay in that direction, the arrow shifted with us. When we took a couple steps, the map changed to show a smidge more on one side, less on the other. A small gold-stamped device in one corner let us change the map's resolution from just a few streets to the entire city, with the widest avenues shrinking to needle-thin lines.

I whistled. "Fancy."

"It's the new techno-ink-magic. Let's go."

According to the map, the train station was near the city center. The student dormitories were in the southwest quadrant of the city, thirty *li* away.

We didn't have enough money for the tram, so we set off on foot. Our trip across the city took five long miserable hours. Sure, the magical map was clever and handy. More than once, the ink lines blinked at us if we took a wrong turn. But it couldn't conjure us from point A to point B in two sneezes. We trudged through the crowded streets, while the sun blazed down on our backs. Electric trams glided past. Bicycles clanged bells in warning as their riders wove in and around slow-moving pedestrians. Once a parade of monks strode by, clanging cymbals and bells, and waving bundles of burning incense. I saw a few carts drawn by mules or ponies. I saw a lot more carts drawn by people. One stopped next to us. "Want a ride?" the man said. He was a massive man with thick arms and legs. Sweat gleamed from his face, as though he'd been working hard all day.

"How much?" Yún said.

The man glanced at our paper and named a price so high, I squeaked.

Yún shook her head. The man spat on the ground and lumbered on.

The sun was slanting down toward the rooftops by the time we reached a pair of iron gates set into square stone pillars. Tall buildings built from smooth golden stonework loomed over the gate. Inside, dozens of young men and women dressed in scruffy trousers and tunics hurried back and forth with books under their arms. When we checked our map, the arrow vanished and we read the words, *Destination Reached*. Then the sheet went blank on both sides.

We tried the gates, but they proved to be locked. I called out to a student inside. He only stared at me and kept going.

"Maybe we need to summon her," Yún said.

She pointed to the stone pillar on our right. It had a small metal plaque pierced by dozens of holes, just like the speakers in the train's vid-screen.

I coughed and cleared my throat.

"Identity, please," said a man's gruff voice.

"My name is Kai Zōu and I—"

"Identity, please," the voice repeated.

Yún motioned for me to let her try. "We are here to see Princess Lian Song Li."

The metal speaker clicked and buzzed a few moments.

Then, "Invalid response. You have one more attempt. Thank you."

One more attempt? I opened my mouth to give my name, when Yún dragged me away. "What's wrong?" I hissed.

"I'm not sure, but I think if we make too many mistakes, they'll send the watch after us."

"But we have to find Lian."

"I know. But we can't find her if they arrest us."

I scowled. Inside my shirt, the griffin was poking me with his claws, clearly upset by our argument. I rubbed its head and tried to think. We had money—some—but no rooms. And the sun was setting. It occurred to me that we hadn't needed to think about watch-demons since Lóng City. Who knew what kind of horrible patrols the emperor of the Phoenix Empire loosed to guard the streets of *his* capitol?

Chen? I whispered, wondering if my spirit companion had returned.

No reply.

All of a sudden, the gates swung open and a crowd of students streamed out. Most of these were scruffy, too, but a few were dressed in elegant silks or woolen tunics and trousers, some of them with magic flux woven into the threads.

One of them glanced at us, then whispered something to the girl next to him. They laughed.

"Excuse me," Yún said. "Excuse me, could you tell us where—"

"Beggars' Quarter is three districts over," the first student said.

My hand curled into a fist. Yún gripped my arm and yanked me behind her. "We're looking for Princess Lian Song Li," she said to the student. "Could you please help us find her?"

He stared at her. His mouth twitched in amusement. Yún stared back. His glance slid away. "Come on," he said to his friends. "Let's get away from these slugs before we get slime on ourselves."

He and the girl minced away. Most of his companions followed, with only a few curious glances in our direction, but one young man remained behind. "You go on," he said to the others. "I'll walk home tonight."

The crowd drifted off. Our new friend (if you could call him that) studied us silently. I could tell he wasn't impressed. We were scruffier than the scruffiest students, our clothes dusty and stained from camping in the mountains, and if we'd taken three baths each in that fancy wind-and-magic train, you sure couldn't tell now.

"You're looking for Princess Lian from Lóng City," he said finally. "Why?"

"Why should you care?" I said.

"Maybe I know her."

Yún returned his gaze calmly. "The princess is our friend. We bring her news from home."

"Anyone can bring news. Can you prove that you're her friends?"

His face was pleasant enough. Ordinary and maybe he knew how to laugh. But right now, his eyes were narrowed and he stood stiff and cautious. A worm of cold worry crawled up my spine.

"What about you?" I said. "Why should we trust you?"

Now he did laugh, but it was a short unhappy one. "You can't. My apologies for my presumptions. If you will excuse me, I must hurry homeward. Twilight falls slowly in the southern plains, but it does fall. Don't let it take you by surprise."

Already he was edging away from us.

Then it came to me, a way to see if he really did know Lian.

"Wait," I called out. "Do you know the story of her heart's desire?"

The student spun around. Stared at us with an expression caught between curiosity and apprehension. "I do," he said cautiously. "What of it?"

"Then you know the names of her friends."

His expression eased, but only slightly. "Kai Zōu and Yún Chang." He spoke softly, more to himself than to us. "Yes, I should have known. But what kind of news do you bring?"

Yún shook her head. "It's private."

Another sharp assessing glance. "I see. Well, you won't find the princess in these dormitories. She used to have rooms nearby, but several months ago, the emperor invited her to live in the Imperial Palace. An honor that she could not refuse, you understand."

"And where is the palace?" Yún asked.

"Too far away for you to reach before dark, I'm afraid." He paused. "My rooms are poor, but I would be honored to have you both as my guests tonight. I live just a few districts over."

"With the beggars?"

The young man flushed. "I apologize for my companions. But yes, I live with the beggars. It comes in handy for my work."

I didn't understand, and I wanted to say so, but Yún was

smiling the same way as when she'd figured out a really complicated equation. "Thank you," she said. "We accept. Do you mind griffins, by the way?"

His eyes widened. "Um, not at all."

"Good. Kai?"

I glared at her. She glared back. "Very well," I muttered.

But as I trotted behind the pair, I found myself recalling Yún's warning about coincidences. Sure, we'd been lucky to find a friend and shelter so easily. Someone who even knew Lian. But was it a coincidence, or something else?

11

OUR NEW FRIEND INTRODUCED HIMSELF AS QUAN Dei Tsang. He was a medical student, he said. Or rather he had been. Having taken his degree two years ago, he had applied for a research position to study diseases and their cures. While he waited for an appointment, he attended lectures and earned cash by tutoring students.

"Do you really live in the Beggars' Quarter?" I asked.

He shrugged. "The rent is cheap. And I find it useful."

Useful?

We reached the main boulevard, which was crowded with bicycles and carts and electric trams. All questions had to stop as we threaded our way through the chaos. Quan led us uptown a couple of blocks, then ducked into a narrow opening between two tall buildings. It was like a tiny slice of quiet in that noisy city. There was barely enough room to walk single-file. My boots made a soft padding noise that whispered from stone and brick walls.

The passage opened into a wider lane edged by rows of tiny shops—butchers and candle makers, tailors and fishmongers, astrologers and scribes—all with brightly colored awnings stretched down to bamboo poles. The sharp scent of curries and peppers hung in the air. The neighborhood reminded me of the bazaars in Lóng City, especially the hawkers accosting passersby. There was even one old man guarding tanks of live fish and eels. I stopped by one and saw several ugly prickly creatures scuttling along the bottom.

"You like magic crabs?" the man said.

As I watched, one crab excreted a small pile of glowing ... dung.

"They look ugly," I said.

He nodded, as though pleased. "Very ugly. That means their magic is more powerful."

I shot him a suspicious glance, but he seemed to believe what he said. I shifted my attention back to the tanks. One fish—a paper-thin, black and orange triangle—paused in front of me. The next moment, it had darted forward and snapped another fish in half. One piece disappeared into the larger fish's gullet. The second floated down to the tank's floor. A smaller crab scuttled from behind a pile of rocks. A bright glitter filled the tank. When the water cleared, the fish had vanished and so had the crab.

"Was that magic?" I demanded.

"Magic crabs make magic," the old man said.

Yún gestured for me to hurry up. Quan had already crossed the square to another narrow opening. Was that how districts divided themselves? No time to ask, because Quan was urging us through the alleyway, which emptied into a maze of backstreets.

Once more the neighborhood had changed. Instead of shops, we saw rows and rows of tumbledown houses, with trash blowing over the mud-packed streets. Tired old men and women sprawled on the front porches. Some of them knitted or mended clothes as they chatted together. None of them looked anything like Quan's rich friends from the university, but he didn't seem to notice. Whenever someone accosted him, he stopped to ask about old grandmother's cough, or the sores on uncle's leg, or how many eggs they had left in their icebox.

The sun had disappeared behind the rooftops by the time we halted in front of a narrow brick building. Steps led up to a wooden door with a metal box over the latch. Quan placed his palm against the box. Magic rippled through the air, then I heard a loud *click*. Yāo-guài chirped with excitement.

Quan smiled at the griffin. "He likes magic."

"He's just hungry," I said. "The only meal he likes better than magic is fresh meat. *Rich* meat, if you know what I mean."

Quan's smile turned extra bland. "I shall take care, then."

He ushered us into a shabby entry hall. The moment we entered, a trio of small glass globes flickered with pale light. *Hü*, motion detectors. I hadn't expected to find those in a beggar's district. The current was weak, however, and the lamps flickered annoyingly as we climbed up the four flights to Quan's rooms. The smell of cooking curry, wet diapers, and the sharper stink of old urine filled the stairwell. The top landing, however, was painfully clean.

Quan pressed his hand against another of those metal boxes. The air flickered with uncertain magic and the door swung open.

"My home," he said, standing to one side.

Yún entered first, tall and straight and graceful, as if she had not been wandering Phoenix City with a backpack over her shoulder. I followed, weary and stumbling and not afraid to show it. We found ourselves in the middle of a plain entryway, with bare wooden floors and battered pieces of furniture.

No, this *was* the main room. A small alcove off to one

side served as a miniature kitchen, with one counter stacked high with cook pots and dishes, spice jars, and what looked like a mortar and pestle. Another alcove contained a wash-stand and pitcher. Bookshelves and cabinets lined the rest of the rooms, except for one door and a large window overlooking the alley below. I deposited the griffin on the nearest chair. He grumbled at being put down, then settled into the chair and began to pick at the loose threads with his beak.

Quan came last and bolted the door behind us. "I apologize for my poor rooms. But they are more comfortable than the city's free shelters."

"More comfortable than the dormitories?" Yún asked.

"Cheaper," I said.

Quan flushed. "I have my reasons. If you will excuse me a moment."

He disappeared into what looked like a closet. No, that was his bedroom. I smirked. Yún smacked me on the shoulder. "Be nice," she whispered.

"Why? He's a stuck-up rich man pretending he likes the poor."

"Maybe so. Be polite anyway, until we find out *why* he wants to help us."

Aha. Now I understood.

Quan reappeared with cushions and blankets, which he stacked in one corner. "I don't have much," he said. "But I can offer you tea while I make dinner."

He took a square metal box from one of the cabinets. It turned out to be a burner powered by magic flux. Quan cleared off his desk, uncoiled the thick gray cord, and inserted the plug into a wall outlet. He filled the kettle, then set it on the burner, which hummed and fizzed with current. My skin prickled at the sight.

Magical locks outside and in. Magical lamps in the corridor. Motion detectors and outlets. How did such a poor neighborhood rate the special connections you needed for the current? I glanced toward Yún and mouthed the words *too much magic*. She nodded but signaled for me keep quiet.

"So," she said, "how do you know Lian? Did our princess decide to study medicine?"

Quan looked puzzled at first, then laughed. "Hardly. We met in lectures. Magical Philosophy and Ethical Applications. Would you like sugar for your tea?"

Yún made a face. "Who puts sugar in their tea?"

"Barbarians," Quan said. "We had several exchange students from tribes in the far northeast. Interesting customs. One of my cousins lives in the outer provinces, and he tells me the most outrageous tales. Of course, he could be exaggerating."

As he talked, he measured tea into a small teapot decorated with dragons that intertwined into a pattern making an even larger dragon. Soon he was pouring tea into three cups that looked as though they'd been cracked and mended several times over. A poor man, but I recognized the dishes as coming from a once-rich household. And the tea itself turned out to be a rare and delicious blend from the southern coastal cities. It had a delicate smoky flavor that chased away all my miseries in spite of myself. Quan explained that another cousin who lived on the coast sent him regular shipments. Meanwhile, Yún continued to ask polite questions about Quan and his studies, which he just as politely deflected.

She's right, I thought. *He's hiding something.*

We finished our tea. Quan smiled, but I could tell he was embarrassed. "I promised you dinner. There is only one difficulty." He paused, cleared his throat. "You see, I meant to visit the markets today, but—"

"But you stopped to talk with us," Yún finished for him. "Never mind. We have some leftovers from the train. Show me what you do have. Let's see what we can cook up."

Quan supplied rice, eggs, fresh leeks, and one lonely onion. We supplied our cartons of twice-cooked beef. It wasn't easy, cooking for three (plus one hungry griffin) in that makeshift kitchen, but one burner, three pots, and two skillets later, we had a heaping bowl of what the snobs would call an unclassifiable meal.

As we cooked and ate, Quan told us funny stories about the university, his cousins (he had a hundred, at least), and Phoenix City itself. He never mentioned Lian again, nor did he talk about the emperor or his court. I expected Yún to ask more questions, but she didn't. She laughed at Quan's stupid jokes and convinced Yāo-guài to accept tidbits from our host's fingers. Only when Quan happened to glance away did I catch the calculating look in her eyes, and I knew she had not forgotten her own warning.

Once the meal was over, Quan nodded toward the stacks of pillows and blankets. "My bedroom is yours," he told Yún over her protests. "I remade the bed with clean linens. Kai and I will be comfortable enough out here. The floor isn't as hard as it looks."

Yún glanced at me. I rolled my eyes. Reluctantly, she withdrew with our griffin. Quan set to work, laying out the cushions and blankets. I scowled at him. *Are we supposed to like you now?*

He glanced up and smiled pleasantly. "Doesn't that hurt your face?"

That only made me scowl harder. "Why are you being so nice to us?" I demanded. "We don't have any money, and we aren't powerful nobles back in Lóng City. Anyway, what were you doing with those snobs from the university?"

"My father taught me to be helpful. It was a rule in our household. Besides, I remember when I first came to Phoenix City, years ago. Someone helped me then. It's my turn now."

I opened my mouth, shut it. Maybe that was enough to explain his kindness to us. Maybe, I thought, there was such a thing as a good coincidence. Maybe I should just keep watching.

IN SPITE OF everything, I slept like a twice-dead griffin. Once, close to dawn, I drifted up from muffled dreams to find Yāo-guài nestled under my chin, his feathers tickling my nose. His breath was warm upon my wrist, and I could feel a steady heartbeat against my chest. Dead or revived? But sleep rolled over me once more, and I sank back into never-dreams.

Later, much later, I woke again to the murmuring of voices. Bright light slanted through the window shutters, and from far away came the familiar noises of early morning street traffic. *Not yet,* I mumbled.

A heavy weight thudded on my back. The griffin gave a bone-shaking screech and pecked at the back of my head.

"Time for breakfast, Kai," Yún called out.

Bleary-eyed, I sat up.

Yún and Quan were both disgustingly wide awake. Yún was making tea, while Quan searched through the narrow closet that served as his pantry, muttering. "Rice, smoked fish, I thought I remembered buying more groceries last week. Ah, Kai, you're awake. If you'd like a bath, you should hurry before the hot water runs out. The tub is just down the hall."

Yún tossed a towel at me. "Take Yāo-guài with you He's stinky from yesterday. I think he's molting, too. Here's a comb."

"What about soap?"

"I left some by the bathtub."

I eyed the griffin. She was right. Yāo-guài looked pretty shabby. No palace guard would let us inside with him the way he looked. Swallowing my grumbles, I captured him and stalked down the hall.

The bathroom was more like an extra-large closet, completely filled with a gigantic iron tub. A small sign listed the invocations to use for turning the water on and off, and adjusting the temperature. *More magic,* I thought uneasily, and of a kind I never expected to find outside a royal palace. You couldn't use up magic flux, according to my mother, but you could wreck the currents by sucking away too much at one time.

Pretty soon I was too busy wrestling with a very uncooperative griffin to worry about magic or its misuse. By the time we finished with our baths and got back to the room, Yún and Quan had laid out breakfast. There were bowls of rice and curry, and a stack of yeasty cakes. Quan must have nipped out to an early market, I thought, as I gobbled down a handful.

Quan watched as Yún fed bits of rice and beef to Yāo-guài. "You say he was dead?"

"Dead and stuffed," I said. "My mother bought him from a wandering junk man."

"Interesting," Quan murmured. "There are some odd qualities about the magic, almost as if someone had cast several spells at once. Would he let me examine him?"

"Try it," I said.

Quan and I exchanged pleasant glances. His eyebrows lifted, clearly suspicious, but he held out two fingers to Yāo-guài.

The griffin gently nibbled at the offered fingertips. Its eyes gleamed and it snapped.

Quan jerked his hand back and sucked on his fingers. He studied the griffin with increased respect. "I see where you got the name," he said. "Little monster."

Yún chuckled. "It's the fish oil on your fingers, I think."

"Are you sure?"

"No." She gathered Yāo-guài into her arms. "Now, what about Lian? We need to talk to her right away. Kai has a talk-phone, but we've had trouble using Lian's number."

"And I bet the wizards here spike the lines," I added.

"They do," Quan said. "Let me think."

He rubbed his bitten finger absentmindedly, as though he were running through a dozen or more possibilities. *Like a doctor making his diagnosis,* I thought. *Or a spy figuring through which plans would work and what to do if they didn't.*

No, not a spy. A nobleman used to courts and intrigue.

"We could send a message," he said at last. "By hand is best."

"A courier?" Yún asked.

"No. I have some friends I trust."

He brought out a writing kit and paper. For a moment, he frowned at the paper, then brushed a note swiftly and sloppily. The message, which he showed to us both, told Lian that a friend in Lóng City had sent her a gift she had long desired in her heart. If she wished to accept the package, she should arrange for the messengers to be admitted to the palace. I also noticed he didn't sign the message.

The note went to a child in the courtyard below. Thereafter, Quan told us, it would make its way across the city to a certain trusted runner inside the palace.

"What if you can't trust this runner?" I asked.

"I can. She won't say anything. I know her."

Yún's eyebrows lifted. "Another cousin?"

"I have several," Quan said mildly.

His answer did nothing to ease the anxious twinges in my stomach, but I couldn't argue without giving away our news for Lian. And no matter how friendly he was, I couldn't quite trust him. Once we reached Lian, we didn't have to.

Two hours later, the reply came back: *Bring me the package at once, please. I will make certain the gates open to you. Lian.*

The trip took an hour by tram, in between stops and transfers and blockages. Quan had politely insisted on coming, even though Yún insisted back—not quite so politely—that it wasn't necessary. Most of the time, I pretended to doze in my seat, but I was watching Quan from half-closed eyes. Something had changed. He wasn't the stiff, cautious young man we'd first met. He looked nervous, and that made me nervous, too.

The tram jerked to a halt in the middle of a crowded square. At the north end, a high wall stretched the entire width of the plaza. Behind it came a series of huge build-ings, fat towers, and skinny towers, all of them capped with gold-plated roofs shaped like fancy pastries. From every-where at once came the strong, taut sense of magic. Those were no ordinary protection spells. Those would pluck any thought of danger from my mind and crisp my body to ash before I could even clear my throat to work a spell or plan a misdeed.

The palace.

Quan tapped my arm, recalling me. "This way."

He took us along the wall and around the corner to a smaller gate flanked by dozens of guards. All of them were dressed in sober gray. All had the imperial insignia of a blaz-ing phoenix embroidered over their chests, and the usual assortment of stun pistols and daggers. Several, those with gems above the insignia or embedded in their ears, carried long curved sabers.

Quan approached the senior guard and bowed. A flash of electronics from the guard's eyes told me our images were being recorded. Nervously, I shifted on my feet until Yún hissed at me to keep still. Quan was talking to the guard, but his voice was too low for me to make out the words. Then I heard the words "gift" and "package."

The guard beckoned us to approach. "Show me this gift," he said.

"It's a magical beast," Quan said smoothly. "Apprentice Yún?"

Yún took the griffin from inside her shirt and let the guard examine him. Yāo-guài hissed and ruffled his feathers, but allowed the guard to look him over, only snapping once when the man lifted his tail.

"Very well," the guard said, returning the griffin to Yún's arms. He flicked open the talk-phone on his wrist and spoke some nonsense words. Coded instructions, I guessed, because a runner appeared almost right away.

First, we had to stop inside a small stuffy room, where more guards recorded our faces and fingerprints. After that, the runner took us through a small set of doors into a very plain corridor—a service passageway, from the looks. Gray stone walls. Gray stone floors. The air felt warm and close, as if we were a hundred *li* underground. A series of lamps overhead slowly rotated on their stems, following us as we passed by.

The corridor ended in an empty room with low ceilings and a railing around its three walls. The minute we stepped inside, a door slid shut behind us. None opened in front.

"Where are we?" I asked.

"Magic lift," Quan said.

"But we're—"

The runner pressed a series of buttons on a small inset panel. Abruptly my stomach dropped to my toes. I lurched sideways, just in time for Yún to lurch into me. Quan and the runner had both braced themselves against the wall.

One sudden stop. Another lurch toward the side. My ears were buzzing from all the magic, my insides were crawling up through my throat, and all I wanted to do was pound on the door and scream for someone to let me out of this hideous trap.

With another whooping change of direction, the magic

faded slowly away, while it felt as though the room was sliding slowly across a level surface. I swallowed my stomach back to its proper place. Yún didn't look any less unnerved than I did. The wretched griffin, however, was chirping in excitement.

The same doors slid open to reveal another corridor.

"Did we actually go anywhere?" I croaked.

"Quite a distance," Quan said. "Up five floors and across half the palace."

To my relief, he wasn't laughing at either of us. The runner had that blank servant's expression that said he'd tell the story later to his friends. Probably with lots of exaggeration and jokes about the poor mountain peasants from up north.

"This way," Quan said.

"You say that a lot," I growled.

Yún smiled queasily, as though she hadn't recovered yet. "Slowly, please."

We followed the runner past several large courtyards filled with blossoming trees, along a sunlit gallery, through more halls and chambers. Finally, we stopped before a small set of doors, decorated with tiny enameled panels depicting folk tales of the mountain kingdoms.

The runner touched a wall panel of silver webbing. Soft chimes sounded from within. Very quickly, a woman in the emperor's livery opened the door. "The princess expects you," she said, gesturing for us to enter.

We came into an airy, six-sided entryway. I only had time to take in the silk hangings; the miniature fountain carved from a block of jade, with more jade figures set all about its rim; and a scent that reminded me of mountains and home, before a voice called out. "Kai! Yún!"

Lian ran toward us. She hugged Yún first, me next. "I'm so glad to see you," she said fervently. "I've missed faces from home. I missed yours." She hugged me again, so fiercely it left me breathless. My throat contracted as I realized we would be bringing her no good news from that home she missed so much.

A musky scent tickled my nose. A fox-shaped shadow glided past us. Jun, Lian's fox-spirit, circled us once and paused, her nose pointed toward the doorway behind us. Her muzzle wrinkled into a snarl.

Abruptly Lian drew back. Her gaze traveled past us to Quan. All the joy vanished from her face. "You," she said. She drew up stiff and straight, once more the cold, remote princess I remembered from the first time we met.

Quan flinched. "Your Highness."

"You did not write that note," Lian said. "I know your handwriting. Or were you lying with your brush? The way you lied to me before, with words and deeds."

"Lian, I wasn't lying. I—"

Jun cut him off with a growl.

"Go," Lian said coldly. "Thank you for bringing my friends, but go."

Quan's face flushed. He swept into a deep bow, his manner as formal as Lian's. Without another word, he backed out of the entry hall. Jun flickered out of sight, back to the unseen world of the spirit companions.

Lian waited, her hands pressed together in front of her chest, until the outer doors closed. She released a long breath and turned to us, her expression still remote. "I apologize for such rudeness," she said. "It was . . . he was . . ." She dismissed whatever she was about to say with a swift sweeping gesture. "Never mind him. Tell me why you've come to Phoenix City. I'm quite, quite happy to see you, but it's so strange."

Yún glanced at me. I opened my mouth, but my voice

died inside my throat. After a long moment of silence, Lian stared from Yún to me, then back. "The message said you had news," she whispered. "What is it, Kai?"

There was no way except the straight one.

"Your father is ill," I said. "They believe he is dying."

12

LIAN STARED AT ME. "MY FATHER? DYING?"

A woman popped into sight from behind a painted screen—another servant dressed in the emperor's livery. She bowed quickly and vanished through a doorway. I heard the susurrus of voices in another room, the *hiss* of slippers over bare tile, as those other servants withdrew to some farther set of rooms. The gossiping had started already.

Lian's expression seemed to close in on itself, as if she was thinking the same thing. "Please," she said, "come with me. We must talk more."

She swept through the arched doorway, her robes gleaming like a waterfall of blue and silver. Yún and I glanced at each other, then hurried after her.

Lian took us without pause through a series of exquisite rooms. Watercolors hung from the walls. Fantastical creatures built from wire and priceless gems curled around the lamps overhead. And everywhere, just where you might want to sit, were benches covered in brilliant silks of jade and indigo. It was like walking through a fairy-tale treasure house.

I'd hate it here, I thought. *Nowhere to kick off your sandals and get comfortable.*

Not exactly nowhere. Lian brought us to a small room, off what looked like her bedchamber. Here were several enormous stuffed chairs, the kind where you could curl up and take a nap. Or sit and read. Or just talk with friends. Oh, and there were books—shelves and shelves stuffed with them. A wide desk occupied one corner, with more books and a few papers scattered over its polished surface. I saw a brush and inkwell, a sheet of paper half-filled with writing. She must have been at work when we arrived, I thought.

Lian paced back and forth between the window and the desk. She swung around, her face no longer blank, but alive with a fierce determination. "Tell me what happened," she said. "Tell me everything."

Yún and I glanced at each other. Yún nodded. *You first.*

Right. The ghost dragon king had appointed me the messenger. With a few stops and starts, I gave Lian the story from the beginning, from the trade negotiations, to her father's sudden collapse at a banquet, to the rumors of plots and machinations at court. Lian nodded a few times—her father must have told her about the negotiations months before—and frowned when I mentioned the rumors. When I told her how the court wizards and physicians were unable to cure the king, her lips thinned into a sharp line.

"Why did no one send word?" she demanded.

"They claimed they did," Yún said. "They said you never replied."

"I received no message. Go on."

I finished up with my mother's disappearance and the ghost dragon king's commands, then Yún took over. She told Lian about our arrival in Phoenix City and how we met Quan. The moment she mentioned his name, Lian's eyes narrowed. "He is an opportunist," she said, her voice going low and dangerous. "He used your innocence to pretend you needed him."

"He was not entirely wrong," Yún said slowly. "We've encountered some odd . . . coincidences."

She named them: the bandits who weren't really bandits; the thief in Golden Snowcloud; the strange magical disturbance in Silver Hawk City, on the edge of the Phoenix Empire.

"Chen and Qi went off to investigate, and they haven't come back yet. That's strange, too."

"Coincidences," Lian began.

"Yes, but there have been too many of them," Yún countered. "Magical and mundane. Kai didn't say before, but he tried a dozen times or more to call you with his talk-phone. He couldn't. The network said your number no longer existed."

"And don't forget about the magic flux," I said. "Snow Thunder City had none at all. A boy told us it would come back in the spring, but that makes no sense."

"It might be connected with the crisis in magic flux shares," Yún said.

Lian waved her hand abruptly. "The magic flux doesn't matter. What matters is that I go back to Lóng City at once."

She clapped her hands. Dozens of servants in the emperor's livery swarmed into the study. A flurry of complicated commands followed—instructions for collecting belongings, fetching trunks from storage, a summons for scribes and runners, and orders to her own maids to lay out her best and most formal robes—then all the servants streamed off in ten directions.

Lian turned to her desk and pressed a series of buttons.

The surface split in two; a very sleek calculor machine rose into the air. She tapped the keys. The vid-screen (made from a strange plastic web) glowed a moment, then its background went dark, except for the image of a man's pale face in the center.

The man bowed. "Your Highness?"

"I request an interview with His Imperial Majesty. An urgent matter."

"Of course. I will inquire." He didn't look surprised. These rooms were spiked, then.

The man consulted another screen off to one side. He tapped a few keys. "His Imperial Majesty will receive you in the Emeralds-of-Heaven audience chamber in half an hour. You may have ten minutes of his time. Does that suffice, Your Highness?"

"A more than generous allotment," Lian said. "Thank you."

She switched off the calculor and returned the machine to its slot. For a moment, she did nothing but stare into the distance, as though Yún and I were invisible.

(As though she sat alone on Lóng City's throne.)

At last, she gave herself a shake. Her mouth twitched into the barest of smiles. "My presence here is different from most other students'. The emperor specifically invited me to stay at his court. I cannot leave unless I petition him. But there is no need for you to concern yourselves," she said, as Yún started to rise. "Stay here and rest. I shall have the servants bring you refreshments."

She clapped again. More servants appeared from nowhere to receive orders. Once she delivered them, Lian herself vanished through a side door, trailed by a dozen maids.

"She's very upset," Yún whispered.

"Upset, or angry?"

Yún eyed the doorway where Lian had disappeared. "She is like her father," she said in soft voice. "Very proud. Which means she would hate to hear me say such a thing."

A collection of servants arrived with trays, bearing tea and pastries stuffed with magic crabmeat. From the next room, we could hear Lian's raised voice. More servants hurried between nearby rooms, fetching piles of clothing, from brilliant emeralds and ruby to sober-hued grays and darkest indigo. Others flitted around with brushes and combs and jewelry boxes. Watching them, I forgot to eat, except when Yāo-guài pecked at my hands.

Sooner than I expected, Lian reemerged from her dressing room. She wore layers of shimmering robes, ivory and emerald green and black, with gems at the sleeves and all along the hemline. More gems sparkled from her hair, which she now wore in a complicated arrangement. "This shall not take very long," she said.

She swept out the door, leaving a faint cloud of jasmine perfume in her wake.

"Very proud," I whispered.

"*Shī*," Yún said, hushing me. "She worries about her father."

Remembering how my mother had grieved for my father, I shut my mouth on any comeback. Yún was right. Lian would not show any tears or anxiety in front of us, never mind the rest of the world. *Āi-āi*. Now I wished I had broken the news more easily, instead of blurting it out, but my words were like kites on broken strings, swooping away from all recall.

Glumly, I stared at the piles of fragrant, no doubt tasty food. "I wish Chen were here."

"And I wish Qi were here," Yún said. "I thought they'd catch up with us by now, but—"

"Maybe they're hunting clues and got sidetracked. Chen does that sometimes."

"Maybe." But Yún didn't look any more convinced than I felt.

She picked up a chopstick and poked at one of the pastries without any enthusiasm.

I sighed and poured myself a cup of tea (which reminded me uncomfortably of Quan's exquisite smoky tea).

We had all changed forever. Me, Yún, and Lian. All the rest of my gang. Which wasn't my gang anymore. Briefly I wished I could recite a magic spell and transport us all back to a time when all we cared about were running pranks and tricks in the Pots-and-Kettles Bazaar. But my mother was right. I wasn't a child any longer. Even the most complicated magical spell in the world couldn't change that.

I miss you, Mā mī.

"Kai, what's wrong?"

Yún watched me with those large dark eyes.

"Besides the obvious?" I asked, then flipped my hand to one side. "Sorry. I'm just worried about Chen and Qi."

I poked at a pyramid of steamed dumplings. No good. My appetite had vanished. Restless, I let my feet carry me into another room off the bedchamber. It was a sitting room, decorated with paintings. They were all pictures of Lóng City, I realized. There was the Golden Market on a feast day; there the main temples and the monks parading in crimson robes; there a view from the high walls, with the whole city poured over the mountainside.

(She misses home.)

(Of course, idiot. So do you.)

(Well, I didn't ask to leave. She did.)

(You aren't going to be king of Lóng City. Just a make-believe Prince of the Streets.)

Dismissing my loathsome inner critic, I passed by the rest of the landscapes and cityscapes to a small group of portraits. The center one was a square of painted silk that shimmered with magic. It was a portrait of Lian's father, Wencheng Li, just as I remembered him from last year. Thin gray hair drawn back into a tight queue. Weary eyes, but not so weary that you missed their intelligence. As I watched, I saw those eyes flicker toward me, then above my shoulder, as though he'd noticed something. He smiled. Maybe Lian had come to watch her father sit. Maybe he was smiling at her.

I jerked back.

That's what I get for snooping. I see too much inside my friends.

I plopped onto the nearest bench. From time to time, a servant glided silently through the room on errands. Next door, Yāo-guài warbled in excitement while Yún spoke to the beast in low soothing tones. Everyone had a task or obligation here except me. "I wish I had something to do," I muttered.

A faint whirring sounded from the floor. I jumped up, startled.

A small square table, the size of a handkerchief, rose from the floor. More gadgets. The table paused. Cautiously, I sat down again. The table continued to rise. As soon as it reached the level of my arm, it stopped again. On top of the table stood an even smaller square box. As I watched, wide-eyed, the box flipped open to display an even smaller vid-screen, the color of creamy new parchment.

Mrrrp, said the vid-screen.

Magic flux rippled through the air as the vid-screen came to life. A thin keyboard unrolled itself from underneath the box and prodded my arm.

There's too much magic in this palace, I thought.

The metal box vibrated. Intrigued, I ran my fingers over the keyboard. The vid-screen shimmered. A stream of images flickered past—so quickly they were more like dots of color and light. I tapped a few more keys. The images slowed, then froze with another tap.

I saw a thousand upturned faces, like a sea of brown dots against an emerald green expanse. I saw a great phoenix worked in gold, suspended from the ceiling. I saw a chamber so vast, it made the palace in Lóng City look like a mousetrap. In spite of the tiny vid-screen, I felt as though I had tumbled directly into another world.

The focus changed; the dots changed to courtiers, guards, and commoners, the camera pausing here and there. It was a silent scene. I saw one courtier lean toward another, but their conversation was inaudible to me. Before I could figure out how to change the volume, the camera zoomed away from them and locked on one man's face.

Kaishan Zhu. The emperor.

The smooth, pale features filled the screen, the eyes bright and intent, the skin like fine silk drawn tight over his bones. An old man—this I could see—but alive with the knowledge of his power.

He was speaking to someone close by. Again, the scene played silently. I fiddled with the controls, but nothing worked. I tapped harder. The calculor buzzed, and the screen flashed the words "Audio Options Not Available."

I clicked off the vid-screen and headed out the nearest door. Right away, a liveried servant popped into view—a stout, muscled woman, who looked as though she didn't want to hear any nonsense.

"Princess Lian," I said before she could speak. "She is currently in the emperor's audience chamber. Please direct me to the nearest lift."

The woman hesitated. Her lips moved silently through a few replies, but then she smiled broadly. "Of course, young sir. Please continue left along this gallery to the next green tapestry. You will see a small service corridor on your left. Take the lift at the end." She rattled off the buttons to push for the emperor's audience chamber.

The lift was right where she said it would be. I slapped my palm against the glowing yellow panel to open the door. Inside, I tapped out the buttons. Just as the doors clicked shut, I heard Yún's voice, calling out to me.

Magic flux filled the compartment. The lift ascended, as smooth as oil rolling over water. As slow as smoke rising on a windless day.

Then slower. And slower.

The floor beneath me gave a funny lurch. I gripped the handy railing—just in time. The magical lift abruptly zipped along sideways, so fast it made my eyes roll backward.

Thump.

That was the sound of my head hitting the walls. I lost my grip and landed on the floor with a second thump. Magic still hummed around me, thick and sharp and smelling strong. It took me at least a minute before I accepted I hadn't died. Another couple of minutes before I could tell the lift no longer moved, up, down, or sideways.

Right about the time I decided to stand up, the lift shuddered. I heard a horrible squealing. The floor opened up; its two halves tilted down and dropped me onto a thickly carpeted hallway. Mission accomplished, they snapped shut. The magical lift zoomed away, leaving me gaping and sick to my stomach.

I was right back where I had started, outside Princess Lian's suite of rooms.

Yún sat next to me. Her face was gray. Her expression jumped between scared and furious. The griffin had disappeared.

Finally, Yún swallowed. The furious expression leaked away, and she just looked ill. "Magic," she said, then swallowed again. "Protection spells."

"I guessed that."

She frowned. "Your fault, Kai. What—"

"Oh, shut up," I said and rolled over to throw up everything I'd eaten.

Yún shouted for help. Above the pounding in my skull, I heard an even louder thunder of footsteps. Doors opened from fifty different directions, and a whole battalion of servants exploded into view. When they saw us, they all sneered in unison and turned to go, but

Yún was having none of that. She shouted some more, ordering them around as if she were a princess herself. In two minutes they'd mopped up the mess, and I was sitting over in one corner, dressed in a fresh tunic and with my face scrubbed clean, while Yún fussed over me.

I swatted her away. "I'm fine. Leave me alone."

"What did you think you were doing? Running around the palace without an escort?"

"I-I wanted to see the emperor. That's all. And don't tell me how stupid that was. I know."

"Not stupid," she said. "Impulsive."

I glanced up to see her smiling at me. The first real smile since that night when she caught up with me in the mountains. We were alone. The servants had all disappeared into their hidey-holes, even the ones who usually loitered around waiting for orders. All I could think about was how much I wanted to kiss her.

Voices—way too close—made us both jump back. The next minute, Lian came striding toward her rooms, trailed by a retinue of courtiers and palace servants. Her eyes gleamed like a mountain eagle's.

Uh-oh.

Lian halted in front of us. The tide of followers crashed into an invisible barrier behind her.

"What are you doing?" she said.

"Taking a tour," I said weakly.

Her gaze flicked from me to Yún and back. "Ah, yes. I should have told you. It's dangerous to wander around the palace without permission."

"So we found out," Yún said. "What happened to you?"

Lian flushed. "Not here," she said in a low voice.

She stalked through the doors. Her followers poured inside. Just as quickly they poured back out and scattered in all directions. Some glared at us as they passed. The rest wore those blank expressions you see in *Courtier Catalog*.

Yún watched them depart, smiling faintly. "Our princess is in a rage."

She stood and held out a hand. Too miserable to argue, I let her pull me to standing. "Thanks," I said gruffly.

"It was my turn to help you," she said. "Come on. We'd better find out what happened with our friend."

Lian waited for us in a parlor. She stood by the window overlooking an exquisite courtyard filled with trees covered with emerald-bright leaves. A narrow patch of cloud-smeared sky showed between the golden towers and spires that reached upward from all around. I caught a whiff of Jun's musky scent, but the fox-spirit remained invisible. Just as well. Jun made me nervous.

Yún and I sat. Lian remained standing, staring down at the trees below, but her expression was remote, as though she were watching a far different scene.

I stirred. "What—"

"Nothing," Lian snapped.

I glanced at Yún, who was studying Lian with a curious expression.

"You met Quan again, didn't you?" she said.

Lian spun around. Stopped. Sank into the nearest chair. "Yes."

We were all quiet a few moments.

"Tell us what happened," Yún said at last. "Not with the emperor. With Quan."

Lian jerked her chin away. I was certain she was about to indulge in a flaming rage, but she only let out a long, unhappy sigh, and all the royal stiffness melted away from her face.

"We met last year in a lecture class, not long after I arrived," she said slowly. "He invited me to join his study group. After that . . . he showed me around the city. When the emperor summoned me to court, Quan could help me there, too. His father had served the emperor, so Quan's family had lived in the palace until he was fourteen. That was when the emperor dismissed Quan's father and sent him to a posting far away. He only allowed Quan to remain behind so he could study at the university. It was easy to talk to him," she added, half to herself. "About studies. Politics. So many things. I . . . I liked his company."

Her gaze dropped to her hands, which lay knotted together in her lap. "But then I discovered his friendship was a pretense. He even—" She broke off and slowly unraveled her fingers from each other. "He asked me for money."

My mouth fell open. "What?"

"He did. He was quite forthright. He asked for money and named the sum."

That didn't sound right. Sure, I thought Quan was a tilt-nosed snob. Okay, not tilt-nosed, and not a snob exactly. Just too smooth and smart for me to trust him. Even so, I found it hard to believe he would do or say anything that rude.

Yún appeared just as surprised. "Did he say why?"

"I don't need to hear his reasons. There are opportunists in my father's court. I learned about such parasites before I turned four years old. I—" Lian shook her head. "I'm sorry. I am more disappointed than I expected."

Another serving of silence followed, this one even more uncomfortable than the last one.

I coughed. "And, um, the emperor. What did *he* say?"

Lian tilted a hand to one side, as though emperors and their decisions were less than important to her at the moment. "He granted me permission to leave whenever I wish. I must obtain the proper travel documents for all of us. That is, if you wish to return with me."

"Of course we do," Yún said. "But—"

Lian jumped to her feet. "No more talk, please. If you will excuse me, there is much I must oversee if we are to have everything ready by tomorrow."

With a swirl of robes, she was gone from the room.

I whistled softly. "I wonder what really happened?"

Yún's mouth twisted into a pensive smile. "Oh, I can guess. Parts of it, at least."

She hurried from the room to join Lian.

Something sharp and small poked at my arm. Yāo-guài clutched at my sleeve and keened. Grateful for the distraction, I broke a piece of flatbread into small bits and fed him.

At least one of us was easy to please.

13

LIAN HAD NOT EXAGGERATED WHEN SHE SAID A royal princess could not take leave of the emperor's court without many formalities. Not only did she need special travel permits for herself and her entourage (us?), but court etiquette required her to send out dozens of letters of farewell to the emperor, his chief councilors, and all the high-ranking nobles of the court, as well as her professors and advisors at the university. It would take all day, I thought gloomily, as I sat in Lian's study, watching Yún wear a circle into the carpet with her pacing. Maybe longer.

A small, round-shouldered man, who reminded me of a mouse with his sleek brown face, presented himself to us with a bow. "The princess extends her apologies. She finds she will be occupied for many hours," he said. "The senior palace steward has appointed you both suitable chambers. I will show you to them, if you wish. If there is anything else you require, you have only to send a runner to notify me."

What I wanted was a midnight train to the border. I knew better than to say *that*.

Yún was better at make-polite than I was. She smiled. "Rooms would be most welcome, thank you. We are weary after our long journey."

"Of course." Mr. Sleek bowed and motioned for us to follow him. He didn't even flinch when Yún whistled and Yāo-guài popped into sight on her shoulder. Mentally, I placed a bet that Mr. Sleek would be Mr. Senior Sleek pretty soon.

Our rooms, it turned out, were in the next wing, down a winding open staircase, then through a dark tunnel. The tunnel brought us into another airy space, this one with doors leading off in six different directions. Six. They liked that number, I thought, gazing around, as the steward's minion explained how to use the palace's internal talk-phone and calculor system.

He indicated the door to our left. "Yours, young sir. And yours"—he gestured to another opposite—"young lady. The door at the end is a fully-appointed bathing room, and this one for dining. You have only to speak to lock or open the doors."

Our tour guide excused himself, reminding us again that

we had but to ring the summons bell if we required more. Yún and I each disappeared into our separate rooms.

I dumped my backpack onto my new bed. The room was tiny, but stuffed full of gadgets. One handle swung out to reveal a basin with sweetly scented running water. Another door hid a small cabinet with a vid-screen and calculor tucked away as neatly as a cat. More fancy devices crowded the shelves and the bedside table, which was no bigger than a handprint. *Jing-mei would like these,* I thought, turning over a glass cube that showed different videos on each of its faces.

Thinking of magic and gadgets, I made another, more careful inspection. Inside a handful of moments, I uncovered six secret microphones. No doubt there were a dozen more.

I blew out a breath. Not that I was surprised. Lian had told me about the hidden cameras in Lóng City's palace. It was something royals and nobles did. The important thing was the emperor didn't trust me or Yún. Which meant he didn't trust Lian.

She probably knows that already. Strike that. She definitely *knows.*

A soft chiming sound echoed from beside my bed. "Kai? Kai, are you there?"

Yún. She must have figured out the talk-system already. "Yes?"

"I'm tired. I think I'll take a nap. Call you when it's time for dinner."

"Okay, but what about—"

A *click* told me she'd cut the connection.

I blew out a breath. What was that about?

(She doesn't want to see you, bright boy.)

(Or maybe that wasn't a real truce and she's still mad at me for no reason.)

Or maybe she just wanted to be alone. After all, we'd spent the past month and more together. Even spirit companions didn't spend every single hour with their humans. They popped in and out of the magical plane. There were times when I had accused Chen of holding secret parties with the other spirits.

Hardly daring to hope, I sent out a whisper-soft call to Chen.

Nothing.

Damn you, Chen. Show yourself!

No answer.

I ran a trembling hand over my face. It had been four days since Qi and Chen left on their search for whatever.

They never had explained; they had both simply vanished. I hadn't worried too much at first. After all, Chen liked adventures. That's why we fit together so well.

(If he won't come to you, maybe you should look for him.)

(As if I could.)

(You could, if you remembered your meditation lessons.)

Only one way to find out about anything.

I settled onto my bed and closed my eyes. My heart fluttered uncomfortably as I took my first breath. Mā mī said that lighting a fire was harder than feeding one. The second breath came more easily; with the third, my thoughts spiraled down inside myself. I was floating between the spirit plane and the outer world.

Chen?

Ghosts and spirits gibbered at me from beyond the rift. I felt the faint traces of those who had died in these chambers—ordinary servants dead from fever, a nobleman killed by the scullery girl he tried to force, an old woman who took her own life with a thin, sharp dagger. I could sense the presence of animal spirits, too, as they flitted between the worlds. But no sign of Chen.

Deeper and deeper, I told myself. Another old lesson recalled—that a human spirit cannot dwell long across the rift—but I would be quick. Just a peek to see if Chen was there, hiding among the slithery shadows. But as I felt my soul dipping and diving closer to the rift, I smacked against a strange invisible shield.

Snow-cold fingers gripped the essence of my spirit and flung me backward. I lurched back into my body, rapping my head against a shelf.

"What the hell?"

Bright points of light circled in front of my eyes, and my stomach was flipping this way and that. Fuzzily, I tried to figure out what had just happened. Something . . . something had stopped me from exploring the rift. But what? And why? I wiped a hand across my eyes and glanced around my small bedchamber. Nothing moved. I sniffed, smelled no sign of recent magic.

I rubbed the knot on my head. *I'll ask Yún tonight. She might understand what's going on.*

YÚN NEVER DID call. A couple of hours later, I broke down and decoded the instructions for the talk-system. They'd been written by a second-class technical writer, I thought, squinting at the manual. Or someone with a terrible sense of humor. Whatever. I finally managed to convince the blasted monstrosity to connect me with Yún.

The system chimed a couple times, then a bland voice informed me the young mistress had requested privacy.

I clicked off the talk-system with a loud, unsatisfying smack of my hand.

Peh. I guess we didn't really have a truce.

I wanted Yún. I wanted Chen. I even wanted that horrible monster Yāo-guài.

Except no one wants me back.

Feeling extra sorry for myself, I ordered an early dinner, which I choked down alone in the dining room. Oh, yeah, I supposed it was delicious, but my stomach hurt too much to appreciate it. Same-same with the video cubes I pretended to watch until late at night. Eventually, I drifted off into a gray, fidgety sleep, filled with dreams about dissatisfied ghost dragons and noisy pigs. About the mercenaries screaming as they fell into the snowy abyss. About Yún's blank expression when she turned away from my kiss, back in Golden Snowcloud.

Eventually, a soft chiming wormed itself into my dreams. A happy, irritating, *persistent* chiming that dragged me up through the sludge of bad dreams to the waking world.

Reluctantly, I opened one gritty eye.

Across the room, a small brass clock chirped. I tried swearing. That didn't work. So much for voice commands. I tried swearing *and* firing a pillow at the blasted thing. The clock dodged me, still chiming. I stumbled to my feet, a second pillow in hand. Maybe I could smother it.

The clock gave an alarmed cry. Six jointed legs sprouted from its sides, and it skittered away from me. I gave chase.

"Stupid, cursed . . ."

Before I could catch up with the damned thing, a slot opened at the base of the wall, and the clock escaped through it. The next moment, something else scuttled into the room. It was a wide, flat, square box—brass, like the clock, but with a dozen tiny clawed feet poking out from all four edges. Once the thing reached the middle of the room, legs extended and popped into straight poles. The surface rolled back to show a tray with a small squat teapot and cup.

I muttered an insult under my breath. Remembered the microphones and cameras. *Okay then. Let's pretend to be polite, if only for Lian's sake.* I thumped down on the bed and poured myself a cup of tea. More creatures appeared from more slots. They skittered around, bringing me bowls of warm scented water, a toothbrush, fluffy towels, and even a couple of bottles of perfume. I scrubbed my face and cleaned my teeth, but ignored the perfume. No use scaring the girls. Then I skinned out of my old tunic and trousers and pulled on the clean ones that a dozen other spiders had laid out on my bed. I still wasn't all awake, but at least I could face Mr. Sleek and his hundred friends.

I punched the button beside my door. It slid open with a whispered admonition.

Yún was waiting for me outside. Well, no, she wasn't waiting. She paced from point to point, her hands clasped behind her back, while Yāo-guài watched from atop a doorframe. Neither of them looked happy, but then I wasn't, either.

"Nice nap," I said bitterly. "Have another, why don't you?"

Yún whirled around. Her eyes were bright with tears. Immediately she drew a hand over her face. "Kai."

(*Peh!* I am such a jerk.)

I didn't even need Chen to tell me that one.

"Yún—"

She made a quick gesture of denial. "Not your fault. It's Qi. I tried to find her. All yesterday. All night. I . . . couldn't."

A waterfall of cold rippled through me. "So did I. I mean, I tried to find Chen. Just once. It—something—threw me back into this world."

"Same here," Yún whispered. "We need to ask Lian about those palace protection spells."

"Or not. We'll be gone soon enough."

She nodded, but her face was clearly miserable.

We rang the bell to summon an escort. A runner appeared in an eyeblink. She took us along a different path—through an airy gallery with ancient statues, up a small back staircase, to another corridor that emptied out beside the princess's door. Once there, she handed us over to a liveried servant who led us into a small sunlit parlor.

The mood of the two people inside the parlor was anything but sunny.

". . . there cannot be an excuse," Lian whispered in a low furious tone. "The emperor himself—"

"Your Highness—"

"Do. Not. Interrupt."

The young man held the sheaf of papers against his chest like a shield, and tried again. "Your Highness, I know of the emperor's wishes. I and my colleagues have spent the night searching for the correct paperwork and seals so that you and your entourage might depart Phoenix City with all dispatch, but I cannot—"

"You cannot conjure the necessary forms from the air.

Yes, I know. Your office is overworked, the most important members of your staff absent to some mysterious conference in the northern provinces. You told me twice already." Lian sighed. "How long, then?"

"If we can—"

"How long?"

He gulped back a breath. "Another day."

Lian stared at him. "Very well," she said slowly. "Tomorrow at sunrise, bring all the necessary permits to me. Or do you require longer?"

"Sunrise," the young man stuttered. "Yes, Your Highness."

"Thank you. You may go now."

The young man sidled past me and out the door. Farther away, another door opened and closed. Meanwhile, Lian flexed her hands and breathed out audibly. "My apologies."

"For what?" Yún asked.

Her mouth twitched. "For being so . . . royal." She sighed. "It's not just the travel permits. The fastest wind-and-magic trains have a worker's strike. They've reduced the number of trains running between Phoenix City and the borders. Even those had no seats or compartments to spare."

"Do you believe that?" Yún said.

"I have no choice what I believe." Lian made a visible effort and smiled at us. "Never mind that. Let us go to the parlor. The servants should have our breakfast ready by now."

We retired into an intimate little dining room, where more liveried servants laid out platter after platter of this useless breakfast feast. Lian herself was polite and attentive throughout the meal—she asked us about our travels and about Yāo-guài—but I could tell she wasn't thinking about griffins or the raw fish and ginger creations the chef had arranged into intricate shapes just for the princess's pleasure.

Yún was just as polite. She answered Lian's questions about home. She asked her own questions about the university, the princess's studies, and life in the Phoenix Court. It was like watching an old-fashioned play, where the actors gave formal speeches instead of just talking to each other. Of course, I knew the reason. Lian and Yún both knew about the microphones and spy machines. After an hour, however, even Yún was yawning.

"Would you like a tour of the palace?" Lian said, at last.

The servants were removing the last of our dishes.

I stopped myself from lunging forward in relief. Barely.

Yún was better. She patted her lips with a scented cloth napkin and smiled. "That would be delightful, Your Highness. Kai?"

"Sure," I said. "The steward said we could ask him, though."

"Nonsense," Lian said. "You are my guests. I shall show you around myself."

An hour later, I had it all figured out. The emperor didn't need any protection spells. He let strangers wander around the palace until their feet dropped off. We saw tiny jewel-bright gardens, grand chambers set about with golden-leaf statuary and marble fountains, and even grander audience chambers. Lian knew everything about them, too. She could recite who had commissioned which terribly expensive tapestry to commemorate what glorious victory, and she could give the history behind every wing, from the dynasty to the architect.

"How do you know all this?" I asked.

"Someone gave me a tour," Lian said. "He—They explained everything to me. Would you like to see the library next? It's small, but very quiet."

Yún lifted her eyebrows. "I like quiet. Kai?"

"Splendiferous," I muttered. "As long as I get to sit down."

The library was a short distance away, down a spiraling staircase and through a hallway lined with old tapestries from the empire's earliest days. Lian led us through a pair of double doors, into a brightly lit entryway. Shelves of books and scrolls rose up to the curved ceiling overhead. Through another pair of doors, past several desks, I could see more bookshelves extending into the distance.

An elderly man approached and bowed. "Your Highness."

Lian smiled—the first genuine smile I'd seen after we arrived. "My friends from Lóng City would like to see your domain. May I show them?"

The man bowed again. "My domain is yours, Princess."

He had once served as the emperor's chief librarian, Lian told us, as we entered the main room, but he preferred to oversee this smaller library, and so the emperor had granted him the favor. If this was the smaller library, then the bigger ones would be larger than all of Lóng City's palace, I thought as I trailed after Lian and Yún. Dozens of scribes and under-librarians and scholars toiled away at their desks, or among the shelves, which must have held thousands of books and scrolls. Everything smelled of ink and leather. And more. I paused, sniffing. Strong magic permeated the air. I recognized special guard spells to keep the books and scrolls safe from decay. Those were easy to identify. But there were others that eluded me.

". . . then there are the archives . . ."

I caught the last of Lian's words and hurried to catch up.

"Here," she said, opening a smaller set of doors. "It's my favorite part of the library."

We came into a small series of rooms, linked together by wide doorways. Locked drawers covered the lower half of the walls, open shelves the upper reaches. I tilted my head back to see a ghost dragon ranged along the highest shelf—a living guardian to go along with the magical ones.

The griffin chirruped. The ghost dragon blinked lazily, its silvery eyes gleaming in the dim light above.

"There's at least one in every room of the library," Lian said. "The king of Phoenix City's ghost dragons signed a treaty, much like the one my father made. Come along, there's a special set of scrolls I'd like to show you."

We passed through five smaller rooms to a large chamber with bright lamps hung from the ceiling. Three ghost dragons stood guard here. At Lian's entrance, the dragons nodded, as though they recognized her.

"Old friends?" Yún asked.

"You might say so," Lian replied. "They are cousins of the ghost dragons in Lóng City. Their loyalty is toward learning, not to the emperor himself." She gestured toward the small square table. "Sit," she told us. "We can talk freely here, but not for long."

Right. I blew out a breath, suddenly shaky, and plopped onto the nearest bench. Yún and Lian sat opposite me, and we all bent forward. Our griffin perched on my shoulder, his claws pricking into my shoulder, as though he too wanted a part of this secret conference.

Yún started, her voice low and urgent. "You think someone in this court wishes to prevent you from leaving."

Lian shook her head. "It makes no sense. Lóng City isn't important enough. And I—I'm just one of thousands who study at the university. Many others are of much higher rank and greater wealth."

"Then why the delays?"

"I don't know. Coincidence. Or bribes from someone in Lóng City's court who has connections here. No one made any objection when I sent half my belongings yesterday to the freight transport company."

"They won't need to object," I said, whispering like the others. "They just need to make sure your stuff never goes anywhere."

"I thought of that," Lian said bitterly. "If they think I care about books or clothes more than my father and my homeland, they are stupid people indeed." Her eyes brightened to a fierce light. "If I cannot obtain my tickets and my papers by tomorrow, I shall walk home."

"The emperor will not permit it."

Quan appeared in the doorway we had just entered. His eyes were ringed with dark circles, like Yún's had been, like mine and Lian's. His hair had come loose from his queue, and he wore the same clothes as yesterday, only now they were rumpled and stained, as though he'd spent the night behind the palace garbage bins. Both his hands were clenched in fists.

Yún gave a sudden jump. I muffled back a yelp. How had he found us?

Lian pushed to her feet abruptly, sending the bench tumbling backward. "You—"

Quan started toward her. She tried to shove past him. He grabbed her by the arm and spun her around. "Listen," he whispered rapidly. "You must listen. I know who wants to keep you in Phoenix City." He glanced over his shoulder. Already a confused noise sounded from the library's main chamber. "There's no time to explain more. Slap my face as hard as you can."

Lian's eyes widened. "Why?"

"Because of this."

Quan slipped one hand behind Lian's neck. Lian stiffened—I thought she might jab him with a fist—then her body melted against his. Quan clasped her other hand and pressed his lips to hers. It was a thorough kiss, as though he were spending a fortune in passion. I had to turn away because it was too embarrassing, too intimate, to watch, but I heard the moment when that forever kiss ended, because Quan gave an audible sigh. Only then did I dare to turn around.

Both their eyes were wide, surprised and wondering.

"Now," he whispered.

I heard the slap before it even registered that she'd moved.

Quan's head jerked back. A dark red spot bloomed on his cheek. Lian herself was breathing hard, and her eyes glittered with emotion. That had not been a pretend blow. Quan gingerly touched the cheek and nodded, as though he'd expected such force. "Be careful," he said softly.

He disappeared through the farther door. Just in time, too, because a swarm of people rushed into the archive room. Some hurried past in chase of Quan; some remained behind to hover over Lian, bowing and fussing and generally doing nothing useful.

"That young man took great liberties." That was the former chief librarian.

Lian stared down at her hands, knotted into fists. "Too many liberties," she repeated in a soft voice. She shook her head. The strange expression cleared from her eyes. "Far too many," she said firmly. "It does not matter, however. He shall not be permitted inside the palace again. I will make certain of that myself. Now, please leave me."

She lifted one hand and flicked her fingers. Everyone else scattered away like ants.

Except Yún and me. We waited, certain Lian had more to say.

Above, the ghost dragons stirred. Lian glanced up. Her gaze caught that of the oldest and largest dragon. He in turn whispered something in that strange harsh language I had come to recognize. The flux shivered. The dragons disappeared.

"What is it?" Yún whispered.

Instead of answering, Lian opened her other hand. I saw a crumpled ball of rice paper. She smoothed the page over the table. The characters were smeared with sweat and almost illegible, but I could just make them out.

If you believe me, meet me behind Scarlet Lotus Noodle House at noon.

14

Yún was the first to crack the silence.

"Do you believe him?" she asked.

Lian made a throw-away gesture. "I don't know."

Yún studied our princess for several moments. There was pity in her eyes, of a kind I'd never seen before, except when she handled our griffin or any other wounded creature. In a gentle voice she said, "Tell us what happened, Lian. All of it."

"I told you what happened."

"Perhaps you misunderstood—"

"I misunderstood nothing. He—It was after—" Lian drew a long breath. "He came to my rooms in the palace. I had not seen him for two days. I had expected—Never mind what I expected. He had promised to visit days before and he did not. Besides, I had learned certain details that troubled me. Another student warned me about Quan. Said he liked to involve himself with wealthy girls. He had already had a relationship with an older woman at court, who favored him with gifts of money."

Lian had delivered this speech while staring hard at the tabletop. Now she met our gazes. Her eyes were bright with unshed tears. "You see," she whispered, "I did not need to hear his reasons for wanting money. I already knew them."

Āi-āi , I thought to myself. No wonder Lian was furious.

Yún was shaking her head. "That doesn't sound like Quan."

"You don't know him."

"I don't. You do." She hesitated. "You haven't asked my advice but I'll give it anyway. Someone ought to hear Quan out, in spite of what he did or what you think he did. He lived in this palace. He knows the court. His father served the emperor. And what about all those cousins of his? Maybe he knows some rumors that you don't."

"I cannot leave the palace . . ."

"Of course not. If Quan is right, and the emperor is involved, he won't allow it. If not, well, you cannot risk his displeasure."

"I'm not a child," Lian said evenly. "I understand the rules of politics."

"Then why argue?" Yún shot back. "You understand politics, but you don't understand—"

"I'll go."

Silence followed my declaration. Both Lian and Yún stared at me. I wet my lips.

Mā mī always told me to think before I talked.

But I was right. I had to be the one who heard Quan's explanation. Yún trusted him too much, no matter what she claimed. And Lian either loved him or hated him, but either way, she'd hear only what she expected, instead of what Quan actually said.

"Yes, me," I said. "The emperor would send guards after Lian. And Yún is better off here, ordering you around and pretending she's not. Besides, no one will suspect me of anything because everyone thinks I'm an idiot."

Yún's cheeks flushed. "Kai thinks Quan is a tilt-nosed sneak."

"Kai thinks that about all nobles." Lian was smiling faintly. It wasn't a big smile, but better than almost-tears. "Kai is right. And you are, too, Yún. We should at least listen to what he says."

We returned to Lian's suite, where an army of minions was packing the princess's belongings into trunks. The only room untouched was her study. Lian went to her calculor and called up a screen with a few taps on the keys. Ten minutes later, a runner appeared with a thick packet stamped all over with official-looking seals.

Lian took out two silver medallions that buzzed with magic flux. "These are your official passes inside the palace," she told us. "Now you can traverse the public wings without an escort. Which is necessary, because I have errands for you both."

She sent Yún back to the library with a list of scrolls and records to borrow. For me, she unlocked her desk and took out a handful of coins. She sketched a second, shorter list and wrapped the coins in the paper.

"These are for you," she said, giving me the packet. "I would like you to go at once to the offices of the Zhang-Yin Freight and Transport Company and request a receipt and bill of lading, which their idiot grandson failed to provide my agent this morning. Some of those tapestries were gifts from my honored grandmother. I would not have them conveniently disappear because the papers were incomplete."

I accepted the paper and coins with a bow. "Yes, Your Princess Highness, ma'am."

Her eyebrow went up. "The list, Kai Zōu," she repeated in

a crisp tone, as though I were a particularly witless servant. "Check those items against the caravan records. If there is any discrepancy, tell them I shall visit their offices myself tomorrow. The coins are to buy tickets and a finder map for the electric tram. Also, a cup of tea after your errand. Now go. And do not dawdle."

The Zhang-Yin Freight and Transport Company was located two districts over, near the merchant and counting houses. Half an hour after leaving the palace, I got off the electric tram in a small public square, surrounded by bland cement office buildings. My map led me down a side street to the caravan company's front doors.

A clerk took my message into the back rooms. He returned with an old woman—the owner. She listened to my fumbling request for the receipt and the bill of lading. I expected her to laugh, but she only nodded, as if she were used to crazy nobles and their stupid demands. She sent the clerk (her nephew, she mentioned) off to write up a new receipt and the detailed bill for their honored customer Princess Lian. A young girl brought me a pot of sweet tea to drink while I waited.

It was a busy shop. More clerks sat at their desks, writing up accounts or whatever clerks do. Other men hauled boxes from one room to another. Once a wizened old man stomped in from the street door and shouted that the horses were ready even if his cargo was not. That sent a dozen clerks running in all directions, until everything was sorted out. The nephew reappeared just as I finished my tea.

"Your receipt and bill, honored sir." He bowed.

I pretended to check the receipt. It looked official, so I tucked it inside my shirt. The bill of lading was even more impressive—fifty pages, with neatly brushed characters running up and down each page. Ai-ya! And Lian wanted me to check for missing items?

For the first time, I glanced at the paper she'd given me.

And grinned. The list was not a list, but directions to the Scarlet Lotus Noodle House.

Hü, that was smart. That way no one could trace me from the magical map I'd bought.

Another electric tram dropped me in a public square a short distance from the noodle house. We were closer to the university—I could tell by the number of second-hand shops and cheap eating houses that lined the streets. Also, the crowds of scruffy students hurrying around. On a corner, one of them shouted political slogans, while others passed around cheap pamphlets. I put on my best peasant face and hurried to the shop with the scarlet lotus painted on its sign-board. The clocks were just chiming noon as a waiter showed me to my seat in the back.

I scanned the room. No sign of Quan, so I ordered a bowl of spicy noodles and settled down to wait. Luckily, I fit right in. There were a few students here, but also lots of ordinary working people, dressed in plain good clothes, like me. Some even looked like mountain folks, with their loose trousers and quilted jackets. I ate my noodles slowly, but after half an hour, Quan still hadn't showed.

(Maybe he got bored and left.)

(Not him. He's expecting Lian. He'd wait a century for her.)

(Then why isn't he here?)

(Are you sure here is *here*?)

I almost smacked my forehead. His note said to meet him *behind* the shop.

In case the emperor sent snoops to ask later, I paid my bill and asked where the latrines were. The waiter waved toward a curtain at the back of the room. Down the hallway were the latrines. Just as I expected, another door opened onto an alleyway behind the shop.

And there he was, one tall plain young man, pacing back and forth in the alley.

He'd been pacing so long he'd worn a visible path through the weeds and dirt. My heart jumped in sympathy, remembering Yún and our arguments. *Āi-āi*, it was hard when the person you cared most about shut you out of their world.

Our boy swung around for another circuit. He stopped, and his face went blank. "You."

I made a rude noise. "Yeah, it's me. Lian couldn't sneak out of the palace. She sent me to listen."

Quan's eyes narrowed as he took in the unspoken meaning behind my words. Lian still didn't trust him, not yet. He ran his fingers through his hair and looked distracted, as though he were recalculating everything he'd intended to say. "Come with me," he said slowly. "I can explain everything to you. I hope I can," he added in an undertone.

"What does that mean?" I snapped.

He shot me a startled glance. "Oh, nothing to do with you. It's all so complicated. Simple, but complicated. I—" He shook his head. "I'm sorry. I'm a bit . . . preoccupied today."

Understatement of the year, I thought. "Tell me everything you think is important. Even if I don't understand, Lian will. She's the one who matters."

"That is something we can agree on," Quan murmured. "Very well. Here is what I've discovered over the past month . . ."

As we walked down the one alley, into another and around the maze of lanes that made up this district, Quan told me a lot more than I had suspected. "It's the emperor," he said in a low voice. "Kaishan Zhu. He's the one who wants to keep Princess Lian in Phoenix City."

I whistled. "Are you sure about that?"

"Absolutely. I thought it was odd when he invited Lian into his court and gave her the finest rooms in the visitor's wing. It was just a suspicion, however—from living so long at court myself. I didn't say anything to Lian at the time, because I had nothing *except* suspicion. We were still . . . friends at the time. Just friends," he said softly. Then louder, "I suppose I didn't want to set doubt in her mind without cause. It would only have made her life at court more difficult. The emperor dislikes any sense of criticism, or even simple reserve, in subjects or guests alike."

Once more his gaze turned abstracted, as if he were remembering his own days at court.

"Tell me about this plot," I said. "And how you found out."

Quan nodded. "The plot is simple. The reasons complicated. The emperor invited your princess to court to draw her into dependence. He wants to arrange a marriage between her and his youngest son. As for how I found out, I have second and third cousins employed in the palace. Some are guards. Some are minor functionaries. They pass me rumors from time to time."

"But rumors—"

"—are watered by truth," Quan said impatiently. "The truth is that the emperor wants to expand the empire. He's spent his entire reign doing that. There used to be a dozen small principalities—city kingdoms like Lóng City—along the edges of the mountains. Most still call themselves kingdoms, but the truth—" Here Quan made a face as though he'd bitten a very green peach. "The truth is that those kingdoms have become fiefs to the Phoenix Empire. The emperor showers them with trade treaties, loans for building new roads, all kinds of favors. In return, he receives what he wants most. Their magic."

I'd run out of whistles by this point. "Why does the emperor want so much magic?"

"It's not what he wants, it's what he *needs*. Desperately. Haven't you noticed how much magic the empire requires?"

He babbled on about mega-kilowatt currents and the special transmitters used to funnel the magic flux around the empire. Most of the magic flowed into Phoenix City, but the emperor had plans to build vast dams and holding tanks, so he could replace the wind-and-magic trains with ones running on pure magic. He wanted to build a network of calculors to span the continent, not just the empire.

It's wrong, I thought. *Wrong and dangerous. Magic is like rain. You can't catch a storm cloud and squeeze it dry. Even if you could do that, you'd cause a drought.*

That's when cold washed over me. The emperor had already caused one drought—in Snow Thunder City. Maybe other kingdoms had promised all their magic flux to feed the Phoenix Empire's demands.

"Now the stock markets are in danger," Quan went on. "People thought they could make their fortunes buying futures in magic flux. And that is why he wants this marriage. Once he gains that, it doesn't matter if Lian remains here or returns home. He will load her with advisors—his advisors—and rule through her. And by ruling Lóng City, he will rule its magic wells and currents."

The part about buying futures didn't make sense to me, but even an idiot like me could understand the reasons for taking over Lóng City. *He won't stop with us,* I thought. *Once he conquers Lóng City, he can take over the rest of the Seventy Kingdoms, one by one.*

I shivered at the vision of the emperor's minions scattered all over Lóng City like ticks on a dog. "What can we do?"

"We help Lian escape. I have a plan."

I snorted. "It better be a good one. That palace is stuffed with watching and listening devices."

"I know. I'm depending on you and Yún to help for that part. Once you're outside the palace, certain friends of mine can get us outside the city. They . . . Let us say that they are familiar with certain unofficial routes under the walls."

Smugglers. Okay, that sounded more like it.

"How and where and when?" I said.

"Tomorrow morning. Early. Tell Lian to pretend she's visiting her advisors at the university. My friends and I will wait behind the kitchen quadrant, near the servant gate. Bring nothing extraordinary. No extra bags. I'll make sure to provide anything she needs—clothes, gear, food."

"What about money? We can smuggle that out."

There was the briefest flicker of pain in Quan's normally impassive eyes. "I do not ask her for money."

Okay. Note to self: Get money anyway. Don't tell Hero Boy.

A sensible person would have kept his mouth shut. A sensible person would listen to Quan's plans and trot back to the palace to report to his princess. But as my mother said too many times, I was not the most sensible person in the world.

Which is why I blurted, "Why *did* you ask Lian for money?"

Quan stopped abruptly and stared at me. His face turned dark with anger. No, shame. Then he blew out a shaky breath. "I suppose that's a fair question."

Maybe-so-or-not, but I wasn't going to object.

"It was for a hospital," Quan said.

"A what?"

"A hospital," he said patiently. "For the Beggars' Quarter. I'd raised enough money to rent an old warehouse that nobody was using. Some of my friends at the medical school offered their time, and we had others who donated equipment. We had opened a few rooms for a day clinic, but we hoped to do more. Surgery. A druggist. Then, a month ago, the landlord came to me demanding a higher rent or he'd cancel our lease."

"Cancel? Isn't that illegal?"

He made a dismissive gesture. "There were loopholes. I'm not a lawyer. I can't afford one."

The story made so much sense. And yet it didn't.

"Why didn't you tell Lian it was for a hospital?" I said suspiciously. "What about that woman at court who gave you money?"

Now Quan looked truly embarrassed. He stuffed his hands into his pockets and stared at his feet. "I tried to tell her," he said. "I thought I did. But I was so distracted that I did not express myself as well as I hoped. And. And there were other circumstances. You see, I chose a particularly unfortunate day to ask her for such a great favor. Afterward, she would not hear me, nor would her fox spirit listen to my companion."

I swallowed, thinking of a hundred reasons why Lian would misunderstand a good friend.

(A lover. A very new lover.)

(Yeah, Lian said almost that much herself.)

"If she asks," Quan said softly. "Tell her that the other woman is a friend of my family, nothing more. I asked her for money, yes, but only to help with the hospital."

After a few more moments of us not looking at each other, we circled back to the alleyway behind the Scarlet Lotus Noodle House, talking over fall-back plans and other details. Quan took off to find his smuggler friends. I returned to the caravan offices, then zipped back to the palace on the next tram. My magical medallion got me past the guards without any questions. One of them even told me the best shortcuts between the entrance and Lian's rooms. If only we didn't have to worry about kings dying and emperors trying to take over the world (or at least the Seventy Kingdoms), the palace could be a pretty sweet set of digs.

And if wishes were crickets, we'd never get any sleep, I thought as I rounded the last corner onto the wing where Lian had her quarters.

Right away, I scurried back.

The emperor. Here in the same wing as Lian's suite. Maybe I had imagined it, I told myself.

Cautiously, I peered around the corner and ducked back even faster this time. It *was* the emperor, striding down the gallery with at least a hundred minions trailing after him. A young nobleman dressed in silks and jewels strode next to the emperor. One of the emperor's sons—had to be. Even this far away, I could see the resemblance between them.

(Any bets which one?)

(The youngest, of course.)

Brisk sharp tones echoed from the approaching entourage. Old man. Young man. Neither of them happy. Oh, the words they spoke were all polite, slipping off their tongues like thrice-filtered oil, but I could hear the discord under-neath. Something about marriage, obedience, duty toward the empire. Definitely the youngest son. Were they talking about Lian? Curious, I leaned forward, thinking I could over-hear them better as they walked past.

Emperor and son rounded the corner and stopped.

Hurriedly, I dropped to my knees. My forehead touched the marble tiles as the emperor swept past in a whisper of voluminous robes. Invisible, I was just one of ten thousand invisible servants in this palace. No one noticed me. I was safe. I was—

Two slippered feet stopped in front of me. The scent of musk and sandalwood floated down from above.

Damn.

I held my breath. Whoever it was didn't move on. Some self-important flunky? Or maybe a senior invisible servant who wanted to critique my style in groveling? I dared a glance upward and had to choke back a squeak. Double-damn. It was the emperor's youngest son.

His eyes were dark slits in a narrow face. His scarlet-painted lips were set in a thin line. Magic glittered over his shaved head, making him look more like a skeleton than ever. I'd seen friendlier expressions on a gargoyle.

"Mountain Boy," he said. "What are you doing here? Spying?"

(Play stupid. You're good at that.)

I grinned.

Wrong move. The prince flicked his hand up, ready to slap me.

"Mei-shan." It was the emperor. "Do not torment the servants. I expect better from you."

The prince muttered a curse and stalked away. My breath trickled out. Safe, safe, safe. But then I caught a glimpse of the emperor. He, too, continued down the corridor, but not before letting his keen glance pass over me.

TWO HOURS LATER, Yún, Lian, and I sat around an old battered table in a storage room next to the basement library. Lian had given the excuse that she needed to research tax codes from the Seventh Imperial Reign for a paper. We were there to take notes and run errands. It was quiet here, nothing but scrolls and books and paper dust spinning around in the musty air, glittering in the faint light of a single shaded lantern. The griffin paced back and forth, leaving tiny dusty tracks over every available surface.

Lian listened intently as I reported everything about my meeting with Quan. And I mean everything. What he said, how he said it. What he left out or tried to skip over. When I mentioned the part about the money, she flinched. When I got to the part about why he wanted the money, she sat as still as any mountain.

Finally, I ran out of report. My throat was parched from dust and worry. Yún handed me a flask of water, and I drank. Lian said nothing.

"Do you trust him?" Yún asked after a moment.

The silence went on for almost forever. "I believe him," Lian said at last.

Not an answer to the question, but an answer.

15

Lian sent off a note to her advisor, requesting an interview the following morning. She explained about her father and wished to discuss how she might continue her studies over the winter. She expected to return next spring, and hoped to attend her regular classes once more.

"Very nice," Yún commented. "Very . . . sincere."

"My studies in political rhetoric were useful, then," Lian said drily.

She summoned a runner and gave him the message and directions for its delivery. The runner, an older man in palace livery, promised to return with the reply before sunset.

"Twenty yuan says the emperor hears of my plans within the hour," Lian murmured.

A sucker bet. Yún and I just shook our heads.

The reply came back from Lian's advisor long before sunset. Ten o'clock, the professor wrote. Please to bring notes and drafts for any current research papers, as well as a list of materials available for her studies in Lóng City. His tone made it clear he thought the list would be a short one. Lian's lips curled. "Alas, he would be correct. Our libraries are nothing like the libraries in Phoenix City."

"Are you sorry to leave?" I asked.

She shook her head. "I am only sorry that my father is ill."

There wasn't much I could say to that one. We ate an early dinner together, mostly to satisfy the spies and vid-cameras, then went to our separate rooms and to tense, scattered slumber with ominous shadow dreams.

AT SIX O'CLOCK, the brass clock chimed its alarm. *Chirp, chirp, chirp.* Swearing, I fired a pillow at the cursed thing. The clock chirped louder. Then something bounced off the bed with a rattle of wings. The next minute, there was a horrible crunching noise.

Oops.

I lurched into a sitting position. Screws and broken glass littered the floor. A puddle of dark gooey liquid was spreading over the carpet. It looked like blood; it smelled like oil. Across the room, the griffin clutched a jumble of wires and shiny metal between its front claws. Yāo-guài shot me a triumphant glare, then bit into the clock's remains. I swear the little monster was chortling.

"Remind me to feed you more often," I said.

Still chortling, Yāo-guài set to munching his kill.

At least I'd be long gone before the steward could charge me for damages.

Remembering the spy cameras, I tried to act like this was a regular day. I scrubbed my face, cleaned my teeth. I dressed in my thinnest cotton tunic and trousers, as though I expected to spend all day in the palace, instead of escaping to the northern mountains.

It took some skill (and blood) to separate the griffin from the clock. Yāo-guài hissed and growled, but in the end allowed me to carry him away. As we left the room, I glimpsed the magical tea tray, crouched just inside its slot in the wall. Quickly it ducked out of sight.

Yún waited outside. She gave me a nervous smile.

"Let's go," I murmured.

"Well put," she murmured back.

Lian waited for us in the same small parlor from two days before. Jewels winked from her raven-black hair, and more lights—magical ones—glinted on her dark blue formal robes, which swept in a long train behind her. She looked like a star-filled midnight sky. But when she turned around, I could see the tight set of her jaw.

"Please sit," she said, gesturing to the chairs. To a hovering maid, she said, "You may bring the tea now."

She was silent until the tea service arrived and the maids withdrew. Then she laid an exquisite perfumed scroll on the table. "Read it," she said softly.

Yún and I glanced at each other. "Bad news?" Yún whispered.

"Read it," Lian repeated.

I took the scroll first. It was made from heavy parchment, embossed with the imperial seal of a phoenix wreathed in flames. A faint scent of jasmine and sandalwood wafted upward as I unrolled the sheet.

To Her Royal Highness, Princess Lian Song Li . . .

It was an invitation to a formal banquet that same morning. *More like a summons,* I thought, as I untangled the thick layers of prepositions and subjunctives. That wasn't too bad. We couldn't meet with Quan today, but surely he'd hear through his cousins what happened. We could catch up with him tomorrow . . .

Crap.

. . . further delays to your departure from Our Presence, which are understandably unfortunate for you, but fortunate for us, in that the gods continue bless us with the delight of your presence. Until these matters are resolved, we extend to you an invitation to a hunting excursion at our winter palace . . .

"Hunting?" I whispered.

Lian nodded. "Of a different kind," she whispered back.

I blew out a breath. Obviously, the emperor suspected something. I scanned the rest of the invitation. The emperor expected his entourage (meaning her, plus whatever other unlucky souls he picked) to depart the following morning. The invitation didn't say how long the excursion would last, but those kinds of affairs might last a week or even a month. If Lian's father wasn't already dead, he would be soon, and the kingdom would fall into chaos.

That might be part of his plan, I thought. *He might want to force Lian to accept his help.*

I gave the scroll to Yún, who read through it, frowning the whole time. She handed the scroll back to Lian. "A very great honor," she said carefully.

"One I must not refuse," Lian said. She leaned close and swiftly whispered. "Jun went to find your spirit companions last night. She never returned."

Before either of us could react, she stood. "If you will excuse me, I must go at once to the banquet. I've instructed my servants to bring you breakfast here. Afterward, we shall discuss whether you plan to return to Lóng City, or accompany me to the emperor's estates as my companions."

It had to be a trick that nobles learned, I thought. How to speak smoothly when the whole world is shaking itself into dust around you. But we'd been friends long enough that I could hear the small catch in her voice when she said Lóng City, and how her eyes brightened with anger, when she spoke of the emperor.

(Could the emperor's spy gadgets see and hear what I did?)

(Shut up. Smile at your friend. She needs you to be brave.)

No sooner had Lian gone than servants appeared with dozens of covered platters, carafes of fragrant tea, and even a small dish for Yāo-guài's meal. With a bone-screeching cry, our little monster pounced upon the nearest metal dome, scratching at it with his claws.

"You ate already," I told it.

"The clock?" Yún murmured.

We both managed weak smiles. It wasn't enough to restore our appetites, however. Jun vanished. Chen and Qi missing for days. The emperor tying silken ribbons of politeness around Lian to keep her prisoner. For once I was glad our pesky griffin demanded so much attention at meals. We took turns feeding him bits of magical crab and roasted pork, until he toppled over with a burp.

I wished I could do the same.

Without Yāo-guài to distract her, Yún wandered over to the calculor. She flicked through a dozen channels, before settling on a news vid-cast with several split viewports. I could tell she wasn't really watching, but I could also tell she didn't want to talk.

Restless, I wandered through the suite. Except for Lian's study and the rooms immediately around her bedchamber, it was stripped bare. One small library had a few books on its shelves, but the rest were gone, most likely packed into crates and loaded onto wagons by the Zhang-Yin Freight and Transport Company. Most of the servants had gone, too. Only a couple of maids remained. They were chatting over a pot of tea while they mended what looked like palace uniforms.

In a tiny room I came across an ancient vid-screen and calculor on an overturned packing crate. I dropped onto the floor and tilted the screen down. Flicked on a switch. Magic flux crackled, and the screen wavered queasily before it snapped into focus. Wrinkling my nose against the metallic stink, I scrolled through the programming menu, but my mind wasn't on cartoons or medieval documentaries.

How do we get out? How?

We had to get out and soon. Lian's father was sick. Dying. (Or dead.)

I cursed Kaishan Zhu and all his ancestors. Cursed the gods. Cursed my own bad luck. If we'd only stayed away from Lian, Quan might have smuggled a letter into the palace. Lian might have smuggled herself away from the palace. Quan himself could have helped us escape . . .

Quan. *He* had escaped the palace, the day before.

I flicked off the vid-screen. Stopped myself just in time. Those spy cameras would notice if I went racing back to Yún and told her about any secret passages. I stood up lazily, stretched and yawned, then sauntered to Lian's study.

Yún had shut off the calculor and was staring at the empty walls. She looked tired and frustrated.

"*Hai*, Yún," I said. "Got a question for you, Hotshot Girl."

Her eyes widened slightly. Her eyebrows lifted in curiosity.

"Those scrolls," I said. "I mean books. The ones Princess Lian wanted returned to the library. Didya do that yet?"

Enlightenment showed in Yún's expression. "Ah, yes.

Those books. The ones she told *you* to return. You forgot them?"

"C'mon, Yún." I let my voice slide into a whine. "Remember how she sent me out to that stupid transport company, all for nothing?"

"And what does that have to do with anything? Idiot," she hissed. "Here, here are the books. And while you are mucking and loitering about the palace, here is a list of the scrolls she wishes to study tonight. If," she added, "you can remember to fetch them."

"I'll remember," I snarled.

I snagged three books from Lian's study—ones with cracked covers and stamped with the Phoenix Empire seal— and trotted through the palace labyrinth to the small library. Right away the chief librarian stopped me at the entry door.

"Books," I said, holding them up carelessly. "My royal princess asked me to return these. And she wants me to fetch some different ones. It's for her research paper."

A pained expression crossed the old man's face. "Give me those before you damage them. Yes, the *Essays of Suyin Wei. Philological Observations from the First Empire. Poetry of Cheng-hao Li.* Hmmmm. That last does not appear to be a standard text for the university." He glanced up, still somewhat distracted. "No matter. You say the princess wished to borrow other books in return?"

"These," I said breezily, waving the list. And as the chief librarian scanned the paper, muttering to himself, I added, "She mentioned one or two others. Don't know if she really wants them or not. Said they were in that room we visited yesterday. Do you mind if I look?"

The chief librarian glanced up, and now his eyes narrowed. "What kind of books? Oh, never mind. Go, do what you must. But do not remove any scrolls or books without showing them to me or my chief assistant first. We keep records, you understand."

I poked around the room Lian and Yún and I had first visited. The ghost dragons stirred upon my entrance—I heard a hissing above, like the first faint whistle from a steam kettle—but none of them tried to stop me as I pulled out books, or wiggled the shelves, or kicked the base of the bookcases. More important, none of them gave any alarm.

Much good it did me. The shelves were nothing but wood. And kicking the bookcases only gave me a sore foot.

After fifteen minutes, I sat down on a bench and massaged my toes, cursing. Quan had come from somewhere. But which direction?

I closed my eyes and tried to remember every moment exactly.

I remembered us sitting around the same square table, all of us bent forward and the griffin gripping my shoulder with his claws and listening intently. Quan had appeared in the doorway to my left. Either he'd followed us from outside, or he'd waited in one of the many side chambers we'd passed.

(Didn't matter where he came from. What's important is where he went.)

Okay. Pretend that you're watching an old-time vid, clicking through a single frame at a time. Go back to yesterday again. Lian had declared she would walk home if necessary. You were thinking she looked like a hawk, an eagle, bright-eyed and fierce. Slower. Next picture. Quan shows up and speaks. Lian bolts to her feet. More talkety-talk. (Careful. Slow down.) Angry Lian. Quan desperate. He reached out and pulled Lian into that astonishing forever kiss. Both stare at the other. Click to next. Quan's speaking. Now, he tells Lian. She strikes. Quan darts through the farther door . . .

I hurried through the farther door, following memory.

A corridor continued a short distance, ending in a blank wall. Doors and openings led off to either side. Quan had disappeared right away. He must have, or else the chief librarian's minions would have caught up with him. That meant he'd turned almost immediately into a side chamber.

I made a careful search of the next alcove on my right. A pair of cranky ghost dragons glared at me as I quickly ran my fingers over the bookshelves, then along the cracks between the various cases. No luck. No exits.

To the left, then.

They say you make your own good fortune. Disbelieve in yourself, and the world does, too. Yún and I had proved that last year when we gave the princess her heart's desire, but this was a much harder task. An almost impossible one. For all I knew, Quan had used a secret nobles-only spell, one they hadn't bothered to share with Lian.

I scanned the chamber with fingers and eyes. No luck here, either. I turned to go, trying to quash my doubts. A puff of air brushed my cheek as I crossed the tiny chamber. It took me two more steps before I registered the clues. Breeze. Basement. No windows or doors. Where had that breeze come from?

I backpedaled like a slow-motion monkey until I felt the breeze again. It came from the right-hand set of shelves. Now I could see the narrow gap between two tall stacks. It ran from floor to ceiling.

I pressed my eye to the opening. Shadows flickered in the darkness beyond, and the breeze carried the unmistakable scent of damp earth and magic flux. From farther off I heard dripping water. Yes. Here was Quan's secret passageway.

"A SECRET PASSAGE?" Yún said.

"How else could he get out?"

We'd returned to the library. Yún had told the chief librarian that I had failed to obtain the correct scrolls. If he would permit, she would carry out the princess's orders. She had come equipped with writing materials and, she added, a better understanding of her mistress's requirements than her unfortunate companion, who had been dropped into a gargoyle pit when a young child. To my disgust and relief, the chief librarian believed her.

Now Yún examined the almost-invisible division between two bookshelves. She laid a hand over the gap and whispered a spell.

The magic flux chuckled. Nothing else happened.

"I wish Qi were here." She sighed.

"I wish we *weren't*," I said.

Yún didn't bother to answer Mr. Obvious. She tried a few

more spells, but nothing worked. Meanwhile, Yāo-guài was chittering and chattering emphatically. I hushed him. He snapped at me. I tried to grab his beak, but he escaped and leapt at the bookshelves, trilling loudly. Yún tried to pull him away—he'd latched onto a stack of old papers and bits flew everywhere—but he only snapped and trilled louder.

"Yāo-guài," she hissed. "Stop making so much noise—"

Yāo-guài opened his beak wide and a note rang out.

My ears popped. My insides lurched. It was like standing on the edge of a very tall precipice.

Yún didn't look much better. She clutched her stomach, and her face turned the color of a pasty, pale dumpling. Yāo-guài hummed. A sour stink filled the air, as though a wild animal had passed close by. Just when I thought I would throw up, the humming stopped suddenly and the tension vanished.

Click.

One bookcase slid backward three feet. With a happy cry, the griffin launched himself into flight and soared through the gap. Yún and I darted after him.

And stopped.

We stood in a dim, shadowed corridor. Dust coated the stone-paved walls and floor. Spiderwebs hung from the ceiling in a thick veil to our left. From far off, I heard the sound of water dripping and the *clickety-clack* of beetles scuttling away. Yāo-guài had vanished.

"Now what?" I said.

"We follow those footprints," Yún said, pointing at the fresh tracks in the dust that led off to the right, through the fluttering shreds of more cobwebs.

We followed them through two double bends and left at another intersection. There the corridor continued in a straight line, but the tracks stopped at a hatch set in the middle of the floor. We undid the bolts and eased the hatch open. Yāo-guài reappeared on Yún's shoulder, chittering, then dove into the tunnel. We scrambled down the metal ladder after him.

Magical lamps flickered on as soon as we hit the ground. In some ways, it reminded me of Lóng City's sewers. Well, except these underground passages didn't stink of dung and garbage.

"Escape route," Yún said.

"For nobles."

"Definitely. That explains how Quan escaped. He used to live in the palace, after all. And now . . ." She glanced away from me, and fussed over the griffin. Her lips were pressed together, and she had that stubborn *I know better than you look*. Uh-oh.

"Yún—"

"No. Listen to me, Kai. I have to go after Quan myself. You have to stay here. Think about it. The chief librarian knows I'm studying for my conjuration license. He won't wonder if I spend hours in the library." She smiled weakly. "They might not believe the same about you. So here's my plan. I'll find Quan and explain what happened—"

"You don't know these tunnels, Yún. You could get lost. . . ."

"These tunnels are meant for scared and stupid nobles, Kai. Besides, Yāo-guài can help me. Don't worry about me. The moment Lian comes back from that thrice-cursed banquet, you and she escape through this passageway. Meet me and Quan at the university kitchens. If you don't show by sunset, we'll try again tomorrow morning. After that . . ."

It wasn't necessary for her to spell out more. If we hadn't met up by tomorrow morning, the emperor would have discovered our secret plans, taken Lian prisoner outright, and probably set my sorry, ugly head on display outside the palace walls.

I wanted to argue. I wanted to tie her up with ropes and find Quan myself. Except her plan made too much sense, no matter how much I hated it. I scowled at her. "Bossy girl."

She scowled back at me. "Does that mean you'll do as I ask?"

"You never ask," I muttered, but before she could launch into an argument I held up my hand. "Okay. Just so you know, I hate this. All of it. But I'm not sure we have a better choice."

Yún let her breath trickle out. "Until tonight, then."

She hesitated a moment, then leaned forward and kissed me on the lips. The next moment she had disappeared into the gloom.

I rubbed my hand over my mouth. My lips tingled, and my whole body felt as though I were floating in a sea of magic flux.

(I liked that. I hope she does it again.)

Only one way to make sure. I shook myself back to the present, and the knowledge I had to fool the chief librarian and his assistants long enough to sneak Lian through the tunnels. I climbed back to the dusty corridor and slid through the gap into the library.

Once there, I wrote out an account of what Yún and I had

discovered. I also wrote a bunch of nonsense notes—just in case. When I finished, I tucked the papers into my shirt and glanced at the bookcase, with its still-open entryway into the mysterious corridor beyond. I had no idea how to close it. And no idea how to open it back up. *I just have to hope no one comes back here.* It was a risk I had to take.

I sauntered out. The chief librarian was not around, just one of the clerks. "Hi," I said. "Just going to fetch some more ink for my friend."

No one stopped me. Whistling, I strolled out of the library and back to Lian's rooms.

Over the next few hours, I made three more trips between Lian's suite and the library, pretending to fetch and carry writing materials, more books, and even a pot of tea (which the clerk turned away, saying that liquids were not permitted in the library). When that got old, I set to pacing around Lian's private study.

I was cursing the emperor and his never-ending banquets when Lian reappeared, trailed by three servants. She took one look at me and dismissed them. "You have something for me?" she said, all imperial.

"Notes from Yún." I handed her the sheaf of papers. "She wants to know if she forgot anything."

Lian scanned the first page and frowned. She shuffled through the sheets until she found my account. Her eyes widened and she glanced at me. "Interesting. I find that neither one of you truly understands the research I do here. Wait for me. I shall fetch a few items to bring with me to the library."

In moments, she had changed from her formal silk robes into plain woolen ones. She handed me a heavy bag, which clinked as I took it. Money and jewels, I guessed. I slid the bag inside my shirt and we hurried back to the library.

Only to find out the bookcases had slid closed.

I muttered a string of bad words.

Lian laid a hand over the shelves where the gap should have been. Her breath hissed in surprise. "Very strong guards. But . . . yes, it's an emergency spell. It's keyed to respond to those in great need, but only someone of the palace. Not outsiders. That doesn't explain why . . ."

She murmured a few spells. Nothing happened. Lian cursed and spoke a few words in what sounded like the ghost dragon's language. Still nothing. "That's odd. I would think the spells would respond to their tongue. Perhaps it's keyed to voices or identity, to people who are official members of the court."

Six or seven more spells did nothing. I was ready to pound on the shelves and smash my way through, when a loud *click* made me jump back.

Very slowly, with a faint wheezing noise, one bookcase receded from the other. A plain young man, his hair tousled and a wild look in his eyes, burst through the opening. Quan.

"How did you—"

"Yún told me about the emperor—"

He and Lian both stopped and stared at each other.

"Yún told me what happened," Quan said. "I ran—I came back at once. The passageway doesn't—"

"—stay open for very long," Lian said.

"Yes. Exactly."

Quan reached for Lian's hands. She clasped his tightly. Both of them let out a long sigh of relief. Then they seemed to remember that we were trying to escape from a very angry emperor. We sidled through the gap and ran down the corridor to the ladder. From afar, I heard a distinct *click* as the gap closed once more.

Our tunnel went arrow-straight for a *li* or more. We passed one ladder and half a dozen side tunnels, but Quan ignored them. "Different route," he wheezed. "Longer. Just. In. Case."

In case the emperor sent his soldiers into the streets to fetch Lian back to the palace. Best to keep underground until we got closer to the Beggars' District.

Lian's mouth was set in a grim line. She understood, too. We jogged in silence, while Quan counted under his breath. After six or seven intersections, Quan veered to the left. Things got complicated for a while. A couple more *li*, and we stopped at another metal ladder.

The hatch opened into a private yard with a dirt floor. We were somewhere close to a blacksmith, I guessed, hearing the clang of a hammer on metal. Quan motioned for us to hurry. We followed back alleys into another district, then boarded a rickety tram that dropped us near the Beggars' Quarter. By the time we entered the shadowy lane behind the university kitchens, the sun was slanting toward late afternoon.

The lane was empty. The scent of moldering leaves hung heavy in the cool, damp air. My heart shrank. Then a shadow moved. Yún emerged from a doorway, carrying the griffin in her arms. Her gaze zapped to mine. She smiled faintly, and the terrible tightness in my throat eased.

More men and women appeared from behind half-closed doors. Quan's smugglers. Several carried bulky packs slung over their shoulders. One, a lean and weathered older woman, studied us. Her gaze flickered over me, then settled on Lian.

Lian held out her hand. "Thank you for helping us."

The woman's teeth showed in a thin smile. "I did it for him." She tilted her head toward Quan. "He's tended our sick when no one else cared. We cannot delay," she said to Quan. "It's best if you're outside the city before twilight."

Quan nodded. "We go at once. Lead on, Feng."

Feng took the lead with another woman. Both of them were armed with knives and spiked clubs. So were all the other smugglers. Two of them, short, ugly men as stout as bears, guarded our rear as we traversed a maze of lanes from one part of the university to another.

In the middle of a lonely alley, the whole crew stopped while the bear-men levered a metal grate from the road. *More sewers,* I thought. Down we scrambled, into a gray-lit tunnel. A few moments to replace the grating and we took off at a run.

Feng took the lead. Evidently she knew the way by heart, because she never paused at any intersection. Left and right and left and left. The tunnel took a sudden slant down at one point. We splashed through muck and mud and worse, but instead of slowing down, Feng urged us to run faster. The bricks vanished. Now the walls were nothing more than hard-packed dirt. I smelled a watery scent, unlike the stink I'd been breathing the past hour. Feng slowed, then motioned for us to stop.

A faint gray circle of light showed ahead. The two largest smugglers squeezed past us to deal with the next grate. Feng motioned for us to keep quiet as her minions clambered out. We all waited several tense moments before the younger one poked his head into the tunnel.

"All clear," he whispered.

"Right enough," Feng said. "Now—"

"One moment." Quan turned to Feng. "You remember our agreement."

She shook her head. "You have given us enough already. You are the reason my granddaughter lived through the sweating sickness, and why old Guang over there survived last winter. Go in peace, you and your friends, and may the gods of your ancestors watch over you."

Quan ran his fingers through his hair. He looked like he wanted to argue, but he also knew we didn't have time for that. "Very well. But remember, if you need care—"

"—we go to Xin Tao and his clinic. Yes, we know. Now hurry."

One by one, we crawled through the narrow opening. The smugglers handed over the bulky packs. One went to each of us—the gear and provisions Quan had promised to provide. I shifted mine to a more comfortable position and tightened the straps around my waist. We were well outside the city gates—at least four or five *li* away. The skies were purpling, smudged with inky clouds. The air smelled of wet dirt and imminent rain. Nearby I heard the rill of a stream. In the distance, I saw the brilliant lights of Phoenix City.

Quan touched my arm. "Come quickly. We should reach a good shelter before full dark."

16

WITH TWILIGHT DRIFTING OVER THE COUNTRY-side, we followed the stream until we came to a wooden foot-bridge and a dirt road heading north. "Open roads are dan-gerous," Quan said, "but we'll make better time."

"Where are we going?" Yún asked.

"A village," he answered. "Don't worry. It's safe."

Hü, I thought. I found that hard to believe, but with the emperor sure to send trackers and soldiers after Lian, we had no time to argue. So I jogged onward, stumbling now and then, because the road had turned into a treacherous blank. Yún jogged ahead of me, the griffin clinging to her shoulder. At first I could see them outlined in faint light, then in shad-ows. Now they were invisible. I could only tell their pres-ence by Yún's labored breathing, a rustling from the griffin's wings, and the faint movement of dark against dark.

An hour. Two hours. Rain spattered us, stopped, and spattered again. A stitch caught in my side, and I staggered.

Lian caught my arm. "Quan," she called out softly, "we can't go on. It's too dark."

"Half a *li* farther," came his answer. "We can't stop here."

Thunder grumbled overhead. The clouds spit more rain all over us. Quan moved cautiously, sending back whispered warnings about the footing. Soon we turned off the road onto a side track, which led between tumbled-down walls, into an empty square. I stared around at the circle of looming shapes. Then my foot kicked against something. I bent down and found a broken rake, half buried in weeds and dirt. We had reached a deserted village.

"We can rest until moonrise," Quan said.

"No fire?" Lian asked. "A cup of tea would be welcome right about now."

Quan hesitated. "Too risky. Unless . . ."

". . . we make our camp inside a house," Yún said. "That would hide our fire, and the smoke won't be visible at night."

"Unless the soldiers get close enough to smell it," I added.

Lian shuddered. "Then we make fire just for cooking and douse it right away."

After some searching, we found a house that was nearly whole. We slipped inside one by one, all of us with our knives ready, just in case. Inside, broken furniture and bird nests littered the floor. A mouse skittered away at our approach and, from the smell, more were about. Still, we had four walls and most of a roof.

"Why doesn't anyone live here?" Yún asked. "There's fresh water and the land looks right for good farming—"

"No young people," Quan said shortly. "They all migrated into the city. After a while, the older ones died, or joined their children." He smiled bitterly. "It's the same-old same-old, only it happened faster because of all that magical flux. After all, who wants to stay in a dirty country village when you can choose the emperor's own city a few *li* away?"

I would, I thought.

But then, I was just a mountain boy.

We cleared the rubbish from the kitchen and swept the floor with a broom Lian discovered. Quan unpacked several blankets and laid them over the floor. He also shared out warmer clothing—knitted hats and gloves, a thicker cloak for Lian. It was quiet here. The rain had died off. Far away, a fox yipped. For the first time in days, I found myself breathing easily.

Yún gathered deadwood. Lian came back with a bucket of water from the village well. Together we built a small fire and set water to boil for tea, while Quan dug out two woven containers from his pack. One held packets of loose tea, the other a quantity of cold rice and dried fish. He had even brought strips of dried beef for Yāo-guài, who tore into them with a happy cry. We bolted down our meal, hardly better than the griffin. The tea had a bitter flavor from the tin mugs, but I didn't care. It sucked away the chill in my bones and helped me pretend I was dry and warm.

After we brewed a second pot of tea, we doused the fire. Quan stood and drew a knife from his belt. "I'll take first watch."

No one even pretended to argue. Yún rolled up in her blanket close to the fire. Yāo-guài curled next to her. Lian poured herself another cup of tea and stared out the window, sipping from time to time. A handful of stars speckled the night sky, shedding a faint light through a single round window set high in the dirt wall. Her face was invisible to me, but I could make out the tense lift of her chin. I wondered what she was thinking now.

After a few moments, she sighed and set the cup aside. "You should sleep, Kai."

"So should you."

She gave a breathy laugh. "I will soon enough."

In other words, stop snooping.

I yawned and lay down under my own blanket. Closed my eyes and waited.

Ten, twenty, fifty. I'd reached nearly a hundred before Lian stirred. Her clothes whispered as she stood and glided out the doorway. Moments later, the leather hinges of the front door creaked loudly.

Nothing else happened for a while. Just as I decided it really was time for me to sleep, I heard a rustling in the long dried grass outside the window. Quan or Lian? A stranger? That side of the house looked over the fields. Cautiously, I rolled over and rose into a crouch. My knife slid into my hand and I listened hard. The best gift I had for my enemy was surprise.

More soft-footed rustling that approached our window and stopped.

I was about to wake Yún when a young woman's voice floated through the night air.

"Quan."

Grass crunched as Quan spun around. His tongue must have tripped once or twice, because it took him a couple tries before he said back, "Princess."

A very long pause came next.

"I'm sorry," Lian said softly. "I was wrong. I misjudged you—without any cause. I thought—Well, I made clear what I thought. I wish I could erase those words."

"You don't need to apologize," Quan said very quickly. "Or explain."

"I do. I wronged you, Quan. I knew your character. I had no excuse. I—" Her voice broke off with a catch and quaver. In a lower voice, she continued, "Kai told me why you wanted the money. I'm sorry I didn't listen to you before."

"It doesn't matter."

"It does matter. To me. And I hope it matters to you that I'm listening now."

A silence. A soft breath of exclamation.

That's when I *really* knew I had to stop listening. I coughed. Two thumps sounded on the dirt. Then the noise of rustling grass as two lovers hurried away. The nasty part of me cursed them. Why couldn't they wait until we reached Lóng City? Even better, why hadn't they smooched and made love speeches back in Phoenix City?

(You're just jealous.)

(Of course I am.)

I sighed and rolled over, trying to find a comfortable position on that lumpy dirt floor.

Only to see a gleam from Yún's open eyes.

"He's a good man," she whispered.

"He's an idiot," I said gruffly. "So is Lian."

Yún shut her eyes. It was like the moon dropping from the midnight sky, leaving me in darkness.

(Okay, bright boy. Now what?)

(Apologize.)

(Too easy. What about that kiss in the secret passageway?)

My pulse was dancing around. I ordered it to calm down.

"Yún?"

No response.

The griffin fluffed out his feathers and made soft complaining noises, as if something had disturbed his rest. Gathering up the scattered bits of my courage, I levered myself onto my hands and knees and circled the dead fire to Yún's side. She lay so still, as still as a mountain in winter, I knew she was awake and listening hard.

(Make it good. You won't have another chance.)

I blew out a breath. This was like Chen's laundry spell. Mess up the syllables and rhythm, and things explode.

"Yún . . . I'm sorry. I thought last year that everything had changed between us. And it had, but I spoiled it by being such an idiot. I flirted with that girl from the teahouse. I pretended I didn't care. I stopped talking to you and that might be the worst and stupidest thing, because friends should always talk to each other."

I paused, thinking I'd heard a soft exhalation from Yún, but she didn't stir.

Keep going, I told myself. *Half a spell can wreck things.*

"So," I said. "So I did everything wrong. You're my best friend. You're someone I trust and need and want. And not just as my friend. I . . . I do care, Yún. Very much. And it scares me."

Dead silence outside. Inside, my pulse thundered in my ears.

(She hates me.)

(She's laughing at me.)

Silence was the most eloquent answer the poets always said. I guess I got mine.

I was about to creep away, when Yún reached up to touch my cheek. "Kai. Don't go."

My heart seemed to stop. For a moment, neither of us spoke, neither moved. All I could think was how soft and warm her hands were and why had I spent so many months shoving her away when I all wanted was to hold her tight against me. Then Yún shooed away a protesting griffin, and I was sliding down to press my body against hers. Our mouths fumbled around before we matched up into a long, hard, tooth-clicking kiss.

The taste of honey, the warmth of fire, the zing of magic.

"I love you," I whispered.

(Was that really you?)

(Yeah, me.)

(Say it again. Before she thinks you were lying.)

"Yún, I—"

The outer door crashed open. The next moment, Quan was shouting for us to grab everything now, now, *now!* Lian had already snatched up her blanket and was stuffing it into her pack. Yún shoved me away and buttoned up her shirt. The griffin launched himself into a flurry of dust and feathers and high-pitched screeches.

"Can you quiet him?" Lian asked. The moon had risen high enough that its light flooded our room. Her hands were shaking. Her eyes bright and wide with terror.

"The emperor's soldiers?" I asked, breathless.

"Hundreds," Quan said. "Soldiers, mages, and trackers." He scooped the pots into his pack. Kicked dirt over our dead fire. It wasn't enough, I knew. Not if trackers made any search of this village. But it was the same kind of panicked thoroughness that drove all of us to pick up every bit of gear or clothing, even as Yún tried to capture the frightened griffin.

She snatched at him blindly and captured one leg. Yāo-guài screeched even louder and raked her with his claws. Yún let go with a yelp. Yāo-guài zoomed through the window and vanished in a glitter of magic.

"Yún." I dropped to my knees next to her.

"I'm fine."

"No, you aren't." I ripped a length of cloth from my shirt and bound it around her bleeding arm. "You need washing and a healing. Can you manage until we reach a safer place?"

Her gaze swept up to meet mine. "Of course."

"Hurry," Quan hissed.

We grabbed our packs and ran. The soldiers came from the direction of Phoenix City, Lian told us. She and Quan had detected the first questings from the mages, then heard the tramping of many, many horses. But we had to assume they'd sent out sweepers and trackers in a great circle.

"How did they track us?" Yún whispered. "The smugglers?"

"Not Feng," Quan said shortly. "Maybe you were followed."

"No," Lian said. "That's impossible. We—"

She stopped. "Yún. Kai. Your medallions."

Of course. Those medallions came from the emperor's wizards.

We ripped the medallions from around our necks and hurled them as hard as we could toward the invisible soldiers. Then we took off again with Quan in the lead. A full moon emerged from behind a mass of clouds to illuminate our path. We could see the rough ground, the patches of tall brittle grasses, all limned in silver. The moonlight meant we could run faster without stumbling, but it also meant the emperor's soldiers could spot us more easily.

A voice shouted behind us. I felt the sting of magic. Quan immediately angled toward the northeast, toward a great black shadow on the ground that swayed back and forth. Trees.

We dived into the forest. The thick tang of red pine masked our scent. The thorny underbrush meant we had to creep as slow as worms, unsnagging our clothes from the thorns, testing before we set any weight upon a hand or knee so we didn't give away our position. Quan led us lengthwise through the thicket to a dried up streambed, and motioned for us to drop one by one into its not-so-comforting depths.

Once down, we jogged, doubled-over, until the ground rose to meet the plains again. Quan motioned for us to stop. I fell to my knees, gasping. *Āi-āi.* Surely the soldiers would overtake us. Then Yún leaned against me—just a moment, but enough that my courage flickered high.

"Now what?" Lian asked.

Quan stared ahead, across the gray-lit fields and open plains. "There," he said. "More trees."

I squinted. Moonlight flickered over the open ground ahead of us. Then I saw the feathery outline of Quan's trees. The breeze carried the scent of pine toward us. It would cover ours from the trackers, but what about the mages?

(We can't play hide-and-seek all the way to the mountains.)

A thundering of hooves yanked my heart into my throat.

"Run!" Quan said.

Yún gripped my hand and hauled me to my feet. Lian and Quan reached toward each other. One kiss and they scrambled over the rise and to their feet. Yún and I followed a heartbeat later, pelting toward that small speck of shelter. *We can't make it,* I thought. It was over a *li* to the trees. The soldiers would cut us down long before we reached them.

And then . . .

Light exploded in our faces. Something small and feathered struck my chest. I lost my hold of Yún's hand and tumbled backward. Blinded, I tried to fend off whatever monsters had attacked us. Claws and beaks snatched at my hands. I felt like I was wrestling with a bundle of wind. Someone was shouting—Yún. I wanted to tell her to shut up, remember the soldiers, when my vision cleared.

I froze.

The griffin sat on my chest, its flat black eyes two inches from mine.

"Yāo-guài?" I whispered.

Kai! Kai, wake up!

I knew that voice.

Chen?

A loud grunt echoed inside my head. A wonderful stink of piggy odor rolled over me. *Of course it's me,* said a familiar voice. *Wake up. We don't have much time.*

I shook my head and looked around for my friends. Saw Yún with eyes rounded with amazement. Saw Lian rapt in some secret conversation. Faintly, as though veiled by the layers of worlds, came the flicker of a tall thin crane, a sharp-toothed fox, a blaze-bright creature that I recognized as a phoenix. (Quan? A phoenix?)

Oh, but what stopped my heart was the sight of a smoke-gray mountain cat, her tail switching around in barely contained impatience. The cat spun around and glared directly into my eyes, her own like pale moons on a spring night.

Nuó? I whispered.

My mother's companion spirit gave me a familiar snarl. I winced and shrank into myself.

Meanwhile, Chen was nattering in my ear. *We were trapped in the spirit plane,* he said. *The emperor's doing. Nuó freed us. That horrible griffin led us to you.*

You've wasted enough time, Nuó growled. *We must take them through the gates.*

What gates? I shouted.

The gates to the spirit roads, Yún whispered. *Qi told me.*

I had no chance to demand any answers. My stomach did a hideous hop-skip. Something strange stuck claws into my brain, or at least that's what it felt like. My eyelids fluttered open, but the sight was too horrible to bear—a gulf of inhuman proportions opened below my feet, lit by fire. I clamped my mouth shut at the stink of sulfur and a strong metallic scent that reminded me of magic and blood and intense fear.

A hand pressed over mine. Yún. I knew that shape, that

exact degree of warmth. My panic eased to a more bearable level.

Chen's voice whispered inside my skull, *Do not be afraid. I won't let anything hurt you.*

Even Nuó?

He laughed uneasily. *Even Nuó.*

Liar, I said.

More laughter, this time Nuó's. *Shut up, boy. And follow your pig-creature.*

I felt a tug deep inside my gut. I sensed a large heaving mass next to me—Chen had materialized in his largest form yet, and his shoulder loomed above my head. Instinctively, my hand reached out and clutched the stiff sharp bristles of his chin. Chen grunted in protest, but did not jerk away from me. *Trust me,* he whispered.

I always do.

Night and the plains outside Phoenix City vanished. So did Yún, Quan, and Lian. There was only me and Chen, and the faint musky scent of Nuó, just ahead. I could hear the steady padding of her feet over stone. *Follow, follow, follow,* said their rhythm. Chen's hooves clicked next to me as I trotted through a dark tunnel. Shadows sprang up beside me.

Bright sparks appeared and vanished. Monsters flitted past—ghostly creatures that expanded and shrank and spread out like a living cloud. The stink grew less and less. A new scent overtook it, one of snow and mud and a plethora of smells I could not catalog, except to say I knew them well.

Impossible, I thought.

We are on the spirit roads, Chen grunted. *Nothing is impossible here.*

I opened my mouth to argue—so glad that I had my spirit companion back to argue with—when a blast of wind choked my mouth. Surprised, I fell forward into a deep drift of snow.

17

BLIZZARD WINDS SHRIEKED AROUND ME. IN ONE instant, my face went numb, and a deep ache penetrated my ears and into my brain. I blinked—tried to. My eyelashes were stuck to my face. I rubbed them free with one frozen hand. My brain clicked over into the realization that we were in the middle of a snowstorm, in the mountains, in the pitch-dark depths between midnight and dawn.

Stand up, Chen urged me. *You'll freeze.*

Too late, I snapped. But it was so, so good to hear Chen's voice.

A hand closed over my shoulder and hauled me upright. Quan shouted into my poor abused ear that I must start walking. *I know, I know*, I thought. Gloves, but no boots. Our cloaks too thin for the dagger-sharp mountain winds. I pulled my collar high and tugged my knitted cap over my forehead. Snow had already slithered into my shoes and soaked my socks. We would die in minutes unless we found shelter.

Then another body lurched into mine. "Kai. Oh, Kai, you're safe."

Yún pulled me into a tight hug. I clutched her even closer. We were both babbling, *It's you, you, you, you,* while our spirit companions grunted and roared and shrilled at us to stop the love-talk and march, dammit.

"Quan? Kai? Yún?" The wind snatched at Lian's voice.

"Here," Yún said. "All safe."

"I have Yāo-guài," Lian said. "Quan?"

"Here."

We leaned close, head to head, our arms linked together, our hands tucked into our sleeves, creating a small bubble of temporary warmth, while around us the storm pummeled the mountainside. Yāo-guài poked his head out from Lian's shirt, ruffled his feathers, and dived back inside. *Lucky monster,* I thought, shivering. This close, I could sense Yún's crane-spirit, Lian's fox, and the shimmering phoenix that belonged to Quan. Overwhelming everything was the presence of Nuó, my mother's mountain-cat. A tremor passed through all the other companion spirits, the humans as well. Only then did it occur to me that my mother must have sent Nuó to us.

Where is she? I demanded.

Safe, the cat grumbled. *Safer than you.*

Then why did you dump us here in a blizzard, you stupid piece of flea-bait?

Nuó hissed. *Shut up, stupid boy. Forget your mother now. Follow me to the light.*

Her presence vanished from my brain with a loud *pêng*. A wave of musk whipped around me, jerked my attention away from the circle of my friends. I lifted my head—a blast of wind hit me in the face. My eyes blurred with tears that froze immediately, but I'd caught a glimpse of Nuó's figure striding away, the snows parting to either side, like soft cake split by a knife.

"*Ai!* The light!" Yún shouted. "There! I see it!"

She pointed upward and to the left, in the direction where Nuó had vanished.

The light was hardly more than a smear of dirty yellow, flickering in and out between the streamers of snow. I rubbed my hands over my eyes. Now I could see another smear of light close to the first one. Could it possibly be a shelter?

A squawking, gabbling noise broke out next to me. It was Lian and the griffin.

Lian cursed and struggled. She looked as though she were wrestling with her clothes.

"Stop it, you wretched little monster—"

Yāo-guài broke free and soared after Nuó. Glittering magic trailed behind the griffin, like clouds of golden sun motes. The magic illuminated a series of broad cat-prints in the snow.

Quan and Lian were already trudging ahead, bent against the bone-freezing wind. Yún gripped my arm hard and dragged me after them. But it wasn't fast enough. My hands were stiff inside my gloves. Pinpricks of fire ran through my veins. I could tell the fire would soon fade into numbness and frostbite. *Half a* li, I told myself, staring at the beckoning light. *Less than that.* I ordered my body to keep going, but my feet felt disconnected from my legs, two clumsy lumps of nothing.

With a dozen more painful steps, the blurred lights sharpened into rows of bright squares. Around them, I could make out the outline of a sizeable building.

Relief sent me staggering ahead of the others to the inn's heavy wooden door. My useless hands fumbled at the latch. No good. Then a warm animal breath curled through my hair and down my neck.

Allow me, said Nuó.

She pressed one great paw against the door. The latch shattered into bits. The door banged open so suddenly I fell into a heap. The next moment Yún, Lian, and Quan spilled over me. We untangled ourselves and crawled toward the stone hearth, snow dripping and melting from our clothes as we went.

"*Ai-ya!* Who are you? What are you?"

A small round man charged through one of the side doors, waving both hands in circles. He was dressed in a gown and slippers. His hair was gray and pulled back into a tight, old-fashioned queue.

"Out! Out!" he shrieked. "I have no room for beggars!"

Yāo-guài swooped in from nowhere. The innkeeper shrieked even louder. He snatched up a fire poker and swung it around his head. Yāo-guài dodged the poker. His shrieks were even louder than the innkeeper's, and the griffin was throwing off sparks of magic. Yún and I dragged each other to our feet.

"Yāo-guài! Stop it!"

Yāo-guài soared up to the ceiling and clung to a wooden crossbeam, scolding us all furiously.

Quan laid a hand on the innkeeper's arm. "Honored sir . . ."

The innkeeper shook off his hand and waved the fire poker in our faces. "*Hai!* Beggars! Thieves! Begone! I have spells against you."

"But honored sir, the laws of hospitality . . ."

This was going nowhere. Apparently, Lian thought the same thing. She stepped in front of Quan, her expression the same haughty look I remembered from our first meeting. "You will give us shelter," she said. "Or you will answer to my father the king."

"Liar," the man breathed. "Silly wench, to think I'd believe—"

Another door crashed open, and a new person stalked into the room. He was short. Dressed in an extravagant silk robe over an even more extravagant woolen dressing gown. All along the border and hem were stitched spells for warmth and comfort, and as the robe swirled around, magic flux glittered from special threads woven into the cloth. I was so amazed by the man's clothing, I didn't even bother to look at his face or really listen to his voice as he delivered a grand tirade about the noise.

"It's annoying enough that I'm trapped in your miserable inn until the storm breaks. Now you think to entertain me with arguments in your common room. Who these people are—" He swept his arm around, as if to take us all in, and his voice squeaked to a stop. "Kai?" he bleated.

It was the bleat that recalled me.

"Danzu?"

Danzu glanced wildly from me to my companions, from the griffin to Quan to Yún. When he got to Lian, his eyes stretched wide open and he made a noise as though he had rocks in his throat. "Your—I mean—"

"We need a private room," Lian said calmly.

"Yes. Yes, of course. Right away." He rounded on the inn-keeper, who'd watched this whole exchange with flapping lips. "You. I want a private room with a fire. Hot tea. And I mean *scalding*. Soup and blankets and dry clothing. And two chambers with hot baths. Right away, or I shall report you to my uncle and the rest of the merchant's guild."

I couldn't tell what discombobulated me the most—Danzu giving orders like a merchant king, or the innkeeper bow-ing and babbling and running to obey those orders. Soon enough the inn's servants herded us into a spacious private chamber with a roaring fire, dry clothes, and a vid-screen piping soft pre-recorded music. Two more chambers had been made ready, their bathtubs brimming with steaming scented water.

We took turns soaking until feeling returned to our fin-gers and toes. In the meantime, Danzu had sent word to the kitchens. More servants appeared with platters of barley pilaf, flatbread stuffed with lamb's meat and spices, and pots of fresh tea. Danzu hovered over us—Lian in particular—asking if we were warm and comfortable, assuring us that he would beat that miserable innkeeper if we were not satisfied with our meal. He had changed from his robe and morning gown into an equally elegant tunic and trousers. Now that we weren't frozen and dying, I finally realized how strange it was to find him outside Lóng City, away from his new street gang.

Suspicious, I stared at him. "What *are* you doing here anyway?"

He coughed delicately. "Business."

"Oh, right. Street rats and smugglers always prance around in blizzards—"

"I am *not* a smuggler—"

"Quiet!"

That was Yún.

My mouth snapped shut. So did Danzu's. Old habit dyed into our skins.

Yún glared at us. "Stop fighting. Stop acting like stupid brats. Okay?" She exhaled slowly, as though her own temper weren't so calm. "Good. Now. Danzu, tell us why you're out here. Better, tell us where *here* is."

Danzu's mouth dropped open again. "Um, we're in Lake of the Blue Jewel."

Lake of the Blue Jewel was a tiny city-kingdom northeast of Lóng City. That meant we were less than half a day's journey from home. I frowned. Why hadn't Nuó dumped us outside Lóng City's gates? Or even in the palace itself? Or maybe . . .

Lian had that thoughtful look, the one that said she read more from our circumstances than I could. "It's lucky we met you," she said. "As the philosophers say, it is always better to enter a conflict with knowledge. You know I've been absent from Lóng City almost a year. Please tell me how the kingdom sits these days."

Danzu took a minute to answer. He was going to break terrible news, I knew it. Lian must have suspected the same. Her expression never faltered, but I could see how the pulse at her throat fluttered.

"Your father is alive," he said.

(Lian let an almost soundless exclamation escape.)

"He's very sick," he continued.

(Her fingers tightened around Quan's hand.)

"He can't talk," Danzu went on. "And the physicians don't let the councilors and ministers spend much time in his chambers. They say . . ." He stopped and turned dark with embarrassment. "It's just gossip, your Highness. Nothing worth bothering about."

"Tell me what they say," Lian said. "I must know."

Her gaze locked with his. Danzu flinched and licked his lips. My own heart thumped in sympathy. It was easy to think of Lian as a friend. Never a commoner like me, never someone ordinary, but a companion in flight from the evil bad guys. It was easy to forget that she was a royal princess, the heir to Lóng City's throne.

Except now, when you could see a hundred years of responsibility in her dark eyes.

Danzu looked absolutely queasy by now. He blew out a shaky breath, and when he spoke, his voice wasn't anything like the snarky kid I knew. "They say . . . They say the king is trapped in spells, your Highness. Some say it's because he allowed you to study abroad. Children should not dictate to their elders, and all that. Some—a lot more—say you abandoned your city and your throne for the Phoenix Empire. They say that is why you never answered the Guild Council's messages about your father."

"I never received those messages," Lian whispered. Her expression smoothed out into a royal mask. "What else?" she said. "The council cannot do anything without my father's consent, or mine. Or . . . No, you heard more?"

"It's the Guild Council," Danzu said. "They intend to hold a special conference next week to . . . to . . ." He took a nervous swallow. "To decide who takes the throne."

The Guild Council had that power, written into Lóng City's laws centuries ago, ever since they ended the Interregnum and allowed Prince Xiang back on the throne. Only one queen—Queen Mae-wan, the grand-niece of Prince Xiang—ever tried to overthrow that law. Old tales say the ghost dragons joined with the Guild Council and turned Mae-wan into the very first gargoyle.

Quan clasped her hands within his, and she leaned toward him in whispered conversation. For a moment it was as though they had closed out the world. I wished I could read the story of their past year together.

I wasn't the only person watching. Danzu eyed them closely, as though trying to figure out how to make a profit from this new secret. Then his gaze caught mine. I scowled and drew one finger across my wrist. Danzu shrank into his chair, more like the street rat I knew from the old days. Okay, so he'd changed, but he was still the same old Danzu underneath.

"Danzu," Lian said, recalling us both, "I have yet another favor to ask you. I must reach Lóng City before the Guild Council meets. And I would do so quietly. Do you understand?"

Danzu smirked. "Absolutely, Your Highness."

"Can you convey us into the palace by tonight?"

He whistled. "Tonight?"

"As discreetly as possible," Lian said.

The smirk faded. Danzu plainly was struggling between the honest answer and one that made him look good. "I, ah . . . no. I can't," he said. "Lóng City, yes. Maybe. Not the palace. However, I do know someone who knows someone else who certainly can."

Hü. Sure. It was the old days all over again, with Danzu bragging about his so-called connections. I scowled. "Don't listen to him, Lian. He's not—"

Yún jabbed me with an elbow. *"Shī,"* she whispered. "We can trust him."

Grumbling, I rubbed my sore ribs. Lian smiled smoothly to me, then to Danzu. "Very well. I place myself in your hands. Please do not disappoint me."

HER WORDS MUST have frightened Danzu more than Yún or I ever could. He dashed off, leaving us to devour every speck of the magnificent breakfast. Servants reappeared with a second course of sweet cakes and more tea. We were finishing that off when Danzu came galloping back in.

"I've arranged everything," he told Lian. "We will reach Lóng City by darkfall. I guarantee it. Whether I can smuggle you inside the palace depends on my client and her friend, er, friends—"

"Which clients?" Lian asked.

Danzu hesitated. "I'd rather not say yet. But you can trust them, your Highness. I swear it."

"He's right," Yún said.

That seemed to surprise Lian. She stared hard at Yún, who shrugged.

"What about the blizzard?" Quan said.

"I, ah, have some magical spells in reserve," Danzu said. "Tricks from my uncle."

More bragging. Well, Lian would find out soon enough if he was lying.

In the stables, two large covered wagons stood in the middle of the floor, surrounded by a dozen servants who were busy offloading crates, unpacking them, and transferring items wrapped in brown paper into reed baskets. Danzu waded into the chaos, shouting orders to transport those baskets carefully, *carefully* now, to the inn's storage rooms.

"You trust this innkeeper with your special consignment?" I asked him as he passed by me.

"He's good enough," Danzu said in an undertone. "Besides, I'm not leaving everything behind."

He evicted the last of the stablehands and servants from the stables. A few men remained behind—the wagon drivers and two leathery-faced guards with ugly-looking weapons sticking out of their belts and boots. They hoisted the empty crates back onto the two wagons. Quan and Lian climbed into one wagon, each into a separate crate. Yún and I went into the second wagon, with the griffin stuffed into my shirt. Danzu's men handed us packets of cooked beef and dried apricots, a flask of hot butter tea and another of plain water. Then they packed fresh straw around us and wrapped the crates in thick blankets. Danzu had thought of everything.

Finally, the men closed up the crates and hammered the lids in place.

My stomach fluttered for no particular reason. *We escaped the emperor's palace,* I told myself. *We got away from his soldiers and trackers. We traveled the spirit roads and lived through a blizzard. All we have to do is get inside the Lóng City palace.*

Now came the final preparations—men leading horses from the stables, heavy footsteps tramping over the stone floor, a jingling as the drivers harnessed their beasts, and at last a penetrating creak as the stable's outer doors opened. One of the drivers cursed the cold. Another one laughed and predicted how soon they would all have a drink of hot brewed ale in Lóng City's best taverns.

Danzu gave a shout. Magic flux streamed through the air. My chest went tight and the world shrank. Then a short sharp snap traveled through me. Warmth rolled through my crate, carrying with it an electric scent, mixed with the rich smell of crushed herbs. Magic. Magic keyed to a few words that any fool could unlock.

Ai-ya. *Some trick,* I thought.

And you didn't believe him.

Chen, softly chuckling.

The wagon jerked forward, throwing me against the crate's side. Yāo-guài chattered angrily. Stroking the griffin's feathers, I yawned. The blankets and straw were like a cocoon around me. The unnatural warmth from Danzu's spell made me sleepier than ever. My eyelids sagged shut. It had been a long day.

Sleep, young one, said a familiar gruff voice.

Chen?

Someone laughed. Not Chen, but I was too sleepy to care. I drifted off to sleep. To dream of warm cotton oceans, and hot soup, and a stickle-pig nibbling at my fingers. Hungry stickle-pig. It poked and prodded and tickled with one pin-sharp tooth, almost like a beak.

Yāo-guài bit down hard. I woke with a yelp. "What—"

Shī, shī, Chen said. *We're inside Lóng City. We just passed the gates. And your monster is hungry.*

Fumbling around, I located the packets of food Danzu had provided. Yāo-guài kept up a soft trilling noise until I thrust a handful of meat strips at him. Yāo-guài gobbled them down so fast, I thought he'd choke. The little monster finally settled down with a thick strip between his claws, chewing away, the way a cat chews a freshly caught mouse.

Happy now? I asked.

The griffin made a noise that sounded like *nom, nom, nom.*

The wagon rattled slowly over cobblestones, up an incline to the next terrace, then along a level road with smoother paving stones. At first, the noises outside the wagons were louder—people on foot hurrying home before nightfall, dogs yapping, the noise of metal scraping against stone as someone cleared their steps. These soon dropped away as we turned up another steep slope. The horses strained to pull the heavy wagons. Probably these were draft horses, used for hauling freight. Where and when had Danzu bought them? He made it sound as though he'd been in business a long time—ever since we won our reward. And Yún hadn't acted surprised. In fact, she'd mentioned something about Danzu weeks and weeks go, when she first showed me those expensive maps for the mountain roads.

Maybe I don't know my friends at all.

Maybe you just need to listen harder, Chen said.

I started to tell him to shut up, but the wagon jolted to a stop. Yāo-guài screeched, and we both tumbled on our sides, scattering beef strips and packets everywhere. By the time I could sort everything out, someone was tapping at the crate's lid.

The lid fell open. I blinked at the sudden change from smothering dark to light. Even if that light was dim and uncertain.

A hand grasped my arm. "Come along."

Whoever that was hauled me out of the wagon. My legs, numb from the long day's trek, folded under me. I hit the cold stones of the courtyard with a thump. Yāo-guài gave a squawk and fluttered around me, fussing.

"D'you need help?" the man asked.

It was one of the drivers, I remembered. I shook my head and hauled myself to standing.

We were in a tiny, paved courtyard dusted with snow. Shadows pooled over the bare stones. There was a clean, cold scent in the air, mixed with the smells of horse and leather, a fainter one of crushed herbs and the electric fire of magic flux.

The driver helped Yún climb out. Another was doing the same for Quan and Lian. High overhead, dark clouds smudged a steel-gray sky. It couldn't be more than late afternoon. Snow trickled down from the clouds. Unlit lamps hung from the walls. The courtyard itself was bare, except for several clay pots where someone might plant flowers in the summer. There was a low iron gate—the one we'd just come through—and a pair of heavy wooden doors on the other side.

"Where are we?" I asked.

The doors swung open. A short slender figure marched out. "Danzu, you miserable idiot. You're late! Three days late! Where are my goods?"

"Hello, Jing-mei."

Jing-mei spun around. Her mouth dropped open at the sight of Lian. "Princess?" she whispered. "Is that really you?"

18

"It's me," Lian said.

Jing-mei stared from Lian to me and Yún. When she got to Quan, she paused. Her lips moved silently, as though she wanted to ask a thousand questions, but could not decide which one to pick first. Then she caught sight of Danzu, who was ordering the drivers to unload the rest of the crates.

"Explain," she said shortly.

"Emergency," he said, breathless. "Your shipment is safe. Truly. I left only a few crates in storage in Lake of the Blue Jewel."

"The jewelry? The special holo-glasses? The essences of southern winter? You know those require warmth, special handling—"

"Not those," Danzu whined. "The cheap stuff."

"I. Do. Not. Sell. *Cheap* stuff, Danzu Qián. What have you thrown away from my shipment?"

"Nothing. I swear it. Ask the princess."

Jing-mei drew a deep breath. Her expression reminded me of a watch-demon momentarily denied its prey. Except that watch demons had no faces, nor eyes that glittered with rage. She muttered something that sounded very much like "I'lltalktoyoulateryoumiserabletoad," then turned to Lian. "My apologies, Your Highness."

"The apologies are mine," Lian said smoothly. "I ordered Danzu to convey me into Lóng City in the most discreet fashion he knew."

"Smuggling," I murmured.

Danzu and Yún glared at me. Quan shook his head. Only Jing-mei offered me a tight smile.

"I understand completely," she said to Lian. "Come inside so we might discuss the matter. Let *Danzu* manage the horses and his shipment."

She and Danzu exchanged angry smiles. Jing-mei apparently won, because Danzu shriveled inside his elegant cloak and turned back to the wagons and his crew.

Jing-mei smiled more sweetly (was this really the same bubble-headed girl from my gang?) and led us into a cavern of a room. She brushed her hand over a gray mesh panel by the door. With a hiss, light poured from shaded lamps overhead. I blinked at the sight of row upon row of crates, stacked almost to the ceiling. The air here was much warmer than I expected. Then I remembered Jing-mei scolding Danzu about delicate electronics. This was her warehouse for her special consignments. She kept the goods safe with magically warmed air.

She must be richer than I thought.

Not rich. Clever, Chen said quietly. *There are magic flux wells underneath these warehouses. She's tapping into them.*

Was that legal? I wondered.

Lian too had obviously noticed. Her eyes narrowed at the pipes and vents, the flicker and twitch of magic flux currents. Normally, a person paid fees to the royal wizards for regular access to the magical flux within our kingdom. I'd seen the bills when I first explored my mother's papers. The wizards might not care about one-time, sometimes, once-in-a-while access. This setup, however, was a lot more than once-in-a-while. Lian sent a questioning glance toward Jing-mei, who smiled nervously. Heh. Probably not legal. This could prove interesting.

At the opposite side of the warehouse, a winding staircase brought us up two flights to a small landing. Very plain, except for a complicated set of locks on one door. Jing-mei used a series of keys, then laid her palm against the latch. The lock clicked open, and she gestured for us to come inside.

It was the same apartment I remembered from two months ago, but with a few differences. A broad desk crowded the tiny back room, its surface covered with accounting books, a shiny new calculor in the middle. All the trinkets and gadgets had disappeared from the hallway and nearby rooms. She must have moved them into that enormous warehouse.

"Come with me to the kitchen," Jing-mei said. "I can brew some tea. And we can talk."

Jing-mei managed to seat us all around the table, but barely. Lian and Quan tucked themselves into a corner, closer than absolutely necessary. Yún hesitated, then did the same next to me. Yāo-guài paced the tabletop, chittering with excitement and pleasure that we'd left the cold, dark wagons behind. I'd expected Jing-mei to chitter back, but she merely patted him on the head absent-mindedly in between whisking cups onto the table, setting a kettle of water to boil, and sending curious glances toward Lian and Quan.

"So who are you?" she asked Quan, as she measured tea from a canister into an elegant teapot.

"My friend," Lian said firmly. "We studied at the university together."

"Our rescuer," Yún said even more firmly.

I rolled my eyes, which brought a laugh from Jing-mei. "Very well. None of my business. But you came to me for help. Tell me everything that happened."

Lian exchanged a glance with Quan. "*Everything* will take some time."

"Better to arm your warriors, than to fall victim to excess caution," he murmured.

She smiled. "Very true. Here is what you must know," she said to Jing-mei.

She told Jing-mei about the Phoenix emperor's plans to force her into marriage with his youngest son, and about the treaties the emperor used to drain other mountain kingdoms of their magic flux. How Quan arranged for our escape, how the emperor's soldiers nearly captured us, and our unexpected rescue by Nuó.

By the time she finished, the water had boiled, and the tea had steeped.

"I suspect there are those who would prevent me from reuniting with my father and answering the Guild's accusations," Lian said at last.

"I believe you are right," Jing-mei said as she poured tea for all of us. "It's true the Guild fears you've deserted your responsibilities. *I* happen to think certain factions within the court are feeding those rumors for their own advancement. Which means you cannot simply announce yourself to any guard safely. Let me call someone who knows more about the palace security than I do. . . ."

She plucked a silver disc from behind her ear, tapped it with her thumb, and spoke Gan's name. Magic blossomed in the air. A pale circle of light appeared in front of Jing-mei's face.

"Gan," she said, "we need you here right away."

Where? said a ghostly voice.

"Same-old same-old. We're having a surprise party with some old, true friends."

A long pause. *Right,* said the ghost-voice. *I can be there in maybe-so five ten minutes.*

"Good enough. Thanks."

Jing-mei tapped the disc again. The light blipped into nothing, and she tucked the disc behind her ear. The fancy device reminded me of Deming the waiter and his magic-powered glasses, the ones that let him transmit orders directly to the kitchens. This had to be the same kind of micro-receptor-transmitter technology, but much fancier and much more powerful.

Jing-mei caught me staring. "It's just a new toy. All the courtiers love them."

"You could make a fortune selling those in the Phoenix Court," Quan said. "Where did you find a manufacturer?"

"Trade secret," she said, with a mysterious smile. "And Phoenix City is a nice market, but I hope I can make a fortune right here."

So that's how she'd spent her share of the reward. She sniffed out the latest toys or trinkets, then sold them for a huge profit to rich nobles. Danzu did the grunt work, transporting the goods from wherever—maybe even from Phoenix City. Merchant and businesswoman. It was hard to take in how much my friends had changed in just one year. But in a strange way, they were still all part of the same gang, each helping the other.

"What is Gan's job in all this?" I asked.

Yún and Jing-mei shared a look of sour amusement.

"Stiff stick," Jing-mei said.

"You aren't being fair," Yún murmured.

"Well, no. We can talk about that later. Ah, here he is . . ."

Bells were chiming through the apartment. Jing-mei hurried away. Soon, I heard Gan's deep slow voice from down the corridors.

". . . caught the express transport before it left the guard station. Gave them some excuse about my captain sending me out to investigate a disturbance, but I don't think—"

"You think too much," Jing-mei said.

"Very funny," Gan said. "So which 'old, true friends' did you mean? Don't tell me Yún caught up with Kai and dragged him back to Lóng City."

"Close, but not quite."

"Don't make me guess, Jing-mei. My sergeant says I'm up for review and I—"

Gan rounded the corner and stopped. Tick by tock, he took in my presence, then Yún's. The griffin snagged his whole attention, but only for a moment, because all of a sudden he recognized Lian and his mouth fell open.

"Hello, Gan," Lian said.

Gan collapsed onto the nearest stool and blinked at all of us. Finally, he croaked, "Princess? When did you get back home? And why are you *here*?"

Why not at the palace, he meant.

"I need your help," Lian said. Once more she told the story of our escape and her suspicion that someone, or several someones, had conspired to overthrow Lóng City's king. Throughout her account, Gan continued to blink and make unhappy noises in his throat.

"We believe the conspirators were paid by the Phoenix emperor," Quan said.

"And who are you?" Gan shot back.

"A doctor, student, and former subject of the emperor," Quan replied without hesitation.

He left out the part about being Lian's beloved, I said to Chen.

That comes later, Chen grunted.

I pressed my forehead against my hands. Later. I could only hope there was a later. Right now, all I wanted was a warm bed. My head ached, and the nap I'd had in Danzu's wagon wasn't nearly enough. Yún leaned close and poured me a second mug of tea. "Courage," she said. "We are almost done with the adventure."

"Oh, yeah, but what *kind* of end?"

She smiled and patted me on the arm. Meanwhile, Lian was explaining to Gan exactly what she hoped to accomplish that evening. She wanted to reach her father's bedchamber without any guards sending word to the Guild Council or any member of court. Just in case.

"Is it possible?" she asked.

Gan frowned and kneaded his hands together, as though testing the lumps and flaws in the bundle of clay that was her request. "It's not a simple matter," he said after a couple moments.

"You mean it's not simple if we fail," Jing-mei said.

Gan opened and shut his mouth. "I mean it's not simple."

Lian flicked her hand in a sharp gesture. "No arguments, please. Gan, tell me at once if you cannot manage such a task. I will not blame you," she added quickly. "I understand that your reputation and career would suffer—"

"It's not that," Gan said sharply. "It's . . . I must think how we can do it. You see, in the past month or two, the commanders have changed our routines. Anyone wishing to enter the palace must present three kinds of credentials, all of them approved by the Minister of Inner Harmony. My commanders say it's because everyone's afraid for the king's safety. I think it's because they don't want any witnesses to what's going on."

"And what is going on?"

Lian's voice dropped to a frigid whisper. Gan shivered (we all did) and wiped his forehead. "Your father is ill. He cannot speak. He does not eat anything but a few spoonfuls of soup. Most of the court physicians have been ordered away—all except the two most senior. Oh, and one physician who came with the Lang-zhou City delegation for the trade conference."

Lian gave a soft exclamation. "Go on."

"There isn't much more to say. Three physicians in attendance, all day long. Rumor says . . ." He faltered. "Rumor says your father should have died a month or more ago. They say, either the gods protect him from death, or he's made an unholy pact with demons."

"You didn't tell me that part," Jing-mei murmured.

"We each have our secrets," Gan murmured back.

Lian frowned in concentration. "You can't help us into the palace, I think. Not without someone getting very suspicious, very quickly. What about you, Jing-mei? You say you deliver goods to members of my court. Do you have these new credentials?"

A moment's hesitation. "No, Your Highness. We—Danzu and I have an arrangement with certain officers."

"You bribe them?"

Gan scowled. Yún went tense beside me. Both of them had known about the business, and maybe about tapping into the magic flux, but not the bribes. Jing-mei shifted uncomfortably, her gaze flitting all around the kitchen, anywhere but her friends' faces. Lian waited patiently, her own expression unreadable.

Finally, Jing-mei released an unhappy breath. "Yes. But only to overlook our deliveries. Nothing else. We—"

Lian cut her off with a gesture. "Never mind. Tell me how you enter the palace."

They entered the palace by the stable entrance, Jing-mei explained. Usually between ten o'clock and midnight. Certain junior officers ("bribe takers," Gan muttered unhappily) made certain they stood on duty at the gates. They fiddled with the vid-cameras and sent their underlings on patrol well away from the entrances.

Halfway through her explanation, Danzu appeared. His face turned gray. "Jing-mei—"

"Shut up," Jing-mei told him. Then to Lian, "Once we're inside, we transfer the goods into the freight lifts."

"To which wing of the palace?"

"To a waiting room next to the Royal Audience Chambers for Intimate Friends and Enemies."

Lian's eyebrows lifted in respect. "Very audacious. And clever. You won't find many chance visitors to that hall at night. Your customers visit you there?"

Jing-mei nodded. "It is all arranged, Your Highness."

"Do the junior captains know that?"

"I believe not. *I* have not told them, but there are always rumors."

"Yes," Lian said to herself. "There would be rumors."

"So what's our plan?" I asked. "We walk into the audience chamber. Then what?"

"There are six Royal Audience Chambers, but only one for Intimate Friends and Enemies," Lian said. "My father advised me, as his grandfather advised him, to keep his friends close, but his enemies closer. Therefore, he chose a chamber situated on the floor below his personal suite." Her expression turned grim. "I pity those enemies we encounter tonight."

The next hour raced by. Danzu and Jing-mei went off to prepare a wagon. Quan cooked dinner. Lian and Gan discussed tactics for reaching the king's bedchamber without encountering any guards or other obstacles. Yún and I didn't have much to do, other than keeping our griffin occupied. I felt pretty useless.

I did my part already, I told myself. *I found Lian and helped her escape. Sort of.*

Except it was Yún who brought the maps and money and passports. And Quan who found out the plot and organized his smuggler friends. And Danzu who brought us into Lóng City. Now Gan and Jing-mei would do the rest.

Yún touched my arm and leaned close. "You fought the bandits," she whispered. "You saved my life. You found the secret passage. We would not be here without you."

"How did you—"

She smiled. "I know you, Kai. No matter what you think,

you are smart and clever, just in different ways. And . . ." Her voice caught. "If I were a better friend, I'd tell you that more often."

Her fingers closed over my hand. I almost forgot about all the people around us. Maybe this time it would be okay if I kissed her.

"Dinner is ready," Quan announced.

Peh. I squashed a string of curses. Yún's mouth tucked into a brief smile.

We ate, then trooped down through the warehouse and into the courtyard. The moon was floating low in the skies, half obscured by Lóng City's mountain peak. Our wagon stood in the middle, stacked high with crates and smaller boxes. Someone had lit a torch, which cast a ruddy glare over everything.

Jing-mei pointed to one larger crate with its lid off, which stood near the back of the wagon. "For you and Yún, Princess. Kai, you can pretend you're one of our grunts."

"Not so hard," Danzu said with a grin.

My lips curled back in a snarl. *Later, Goat Boy.*

"What must I do?" Quan said.

"Grunt," Jing-mei said without hesitation. "Danzu and I are the drivers."

"And me?" Gan said.

"You stay here," Jing-mei said. "You can't risk anyone—"

"I can't risk not going—"

Lian silenced them with a sharp gesture. "Gan, Jing-mei is almost right. You must not be seen with people known to give bribes. I want you to meet us in the hall of Royal Audience Chambers for Intimate Friends and Enemies. Wait one hour. If we do not appear, go at once to my father's bed-chamber and tell him—tell everyone—that I have arrived. Understood?"

"What about the watch-demons?" I said.

"Don't worry," Jing-mei said.

Easy for her to say. Seeing her face pale and tense in the torchlight, I reconsidered. Well, maybe not. Either we all died tonight, or she went to prison for bribery, or . . .

I didn't want to think about it. Wishing for good luck made the gods jealous, the old tales said. Better to be a grunt and just follow orders.

We each took our places in the wagon. Lian and Yún climbed inside the crate. Danzu tapped the lid into place, covered the entire lot with blankets. Quan and I squeezed between the crates and the back of the wagon. Gan tilted his head back, studying us all, but Jing-mei in particular. "Good fortune," he said softly.

Her face flushed and she smiled tentatively. "And to you."

Outside the gates we came into a covered street. At the next intersection, Gan peeled off into a smaller passageway used by the royal guards. We continued to a pair of thick iron gates that sang with magic flux. Danzu dismounted briefly and pressed a metal disc into a slot in the wall. The flux scaled upward to a high-pitched tone, then the gates opened.

"What are these?" I said.

"Old King An K'ao built them," Jing-mei said. "After the Horse Guard Rebellion he decided that kings ought have proper tunnels, not those sewers. He ran out of money before he got very far. Then someone poisoned him. Most likely one of the Guild Council. They took over building the tunnels so merchants can transport goods through the city after dark."

We continued on through a pair of gates into a broad tunnel. Flux-powered lamps glimmered to life as we passed. At the next intersection, the tunnel dipped below the level of the city streets, then climbed upward along with the mountainside in long winding loops. Pretty soon, I'd lost all sense of where we could be beneath the city. It was an endless passageway, brick walls gleaming with frost and melted snow. Our only illumination was the soft circle of lamplight which rose and faded as we passed each sconce. A mist flowed over the stones beneath us, stirred into eddies and waves by the horses, then streamed along the side of the wagon.

Quan had let his hand trail the mist. Suddenly, he jerked his hand back. His eyes were wide.

"What's wrong?" I whispered.

"Magic flux," he whispered back. "Stronger than I've ever encountered."

I touched my fingertips to the mist, felt a humming through my veins. Yāo-guài wriggled free of my coat and lapped at the magic flux, making happy chuckling noises in his throat. Fascinated, I watched as his claws shone like silver daggers, his feathers brightened to a burnished gold. His stone-black eyes reminded me of an onyx necklace I'd once seen.

Something nipped at my fingers.

I yanked my hand back with a yelp.

A ghost dragon darted between the wagon wheels and slithered up the side of the wagon. For a moment we were face to face as it stared at me with translucent gray eyes. *Hurry,* it whispered, then dived back into the mist to fade away.

My blood hummed louder. I sucked on my fingers, hoping the legends about their poisonous bites were not true. "Danzu?"

He glanced over his shoulder. "What?"

"Ghost dragons. Are those normal?"

No answer, but he urged his team to a faster pace. The horses were willing beasts; they bent into their harness and hauled us up a series of loops. At the next intersection, they veered to the left, bringing us into a wide underground courtyard. There they halted and dropped their heads.

Lamps in glass cages lined the walls. Ahead, a massive iron gate, guarded by two men and a younger woman. All three wore gray uniforms with the royal insignia of a screaming dragon. The two men wore a row of tiny jewels above their patches. The woman's uniform had an extra row that signified a captain.

"I thought you said junior guards," I whispered to Jing-mei.

"Someone talked," she whispered back.

Or someone had guessed about the peculiar arrangements made by the stable watch's junior officers. Quickly, I glanced around to find Yāo-guài. The griffin had burrowed underneath the blankets, with only an inch of his tail in sight. I pinched the tip, and it vanished.

Danzu hopped down from the wagon and approached the

guards. The captain stepped forward and gestured for him to stop. I bent down to check the knife in my boot. Quan touched my arm and shook his head. Not yet.

The captain didn't give an alarm, but her face was like stone. She leaned forward and started talking to Danzu. Her voice was too soft for me to hear, but I could guess from the way Danzu glanced over his shoulder at Jing-mei. The captain kept talking. Danzu must have said something she didn't like, because the woman scowled and tapped his chest, then pointed at the other two guards.

Danzu trudged back to the wagon. He looked unhappy. "The captain wants a share of our delivery."

Jing-mei bit her lips. "How much?"

"Ten percent."

"Ten—" Jing-mei choked. "Anything else?"

"We're supposed to unload everything. Here. She gets to pick. If she likes what we have, she lets us inside and doesn't report us to the king's guards and the Guild Council."

"But that's—"

"I know—"

"Didn't you tell her—"

"She didn't care—"

"Let her," Quan said quietly.

Both of them rounded on him. "Are you mad?" Jing-mei said.

"We have no choice," Quan said. "We must get into the palace tonight. Besides, if we refuse, she'll have us arrested. And if that happens, *and* the wrong people find out, it might be days or weeks before Lian can convince anyone of her identity."

Or never.

Jing-mei chewed on her fist a moment before she spoke. "Very well. Kai, you and Quan unload the three crates marked with blue stripes. Then bring out the two smallest chests. Danzu, show them which ones I mean."

We obeyed, hauling out the crates as though we were nothing more than thick-witted grunts. Jing-mei and Danzu stood next to the captain. I noticed the two junior officers remained close to the gates, clearly unhappy, but alert. If the captain refused our bribe, we couldn't jump them before they gave a warning with their talk-phones.

When Quan and I finished unloading the crates and chests, we stood off to either side. Jing-mei imperiously ordered Danzu to give her room. She shooed him away toward the gates, then bent over the smallest of the chests. "Here is the finest jewelry in my collection," she told the guard. "But I would be honored if you chose this."

Gold and jewels poured from her hands into the captain's. Magic flux gleamed from the gems and flowed down link by golden link. These were items saturated in protective spells, priceless items that made my breath freeze in amazement.

The captain shrugged. "Not interested."

She said not interested to the miniature vid-screens. She sneered at the silvery disc talk-phones that Jing-mei demonstrated. This was not going well at all. I glanced at my other companions, trying to figure out what we could do.

Quan yawned and stretched, as though working the kinks from his back. That brought him a couple steps closer to the gates. Danzu stared at Quan, then he, too, stretched and shook out his legs. The difference wasn't much, but it put a bit more space between him and the captain. Less between him and the other guards.

My turn.

I yawned and scratched under my shirt. Turned half away from the guards and slid the knife from my wrist sheath into my hand. When I turned back, the captain had rejected the contents of all three chests and half the first crate.

"Junk!" the captain declared. "Who buys this worthless crap?"

I sauntered to the back of the wagon, lowered the front of my pants, and released a stream of piss onto the stones. Behind me, I heard a muffled choking sound from the closest crate. Lian or Yún. Trying not to think of them, I wiped myself and refastened my trousers. Then I turned back to the wagon and wiped my hands on the blanket covering the other crates.

"Yāo-guài," I whispered.

The griffin emerged from the straw, his eyes bright and eager, chuckling softly. Without me saying anything, he wriggled underneath my shirt. I fiddled a while longer, then lurched back gracelessly to my old spot, between the wagon and the gate. Quan had inched closer too, but not much. Danzu was opposite us. And Jing-mei was lifting the last item from the last crate for the captain's inspection.

Time for ingenuity, I thought.

I yelped as loud as I could. All three guards swung around to face me.

Danzu bent down to his boot. In one swift motion, he'd extracted his knife and nailed one guard by the shoulder. Quan downed the second one with a rock to the temple. At the same time, I flung Yāo-guài into the air. The griffin swooped at the captain and snatched the talk-phone from her wrist, then disappeared in a cloud of glittering magic. Before the woman could react, Jing-mei grabbed her around the neck, squeezed tightly, and lowered her to the stones, unconscious. Quan and I took care of the other guards, and soon had them bound and gagged.

"Hurry," Jing-mei said. "We don't have much time before the patrols return."

She searched the captain for keys to the gates. Quan and I released Lian and Yún from their crate. Among all of us, we unharnessed the horses and got them inside the palace storerooms. The wagon we left outside to confuse our pursuers. Then we took off at a run for the nearest stairwell to the upper floors.

We met Gan in the hall of Royal Audience Chambers for Intimate Friends and Enemies. A dozen guards followed him, most of them young, but also one or two senior officers. "Your Highness," Gan said, with a salute. "I brought a squad of loyal men for your protection."

Lian's eyes shone bright with emotion. "I thank you all. I will remember this."

From far off came a thundering, as though a hundred feet galloped toward us. Lian pointed toward a side corridor and a wooden door that screamed servants' passage. All but three of Gan's friends took up positions at the foot of the stairs, their weapons ready. Gan and two others followed us up the narrow winding stairs. In the back of my mind, I heard Chen grunting in eagerness, and a faint whistling from Qi. Jun had turned visible, bristling with anger, her fox tail switching back and forth.

We reached the next landing. A crash and shouts echoed from below. Lian never hesitated. She swung the door open and marched into the room beyond, with Quan a step behind and their companion spirits swarming after them. The rest of us spilled into a brightly lit chamber.

It was just like the vision the ghost dragon king showed me—crowds of servants hurrying this way and that, a line of courtiers off to one side, gossiping, and in the middle, the bed where the king lay. Two royal physicians, surrounded by their attendants, gave orders and counter-orders. And there was a third physician, this one dressed in layers of silk robes. His collar was trimmed with silver lynx tails. His sleeves were embroidered with symbols of health and influence.

Quan shoved through the crowd to the bed. He bent over the thin, old man who lay unmoving underneath the linen sheets and pressed his fingertips against the slack throat. The king's face was as pale as new parchment, his wrists limp atop the sheet. He looked dead, I thought, then gulped to think my ill-thoughts might rise to heaven to influence the gods.

Tense and unmoving, Quan listened. "He lives," he said at last. "Just."

Lian, at his side, released a cry. "Can you save him?"

"I will do everything possible."

Our entrance had frozen everyone. Now shouts went up, the attendants scattered to summon the guards. The third physician, the stranger to Lóng City, tried to drag Quan away from the king. "You idiot," the man bleated. "You will disturb the pattern of my spells. Do you wish to murder the king?"

Lian's fingers closed over the man's arm. "Excuse me. Your patient is my father. *My* beloved father. Make way for the physician *I* choose."

Quan laid his hands over Wencheng Li's chest and closed his eyes. His lips moved rapidly in recitation of healing spells, a staccato dance of syllables that seemed never to repeat itself. And then I caught the pattern, one so very complicated and delicate, as though I watched the pattern of snowflakes in a blizzard. The air around us drew tight. More and more magic flux flooded the room.

Pêng! Yāo-guài materialized at the foot of the bed. His gaze fixed upon the king, he crept closer, panting audibly. Quan paused in his recitation. His eyes widened—I wished I could read his thoughts—then he laid a hand over the griffin's folded wings and recited a new series of words . . .

. . . and the king drew a long breath and opened his eyes. "Lian," he whispered.

"I am here." Lian touched her father's cheek, his forehead. "I was wrong—wrong to leave you, wrong to—I will never do it again."

"Not wrong. My brave daughter."

Quan had stepped back to make way for Lian. He was studying the king with narrowed eyes. A troubled, uneasy look—the look of a doctor who dislikes the signs in his patient. Everyone else had frozen again, so I sidled between to courtiers to reach his side. "What's wrong?" I whispered.

"I'm not certain. There's a strange blankness over his heart."

. . . *a blank, a void, where the sickness eats at him.*

The ghost dragon's words came back to me. "But you cured him."

"Not exactly. Not completely. That . . . thing still eats at him. And there are signs of other magic at work. Magic that heals and doesn't—"

He broke off. *"Hēi!* You, there. Stop!"

He swung around and grappled the stranger physician to the floor. A dozen palace minions threw themselves on the pair. More servants and guards surged forward into battle. Animal spirits materialized from everywhere: pig, crane, fox, and phoenix. Other spirits—from the guards and courtiers—flickered in and out of view. Gan and I waded into the mess, both of us throwing punches. Someone grabbed me around the waist and hauled me away. It was Yún.

"Don't make trouble," she said.

She had a lump over one eye and a bloody nose. My lip split as I grinned at her. Then we turned back to rescue our friends. In a few moments, we'd separated Danzu and Jing-mei from two hulking guards. The stranger physician crawled out from underneath a pile of minions. He was covered in bruises, and someone had ripped the lynx tails from his collar. He looked like he might dart for the nearest exist, but then Nuó appeared and seized his arm in her teeth.

Quan emerged from the chaos. He gripped a chain in one hand. The links were tiny, fashioned out of a whitish-grayish material that made my stomach turn queasy when

I tried to look directly at it. Dangling from the bottom was a twisted mass of the same material. Its shape reminded me of a squashed spider, its legs sprawled in all directions. I noticed that Quan held the chain well away from himself and Lian.

"The spider of death," he said in a thick voice.

Yún turned pale. "Are you . . . never mind. You would know."

Quan rounded on the stranger. "Where did you acquire this loathsome thing?"

The man's eyes popped wide into moon circles. "I didn't. You can't prove it. You—"

"Shut up." Quan squeezed his hand over the chain and spoke a word. A loud *crack* echoed through the chamber and my stomach lurched into my throat.

The thing vanished in a puff of acrid smoke.

Lian cried out. We all turned to see Wencheng Li attempting to rise. He fell back almost at once. When Lian dropped to her knees, he laid a hand on her head. Sweat poured from his face, but he was breathing, deep strong breaths, and there was an angry gleam in his eyes. "Begone," he said to the minions that hovered over him. "I would talk to my daughter. To her alone."

"Take this man way," Gan said to the guards. He glanced at Nuó. "If you don't mind."

Even though Gan was a grunt and no officer, the guards rushed to obey. Soon the crowds had melted away. Jing-mei, Danzu, Yún, and I hesitated, uncertain where to go. All our companions—except for Nuó—had vanished into the spirit plane. Quan remained where he'd been standing, his hand still clutched around what had been a necklace. Slowly, he unfolded his fingers. Ashes floated to the floor.

"You did it," I said.

"Yes." But his expression flitted from confused to more confused. "Nothing can withstand the spider of death," he murmured, more to himself than to me. "And yet the king has lived nearly two months. Almost dead, but not quite. I don't understand . . ."

Another ear-popping *crack* reverberated through the chamber. An enormous ghost dragon materialized, filling the room with its translucent body. Silver scales, like wisps of mist and snow, coiled around us all. My breath hiccupped as I realized their pattern was a magical one. Of course. And yet, I'd never paused long enough to notice before. The king of Lóng City's ghost dragons caught my gaze. His inner eye-lid quivered in a wink for me alone, then he swung his head toward the king. *My friend.*

His voice made the air and stone tremble.

Wencheng Li's eyes fluttered open. "My friend. You saved my life."

Hardly. The dragon's lips curled back in a soundless laugh. *I sent minions. Those two.* He pointed a claw at me and Yún. *Your daughter brought the man who saved you. But until they could breach the many obstacles set by the Phoenix emperor, I asked a great favor of my other old friend.*

His jaws stretched open. A silvery mist flowed out—a cloud of magic flux that slowly resolved into a very familiar figure—a small slight figure, with bright black eyes and a fierce gaze.

"Mā mī?" I croaked.

And fainted.

19

"YOUR MOTHER IS THE MOST ASTONISHING PERSON I know," Lian said.

"All demons are astonishing," I muttered.

Lian merely smiled and poured out two cups of smoke-gray tea. "You must learn to see her as others do."

"As what? A half-demon?"

"Ah, now you are being deliberately obtuse, my friend."

I scowled, but said nothing. It was all part of a grand ceremony, where we sipped our tea, delicately and formally, and kept our voices pitched low, in what the nobles called Everlasting Tranquility. We also wore our stiffest, most elaborate costumes. Lian, with her crown and jewels, could have challenged anyone in the Phoenix Court. Me, I wore a newly tailored shirt and trousers, and a short-sleeved robe decorated with silver threads and golden magic. That was because ours was more than a meeting between two almost-old friends. Today was for the royal princess and one of her trusted advisors.

Oh, yeah, me.

Two weeks had passed since we smuggled Lian into the palace and Quan rescued her father from a slow, miserable death. I'd thought our troubles were over, but I was wrong again. First, Lian had to summon the Guild Council and the king's ministers to explain what had happened in the Phoenix Empire. Yún, Quan, and I served as witnesses. My mother, too, came forward and gave her account. She knew magic was involved, she explained, but she didn't have the key to its power. She and the ghost dragon king had conferred, and agreed that she would remain behind, working spell after spell to sustain the king's life, while her worthless son and her most valuable assistant traveled to the Phoenix Empire to fetch the princess.

"There were plots underway," she'd said, in her driest voice. "And so the ghost dragon king agreed to shelter me from view until the matter was resolved."

Only Mā mī, I thought, could call two months in the ghost dragon king's belly *shelter*.

After the ministers and Guild finished with her, or my mother with them, the court interrogated the false physician. They confirmed what I could have guessed in two seconds—that the man was a spy and agent for the Phoenix emperor, sent to disrupt Lóng City's government, so that Lian would have no choice but to marry the emperor's son. But I guess the muckety-mucks like to have all kinds of ceremony, so they dragged out the interrogation for three days, then opened another session with the ministers and the Guild to report their findings.

Speaking of ceremony, this was another one.

"You have saved my father's life," Lian said.

"Quan did that."

She smiled, a more secretive smile. "True. And he will receive his reward. If he wishes it."

I'd guessed that much, too. "When's the wedding?"

Her gaze, as sharp as a knife, flicked up to mine. "*When* I ask and *if* he accepts."

"Oh, he will. He's not that stupid."

For a moment, I thought I'd gone too far, because Lian's face scrunched into a very odd expression, as though she couldn't make up her mind whether to laugh, or snort, or order me executed by Death of a Thousand Cuts. She settled on merely exasperated. "Never mind about Quan. You are the reason for this meeting."

She touched her palm to a polished silver square set into the tabletop. A servant entered carrying a velvet cushion. On it was a small leather cylinder, with brass caps at both ends. The caps were engraved with dozens of tiny symbols. More symbols were burnt into the leather. Recognizing the official seals of the kings of Lóng City, I nearly whistled.

"Your reward," Lian said, presenting me with the cylinder. "With my word and this device, you are given freedom from all taxes and fees within the kingdom, for your life, the lives of your children, and so unto the distant future. You are named Friend of the Throne, and Brother of My Heart. Your debts are mine. Your sustenance shall be paid from my purse. My faith and loyalty are yours forever."

My hand shook as I accepted the cylinder. "I don't know what to say."

"Try, 'You're welcome, Princess.'"

I regarded her suspiciously. "Isn't that supposed to be 'Thank you'?"

"Not in your case."

I tried several different replies, but it took a while before my voice worked properly. "If I'm your friend, what about Yún? And the others?"

"Yún and I have spoken already. If you wish to know how

I rewarded her, you must ask her yourself. Gan will receive a purse of gold and a promotion. So will the guards he brought. As for Jing-mei and Danzu, they come to me tomorrow for an audience. There are certain matters to forgive. Nothing that we cannot achieve."

Kings and queens spoke a peculiar language, my mother always said. "Forgive" could mean any number of things, from nothing at all, to fines, to much, much worse. But this was Lian, and she would not forget that these two had helped her, even when it meant facing punishment later.

I cleared my throat. "And my mother?"

"She will have whatever she wishes. Though I doubt she will accept much. She is very . . . independent."

"Astonishing," I agreed blandly.

Lian's mouth quirked into a smile. "An excellent word."

We drank more tea, nibbled some fancy pastries. (Pepper pastries. Someone must have told stories. Probably Chen to Lian's fox spirit, Jun.) There were particular protocols for formal visits such as this one, so neither of us hurried. Besides, it was nice to sit in a pretty room, scented with cinnamon and cedar, drinking expensive tea.

"What about your studies?" I said at last. "Are you sorry they ended so soon?"

"Yes. No. I learned a great deal from the university, but I grew to dislike the palace."

We exchanged wry smiles at her understatement.

"You could find another university," I offered. "One without any power-mad emperors."

She shook her head. "My father is old. My duty is here. Also, Quan and I have talked about that. There are a hundred or more small schools all through the Seventy Kingdoms, but no true universities. We might establish our own in Lóng City. Some of those scholars in the mountain schools might join us, and Quan knows others in the empire who are excellent scholars, who need a post. Some of them are cousins . . ."

Quan and his one million cousins. I wanted to envy him. I think I had at one time. He was smart, honorable, brave, and competent. Now? I remembered his face, when he thought he'd lost Lian's trust, and I was glad for him.

Lian and I talked a while longer. Quan had started work on a new hospital for Lóng City's poor. Lian's father had recovered from the magical illness, but his ordeal had left him weakened. Lian would take his place in the trade negotiations when they reopened. She also spent hours with him and his ministers, discussing how to deal with the Phoenix

emperor's displeasure once the snows melted and the mountains were passable.

Eventually, all conventions satisfied, I took my leave from
Lian and the Golden Egg Crate. Lian had offered to order
me a special carriage, but I'd had enough of fancy things. I
walked to the nearest wind-and-magic lift and tossed a ten-
yuan coin at the old woman. The lifts were running half
speed in winter, with more wind than magic. Two easy stops
later, the carriage doors opened and I strolled home through
a drifting of snow to the West Moon Wind District and my
mother's tutoring shop.

She sat at the front counter, ink brush in hand, checking
her accounts with abacus and calculor. One of the shop cats
snored on a sack in the corner. The griffin coiled around her
inkstand, evidently dreaming, because it was twitching and
making soft chirping noises. Yāo-guài belonged to both of us
now, my mother had explained. Our magics had entwined
in that accidental explosion and brought him to life. I wasn't
sure how I felt about that, either.

I paused at the door, and my mother glanced up. Her eyebrows quirked above those bright black eyes. "Staying or
running?" she asked.

We hadn't talked since that night two weeks ago. Mā mī

slept a lot. But even when she woke and puttered around the shop, I found other things to do. Mostly running up and down Lóng City's staircases. It wasn't that I hated her. I just wasn't sure what I'd say. Something angry, probably.

I blew out a breath. "Staying."

My mother regarded me a long moment. "You have some questions for me, I think."

"No. I don't have anything to say."

Her lips thinned in an unhappy smile. "You always were a terrible liar."

When I didn't reply, she sighed and let her gaze drop to her account books. A loose lock of hair fell over her eyes. She brushed it away absentmindedly. With a shock, I realized there were white streaks in her hair where none had been two months before, and the creases from her smile lingered as echoes, as though the skin were too tired to relax.

My mother is growing old.

Old in the usual way. And old from keeping the king alive.

"Why didn't you tell me?" I burst out.

Mā mī paused and lifted her gaze to my face. "I meant to, if that matters."

"But you didn't."

I scowled, knowing I sounded like a spoiled child.

"I didn't tell you because I had no time." Her voice was softer, slower. "I had gone to the market to buy more herbs and a special-order powder. And to make arrangements with Bin Chu and Hai-feng Lo. Not a *li* from the *piaohao*, I noticed two men following me. Amateurs. Oh, some might call them professionals, but I could tell right away. So I lured them into an alleyway and disposed of them. Unfortunately, a squad of royal guards were patrolling nearby and witnessed the event, so after that, I had to disappear myself. The ghost dragon king was quite accommodating."

My lungs squeaked dry. "You killed them?"

My mother made a *tch-tch* noise in her throat. "It was a minor spell, calculated to displace their wretched bodies into an alternate plane of existence. Ah, that reminds me. I really must release them soon. Today, perhaps."

You always said she was scarier than watch-demons, Chen said softly. *Why are you surprised?*

Because . . . because she's my mother.

And she should have her own adventures, no?

My brain hurt at the thought. I rubbed my temples with both hands. "So what about the shop?"

"It can wait. Another month or three. After the wedding."

Gently my mother dislodged Yāo-guài from his napping

spot. She kissed him on top of the head, and he scrambled up the shelves to curl around the old radio. I thought she had finished with me, so I turned to go, but she beckoned me behind the counter.

"You didn't open the safe," she said quietly.

My face turned hot. "We tried, Chen and I."

"Ah. Another item I forgot to tell you. Well, and, you weren't ready before today."

In between her odd tone and the sudden change of subject, I didn't know what to say. I mumbled something about trying the simple spells. She nodded. "Good choice. I did choose a simple one, only not what you guessed."

She laid a hand over the lock and said a name.

My father's name.

The lock clicked; the door swung open.

The safe was stuffed full of scrolls, boxes, and more envelopes. Mā mī extracted an especially thick envelope and handed it to me. "For you," she said. "From your father. He wrote you a letter before going off to war. He wrote several more before . . . before he died. He told me give you them all when you had become a man."

I was too stunned to do more than take the envelope. My blood thrummed, just like when the ghost dragon bit my fingers underneath Lóng City. Mā mī fiddled with another scroll, but then plucked back her fingers, murmuring something about how dreams were best remembered from afar. I wanted to ask what she meant, but her expression had softened to a strange and wistful look.

Silently, I retreated from the front room and crept up the stairs to my room. The light was dim there. Afternoon was falling toward night. Snow pattered against the wooden shutters, interrupted now and then by the *tick-tick* of sleet. A whiff of cold air filtered into the already chilled room. Even as the door swung closed behind me, a magic-powered heater clicked on.

I still clutched the envelope in one hand, the leather cylinder from Lian in the other. I set the cylinder on my desk and lit an oil lamp. By its light I examined my father's packet of letters. It was thick, stained with water and wine and dirt. He had used the cheapest paper. No doubt a soldier couldn't take his finest writing kit to war.

My legs went limp and I sat heavily on my bed.

This is scary, Chen, I whispered.

I know.

My hands shook as I broke the wax seal and lifted the flap.

There were a dozen thick parchment sheets crammed inside. They were just as dirty as the outside, and stiff from waiting ten years. It took me several minutes to unwedge them without ripping the envelope. I laid them on my lap and stared down at the top sheet.

Dear Kai-my-son . . .

It wasn't the letter I expected. But it was the letter I needed right now. My father wrote about a spring day in Lóng City, how the clouds were like great white birds soaring over an ocean of mountains. How the sun glinted off palace and plain red tile roofs alike. How the warmth felt good on his back, how the fresh snowmelt tasted. He was going off to war, he said. And he wanted to fix the good memories of home, of his wife and son, in his mind to keep on the dark nights and in the midst of battle. The day's light faded as I read through all twelve letters. When I looked up, I saw Yún sitting on the floor, gazing up at me. She must have arrived while I was lost in the world of my father's letters. The golden lamplight made her eyes shine like ebony and her skin like polished bronze.

"How are you?" she asked.

My throat hurt. "Better," I managed to say.

"I'm glad." She hesitated. "This is selfish, I know, but . . .

I was afraid that everything had changed once we got back."

Changed—as in, what happened on the road had vanished with our homecoming. I didn't blame her for wondering. All those hours spent running away from Mā mī meant I hadn't spent much time with Yún, either.

I set my letters next to my cylinder and faced Yún.

She is my future, I thought. *If she wants me.*

Then tell her, Chen said.

He was right. Whatever her answer, I had to speak.

"Yún. I have something to say. To ask."

She tilted her head. There was a faint smile on her face. "Then ask," she said.

A tight cord around my heart frayed and burst. I reached out and took Yún's warm hands in mine. Pulled her next to me. She came willingly.

ACKNOWLEDGMENTS

When I sit down to write, it's me and the computer. (And sometimes a cat.) But after that first mad rush of prose, I depend on editors and friends to keep me honest and my story clear. Many thanks go to Delia Sherman, Lisa Mantchev, Shveta Thakrar, Celina Summers, Sherwood Smith, and Fran Wolber for their sharp-eyed critiques and their encouragement. I also owe a great debt to Li Zhao, Anna Shih, and Kelvin Shih for their help with Chinese names and phrases.

A huge thank-you also goes to my editor, Sharyn November, for guiding me to a better book.

And last but not least, I am grateful to my husband and son. You guys make the writing possible.

BETH BERNOBICH comes from a family of storytellers, artists, and engineers. She juggles her time between working with computer software, writing, family, and karate. Her short stories have appeared in publications such as *Asimov's*, *Interzone*, *Postscripts*, and *Strange Horizons*. Her debut adult novel, *Passion Play*, was published in the fall of 2010; its sequel, *Queen's Hunt*, is forthcoming. *Fox and Phoenix* is her first novel for younger readers. She lives with her husband and their son in Bethany, Connecticut.

Visit her Web site at www.beth-bernobich.com.